THE
EMERALD HEAD
CAPER

BY

HAROLD R. MILLER

THE
EMERALD HEAD
CAPER

Taylor-Dth Publishing
108 Caribe Isle
Novato, CA 94949
www.taylor-dth.com

ISBN: 0-9712923-8-8
978-0-9712923-8-3
Library of Congress Control Number: 2002117465

Manufactured in the United States of America

The events in this book are related to fact, although all names have been changed to protect the innocent as well as the guilty. Any relationship between the names in this book and any person real or imaginary is purely coincidental.

Cover by Cardinali Designs

Dedication

Thank you Jan, Nancy, Ana
and '_____' (She knows her name).

■　■　■　■

Books by Harold R. Miller,
listed in the order of the protagonist's development:
Thai Moon Saloon
The Philippine File
The Australian File
The Belize File
The Emerald Head Caper
Universeros
P.I. Adventures in Belize

By Nancy Cardinali and Harold R. Miller
Nitwit

Published exclusively by
Taylor-Dth Publishing

Also available at
www.taylor-dth.com
www.haroldrmiller.com

CHAPTER 1

The shadows played on Penn's face as he raced along the trail. The twisted jungle vines and branches scraped his new trekking clothes, tearing at them, ripping them. At one time, the trail was clear and easily passable, but it was long since forgotten, unused, clogged by decades of old growth. It was hard to see among the brush, the weeds, the fallen trees, and the broken, rotting logs.

Mosquitoes, wasps, gnats, flies and dragonflies, every kind of flying insect common to humid climates flew at him. They hit him in the face. They flooded his mouth when he was careless enough to open it to take a deep gasp of air, winded as he was from running. He spit them out with near panic distaste. He hated creeping, crawling, flying, pests.

"What am I doing here?" he shouted, angry with himself for getting into the situation. He ducked as yet another branch grabbed his sleeve, entwining him as if it were trying to frustrate his escape.

He couldn't use a machete to cut away the brush that tore at him. He didn't have time for cutting and slashing. Or, he couldn't take the time for cutting and slashing, even if he were able to wield his machete, if he had his machete, if he hadn't dropped it in his headlong race to get away.

"The humidity has to be at least 120 percent," he moaned, as sweat poured from his body, soaking his clothes. It was the rainy season in Central America, and everything was wet. He wiped his arm across his forehead, and nearly tripped over a fallen log. Not watching where you're running, even for a second, is dangerous in the jungle.

Without warning the trail ended, and facing him was a river. He came upon it so quickly he nearly lost his balance while stopping. The riverbank sloped gently up from the slow moving, swampy water, and flattened out. It was muddy and sandy.

It might be quicksand, he thought, quickly stepping back to solid ground. In his haste, he barely noticed the ancient Mayan ruins perched over the water less than ten yards away, almost hidden in the growth.

Quicksand wasn't the only problem, though. There was something strange about that river. The floating logs moved upstream.

"Crocodiles!" he shouted in sudden realization. Some of the log-like shapes stopped moving and stared at him with their calculating, unblinking eyes barely above water.

Penn saw crocodiles before in his years as a relic hunter. He even saw them in his earlier days as a private investigator. He saw the crocodiles of the Nile. He saw them in the oceans off Northern Australia where he was nearly chomped on by an Estuarine Crocodile, the largest in the world. He knew how dangerous crocodiles were, but none of them stirred the fear he felt as the largest of these Belizean monsters eyed him. The situation wasn't the same. In Australia he wasn't in a hurry to flee.

He turned back to the trail. He hoped to find another hiding place, or maybe another trail, but there was no escape. His pursuers were near, moving quickly along the same barely marked trail.

He felt the weight of the Mayan ritual dagger and the trinket stuffed in his pants pocket. They were made of gold heavily encrusted with Emeralds. He wondered if they were worth everything he went through to find them, and what he went through to keep them. He was quickly deciding they weren't.

He considered dropping the dagger on the trail when he

discovered his pursuers. He was certain that was what they were after. If he just left it in the middle of the trail, he was certain, they would stop for it and not come after him.

But he couldn't do that. He couldn't force himself to leave the objects of all his efforts. Nor could he turn his back on the obscenely rich collector who hired him to find them, the man who paid him a retainer that was only a quarter of what he would get when he delivered them.

It really wasn't the money, though, he reasoned. Or was he just rationalizing his greed? No, he argued. The truth was he couldn't let his client down. Or, more to the point, he couldn't let himself down. He always kept his end of a bargain, no matter how hard it became to do so.

He let himself down more than a few times in the past, when he wasn't so worried about self-respect, and didn't like the remorse. That was when Lara left him, or rather, that was why she left him. He didn't want to be that person again, so he stuck the dagger back in his pocket and looked around. There had to be another way.

Angry shouts in some strange and unintelligible language erupted from the trail behind him. "Wambe! Wambe!... Negale!" (Faster! Faster! Hurry up!)

Penn had no idea what those words meant, but he was certain the Indians were talking about him.

"Aregeele! Wambe negrili! Tapiri negrili!" (Hurry! We must hurry to catch that Tapir!)

The shouts continued. They were nasty sounding words, and they urged Penn into a frantic search for an escape.

"Oh, come on! Come on!" he almost shouted in exasperation, looking about him at the thick brush lining the trail. "There's got to be a way through this stuff, somewhere." He tried to push aside the branches, but he soon gave up that idea. They were branches with thorns that tore at his hands.

He ran a few yards farther back into the jungle, along the trail, and stopped. His pursuers were in that direction, and they were getting close, too perilously close. He turned around. He thought of returning to the river, of building up enough momentum to leap across it. With any luck, he could clear the water and the crocodiles. He didn't like that idea, but he'd rather face the crocodiles than his pursuers. At least crocodiles were things he knew, things that were predictable.

Wait a minute! He spotted something hopeful. What is that? He raced back another five yards to where the brush parted, slightly. He shoved aside the brush. A tunnel! He peered into the darkness of the tunnel entrance. It wasn't large, but it was big enough to get into, if he kept his head down. It had to be a better choice than the river.

He glanced back along the trail in the direction of his pursuers. If he didn't do something soon, they would be on top of him. He had to make a decision. "I hate tunnels," he moaned in desperation.

The indians shouted again. "Waga nega rumbi. Areegela!" (The monster is here, somewhere. Hurry!)

Penn gritted his teeth, and forced himself into the dark, foreboding tunnel.

Enough light penetrated the growth overhanging the tunnel entrance to allow some vision, once his eyes became adjusted to the change. He was less than a foot's distance inside when his head hit something. A root? He appraised it with a quick upward glance, crouching in nervous reaction. Only a root, he concluded.

He stood up as best he could in the low roofed tunnel, and tried to calm his nerves. He took a deep breath. He immediately he wished he hadn't. The air inside the tunnel was acrid. It smelled of rot and mildew, of the effects of constant humidity, of air without the benefit of the sun's rays, of dead things - rats, snakes, rotting roots.

He choked off a cough as he heard his pursuers again. They were close, continuing their shouting as they ran. He wondered how their long white flower sack clothing resisted tearing by the same branches that tore the special-made jungle trekking clothes he purchased for this expedition. So much for modern textile science, he moaned.

He forced the inane thought from his mind and slowly peered around him. The roots growing through the tunnel walls and down from the top were covered with bugs, with insects, worms, and centipedes, everything imaginable in some entomophobic nightmare.

THE EMERALD HEAD CAPER

"I hate creepie crawlies," he whispered aloud. He shuddered. He forced himself to stifle his desire to shout, to scream. His pursuers were closer. Where were they? Were they in front of the cave entrance? He took a chance and peered between the brush covering the entrance.

He was right. His pursuers were less than five feet away from him. There were six of them. He easily identified them as members of the Lancandon Indian tribe of the dense and remote Guatemalan and Belizean jungles. They were native to the area. To make matters worse, they weren't known for being overly friendly to outsiders, and these six were so fierce in appearance they couldn't have been friendly, even if they wanted. Their brown faces were painted in vivid white designs, and their long, straight, black hair streamed back when they ran. Their appearance struck fear in their enemies.

"Chambela. Non deekee...relzina!" (Where is the tapir?) The leader of the group asked the others.

"Irrega. Non gotcha sequitat unbitchee gompa no catache?" (Hunh?) One of the group responded.

"Relzina!" (The tapir his disappeared. Where could it have gone in such a short time?) The leader demanded.

"Nopsca touchee. Catscasca irranumbulee warrarra. Comatchigo where-abula?" (Darned if I know.) The other indian responded.

"Ooodeekee. Oo-oodeekee. Tapir ooooa." (The Tapir is not here. It must have gone back into the river.) Another commented, gesturing at the river for effect.

Penn cautiously watched them through the vines covering the tunnel entrance. Something dropped on his shoulder. He froze. It took several seconds for him to amass enough courage to slowly turn his head and peer at whatever that something was on his shoulder, next to his face.

It was black and orange. It was as large as his hand, with hairy long legs. Tarantula! It crawled up his shoulder, closer to his face. He hated spiders. He was arachnophobic. He had a fear of spiders, especially tarantulas. He frantically brushed at the monster.

The spider plopped onto the ground, and scurried off into the bottom growth.

Harold R. Miller

Penn was fearful the natives heard the tarantula's fall. He held his breath, listening, staring at the spider's departure, hoping it wouldn't return. It didn't, and at length he pulled his panic-stricken stare away from the spider's path. He let out his breath, wondering if people really did turn blue in such times.

He resumed peering through the growth covering the tunnel's entrance. The original problem was still there. Lancandons! They were a problem he knew wasn't going to be solved as easily as the tarantula.

The natives seemed to be in a violent mood. Some of them carried atl-atls with sling-arrows, and all of them were yelling, brandishing their weapons.

Penn held his breath, fearing the slightest whisper would reveal his hiding place. Then, as if the fates were against him, he heard a long hissing sound. It came from somewhere back in the tunnel. He knew what made such a sound, and he hoped what he knew wasn't going to be what he saw when he slowly turned around.

His eyes went wide. Neither spiders, crocodiles, nor Lancandon indians were anything to worry about any more, not when compared to what faced him. It was a Fer De Lance, and it wound itself around some roots less than three feet away from his head. It hissed at him with its tongue lashing the air, sensing danger. One bite from it, and the Lancandons would cease to be a problem. Everything would cease to be a problem.

The Lancandons were inspecting the trail. They were discussing what they found. They spoke and yelled with animated gestures. The leader of the group gestured back along the trail. "Le! Chambela. Non deekee resina!" (I'm going that way!) He took several steps in that direction.

Several others gestured toward the river. "Oodeekee. Oo-oodeekee?" (Why in the devil would you want to go that way, when we all agree the Tapir has gone in another direction?) They argued.

Penn had no time to listen to any more of their arguing. The viper was drawing back, hissing. Suddenly, it lunged forward.

"Yeeaaaahhhhh!" Penn yelled as he jumped back in fear. He grabbed the dagger relic, and stumbled backwards through the growth hiding the tunnel, waving his arms wildly, slashing at the air, fending off the imaginary attack of the snake.

When he realized he was out of the tunnel, and that the natives were behind him, he stopped. He had to face them now, even if he had to do it hind-side most, because the snake missed him, and that was what mattered at the moment.

It took most of that moment for the natives to focus on Penn's sudden appearance from out of nowhere. He was covered with cobwebs, dirt, and dead roots. He looked fearsome to them, especially when he seemed to have no face, at first, with backward arms waving a knife at them. Some jumped back in surprise. Some turned and ran, while others clutched their weapons for protection. All of them were confused.

"Wagalili? Qweek nopa wagalili? Nogganife? Nugga Tapir?" (What is this thing that is too pale to be human? And what is it doing with that knife? How could the great Tapir, the animal we have been hunting, have suddenly turned into this thing? How could it become this thing that could be human if it weren't so white and pale that it must have been hiding under a log for years?) They stared at the ghostly image in wonder as it slowly turned around. They gasped when they saw its face.

Penn regained his footing as he faced the natives. He had to think. He gulped. He caught his breath, and had a moment of inspiration. He raised the dagger, and threw his arms out in front of him in a defensive manner, wielding the dagger as a weapon.

The natives jumped in surprise.

Penn cautiously backed up.

The natives regrouped. They studied this white monster, again; this oddly reincarnated Tapir. Their curiosity emboldened them to come together and edge closer. They raised their rifles and Atl-Atls, ready to pounce on this thing should it suddenly return to its true shape.

The leader of the natives was curious about the knife the monster used to threaten them. "Rambuleeg," he said to his group. "Rambuleega awalyah moluli." (This monster-thing has to be from the dark side, or it wouldn't be carrying such an odd and old weapon.)

"Oombari. Oombari watsh rambuleega shnigue ula!"

(Yeah. We agree.) The others answered, as they peered at the weapon, edging even closer, even though the monster-thing was backing away, nearing the river.

Penn slowly continued backing, until his feet felt the edge of the mud. He glanced over his shoulder at the river. Several crocodiles floated in the slow moving water. "Now what?" he asked himself

The natives leaned their heads forward. Was this monster speaking to them?

Penn continued threatening them with the dagger. He was sure that as long as he threatened them with it, they wouldn't dare pounce on him. He was certain they wouldn't want to risk destroying it. He was sure of that, because of the way they were eyeing it. He straightened up to the full of his 5' 9" height, and faced them.

They drew back in confusion by this sudden turn of events.

Penn flailed his arms wildly. He shouted. He screamed the most threatening scream he could muster. "Yowoowuuuu!" He hoped it sounded threatening. "Wahba! Wahba!... Wahba!" He didn't have the slightest idea what he was saying, but it sounded good to him.

The natives were taken aback by this sudden vocal onslaught. They regrouped.

To Penn their regrouping was a sure sign of their impending attack. He waved the dagger around again, turned, hesitated long enough to jab the dagger into his waistband, ignoring the wound he gave himself, and leaped for the river, onto the back of the nearest crocodile.

He leaped off the crocodile just as it twisted its snout around to snap at him, and was heading for the second one, thinking he was making good on his Hollywood-ian escape.

But the second crocodile had other intentions. It suddenly submerged.

Penn tried to change direction in mid-jump, but his effort was wasted. He landed in the water with an award winning belly flop.

The natives rushed to the river's edge. They waited to see if this monster-thing would come out of the water, either as the

THE EMERALD HEAD CAPER

Tapir they were hunting, or maybe in a natural brown color, like all humans should be, if it were, indeed, human.

Penn did come out of the water, after nearly a minute. He surfaced six feet from the opposite riverbank, swimming as hard as he could, spitting out water like a breaching whale. He scrambled out on the riverbank, with a crocodile close on his heels. He sprang to his feet and began running.

The crocodile slithered up the bank in pursuit.

The natives witnessed the entire episode. By that time, they decided this grossly pale monster-thing must be evil, or the crocodile Gods wouldn't be chasing it. So they raised their weapons and began shooting at it.

The bullets and arrows shattered the leaves around Penn as he dodged to the right, to the left, and into the jungle to safety.

The crocodile gave up in the flurry of flying leaves, and quickly slithered back into the water.

CHAPTER 2

A semi truck sped along the narrow two-lane highway amid the tall and majestic Sequoias of Northern California. It rolled across the high bridge that spanned the river south of Fort Bragg. Its tires vibrated on the corrugated steel roadbed, creating a low pitched moaning. It was the sound that gave The Moaning Bridge its name.

It was summertime, clear and hot. The truck driver was in a good mood inside his air conditioned cab, and he honked in friendly response to the 'pull the horn cord' signal the three teenagers on the side of the highway gave him with a jerking down of their raised fists.

The teenagers laughed in response to their non-verbal communication with the driver of the long haul rig. As with all teenagers in the idle days of summer, the signaling was generated by a desire to get out and see the country, by the desire to experience more of life, by envy for those who were able to do so.

The teenagers were Chuck, Marcie and Marc. Chuck, who considered himself the leader of the three, was a 17 year-old boy with curly blonde hair. He tried to grow a beard, thinking the curls on his chin would impress the girls – Marcie in particular – but it didn't turn out to his liking, so he gave up the project.

Marcie, the same age as Chuck, had hair the color of a shining carrot blended with wisps of sunlight. It was cut short in keeping with her assertiveness. She admired Chuck, and although her tomboy attitudes about feminine self-sufficiency sometimes interfered, she allowed Chuck to assume the position of leader, since he so enjoyed it. She learned the power of femininity at an early age from dealing with her brother.

Marc was Marcie's twin brother. He, too, had red hair, and kept it cropped close to his head. He wasn't sure he liked it that way, even though the girls in most of his classes enjoyed rubbing their hands over it, feeling the softness of it. He was more easily intimidated than his sister, and often leaned on his sister's intellect to explain things that weren't clear to him.

The happy teenagers were sitting on a fallen redwood tree along the side of the highway not more than twenty yards from the bridge. They watched the passing traffic in idle relaxation, enjoying the new-found freedom gained by their recent high school graduation.

Several more cars and an occasional truck passed them before Chuck finally broke the silence. They were talking before the arrival of the big rig, and he wanted to continue the conversation.

"I've been down there a lot of times, already," he said. "It's easy. All you have to do is climb over the edge on the other side of the highway, and that gets you to the bridge girders." He glanced at Marc, who appeared slightly confused.

"Girders," Marcie explained to her brother. "The metal beams that make up the bridge."

"Oh," Marc smiled in his new-found understanding.

"We can cross the girders all the way to the cave on the other side of the river," Chuck continued. "It's easy. That old pirate does it. I've watched him dozens of times."

"Why do you suppose he keeps going into that cave, anyway?" Marcie asked. Her curiosity was hard to gratify.

Sometimes Chuck found that difficult, especially when her questions were spawned by a sense of reason which confronted his carefree ambitions. "I don't know," he responded with the slightest show of exasperation.

He rekindled his enthusiasm, and continued. "But that's what we want to find out, isn't it?" He hoped his energy would sway the often steadfast young woman. "I asked my dad about the old pirate. He said he's no threat to anyone. He uses him as an extra deckhand when the salmon are running. My dad says he works good, but keeps to himself a lot." He paused to pick up a pebble to throw across the road. "He's a Belizean," he added, hoping to spur the others' interests.

"He's a what?" Marc asked.

"A Belizean," Marcie answered, ever patient, although she was becoming more than slightly interested in Chuck's story, and didn't want the interruption. "You know, from Belize."

"Oh. Thanks, Sis." Marc grinned at his sister. He wasn't sure where, or even what, Belize was, but he didn't want to sound too uninformed. He didn't ask for details.

"I always thought he was from Mexico," Marcie continued to Chuck.

"Yeah. So did I," Chuck said. He paused to think. "I never could figure why he named his boat the Crystal Skull," he continued at length, hoping to pique his friend's enthusiasm even further. He wasn't sure it worked.

"That's kind of eerie, if you ask me," Marcie said. "Who ever heard of a crystal skull? Ugh."

"Yeah," Marc submitted.

Chuck got to his feet. He sensed a stronger lead was needed. "That makes it even more of a mystery, doesn't it?" He stepped forward and peered at the bridge. "We have to get across to the other side of the ravine, under the bridge, to get a look in that cave." He stepped out, heading for the other side of the road. "Come on," he called for the others while darting across the highway. When he reached the end of the bridge, the other two finally overcame their reluctance, and followed.

"The far end of the ravine is too steep to climb down," Chuck said when his friends caught up with him. "So we have to cross the girders to get to the cave." He eyed the bridge girders, and glanced at the ravine they spanned.

The ravine was over a hundred feet deep. The river flowed though it past a small fishing boat harbor set several hundred yards in from the ocean.

Another car passed over the bridge as they peered over the edge, and its tires reminded them of the bridge's name.

"See," Chuck pointed to a cave on the far bank of the ravine, just below the anchoring of the bridge on the opposite side. It was in the part of the ravine that was too steep to climb down. "We can cross the bridge and the river on these lower girders," he added, pointing to the H-Beam horizontal girders that were nearly eighteen inches wide. "They're wide enough for walking. We just have to be careful when we come to the vertical girders, that's all. I saw the old pirate do it lots of times. He just wraps his arms around the vertical girders and sort of inches his way around. He hasn't fallen, yet."

He set out for the end of the bridge. "Come on," he called back when he reached the cement bridge abutment on the side of the ravine. "It's easy," he added, as he descended the cement abutment to the first spanning girder, and stepped onto it.

His friends watched in slight questioning awe.

"See!" he called to them when he reached the first vertical girder. "It's easy. Come on!" He was careful to not look down. It was a bit more frightening than he anticipated, and that was something he certainly didn't want his friends to realize.

Marc and Marcie finally followed Chuck's lead. They scrambled down the abutment to the main girder, then stopped. They peered into the ravine with more than a little trepidation.

"Gosh, that's a long way down," Marc commented, studying a fishing boat plying up the river to a safe haven. "That boat looks awfully small from here."

"Well," Marcie said, half frustrated by her own fears. "Heck. If Chuck can do it, so can we." She reached out her foot to place it on the girder. She carefully put her weight on it, and after forcing her courage, knowing she wasn't going to let Chuck do something she couldn't do, she stepped onto the girder with a show of fortitude.

Chuck stepped around the first vertical girder by carefully reaching his leg and foot around it, then shinnying around it, all the while carefully wrapping his arms around it, lest his foot slipped. "See!" he called to Marcie and Marc. "Like I said, it's easy. Come on!"

Marcie gingerly took a step forward on the girder, not sure she wanted to, but not wanting to be left out of seeing what might be found in the cave. She accidentally kicked some road pavement pebbles from the girder, and watched them disappear in their fall. The river seemed like miles below. She agreed with her brother. The salmon troller seemed like a toy from where she stood.

Chuck was past the second vertical girder, nearly to the center of the bridge span, when the old pirate emerged from the cave. He brandished a rifle, waiving it around in the air. "Hey! You kids!" he shouted in his heavy Belizean accent. "Chu be da gettin' off dis t'ing! Now! I say!"

"Oh, oh," Chuck gulped.

Marc nearly lost his step while still trying to get onto the main girder.

Marcie was almost to the first vertical girder. "I thought you said he was gone on Saturdays?" she shouted to Chuck.

"I thought he was!" Chuck replied, not certain of his information, but sure he didn't want to go any farther in the old pirate's direction. He turned around and scooted back to the first vertical girder as quickly as he could. It took about a tenth as long to get around it in his panic than it took to pass it the first time.

Marcie was already hurrying back to the abutment. She was casting a wary glance at her brother, who seemed to be stuck in his position, staring at the old pirate. Her glance turned to a visual order to get out of the way!

Marc got the hint. He quickly made his way back to the abutment, with Marcie and Chuck hard on his heels, surprised by his own agility, one that only fright can create.

The three scrambled up the abutment to the safety of the road, and were half a block into the redwoods on the trail leading to their houses before slowing down.

THE EMERALD HEAD CAPER

CHAPTER 3

Penn stepped up to the bar in the very exclusive nightclub. It was early evening and the weather was still stifling, but he felt uncomfortable about not dressing nicely when he was in a nice place. That's why he was dressed in formal eveningwear of white dinner jacket and tuxedo pants. His cummerbund and tie were a matching bright red, which he believed was an exciting touch. Without the color, he considered he looked like a penguin, a strutting penguin. Or a flying penguin? Nah, flying is a slang pseudonym for sexual activity. He didn't think he looked like a gigolo.

The bartender, in the red waistcoat and white pants uniform typical of nice cocktail lounges in the most expensive clubs everywhere in the world, came over and addressed him. "Yes, Sir?" the man asked in the most impeccable English to be heard outside Cambridge. "What would you like, Sir?"

"Vodka Martini," Penn ordered with poise. "Make it Stolichnya. Stirred, not shaken. Two Spanish olives."

The bartender nodded, moved away to mix the drink, and looked up. He grinned imperceptibly.

A sultry, buxom, slender woman with neatly groomed blonde hair, slinked herself and her too-small black V-neck evening gown onto the barstool beside Penn. She smiled seductively as she took a cigarette out of her red with silver sequined evening bag, held it to her lips, and waited for a

15

light.

Penn smiled with casual confidence. He decided he would oblige this female bombshell, no matter what she wanted. He removed his gold lighter from his jacket pocket, struck it, and held it under her cigarette. He calmly watched as she puffed the cigarette to life, and removed it from her lips in a slow, sultry manner.

With her white-gloved hand, she grabbed his wrist, the one holding the lighter. She studied the inscription on it. "To Penn," she read in her low, rhythmic voice. "With my sincerest admiration and gratitude for your help." She looked into Penn's eyes. "Signed: James Bond." She completed her reading with a touch of amusement, and let go of his hand while continuing her smile, with her languid eyes half closed in one of those 'come-hither' looks.

Or was it an 'I'd be good for you' look?' Penn couldn't decide which, but he felt a strong preference for the latter.

In rather rude timing, a suspicious man in a black suit entered the club and stood near the door. He scanned the room. He grinned malevolently when he spied Penn and the woman, and stepped forward. His hand reached under his coat to his shoulder holster.

The woman took another slow, long puff on her cigarette. When she finally exhaled, the smoke wafted up in lazy, seductive curls around Penn's face. The red and blue neon lights cast a fuzzy glow through the smoke as he peered into her eyes.

Miami Vice revisited, he mused. Then he needed to cough. Smoking was never one of his habits.

"So, where did you meet James?" she asked."Singapore," he responded, after he sipped his Martini to clear his throat. "I helped him out of a little, ah, aq situation, last year."

"Oh, yes. James is one who can be so... nasty, at times," she said.

Her voice could melt butter, Penn thought. It could thaw an iceberg and use the water to boil an egg. Not to mention all the other clichés. He grinned as he returned the lighter to his pocket.

"How about you?" she asked with a wicked, half smile. "Can you be...?" She let the question drop as she noticed the suspicious man in the black suit step to the middle of the room with a .357 Magnum revolver drawn.

"Can I be what?" Penn asked, confused by her sudden concern for something other than him.

She never answered.

The suspicious man fired his gun. Flame shot from the muzzle. The explosion of the bullet could have wakened the dead.

Penn jumped up in bed.

He was sleeping, covered by a thin sheet. He was in a second rate hotel room in the tropics, with a slowly rotating ceiling fan, and plaster pealing off walls badly in need of repainting.

It was the sunlight streaming through the broken wood slats on the window that made him feel so hot. It was the near white cotton sheet that felt like a dinner jacket, and it must have been the low hum of the ceiling fan that mimicked the sultry purring of the friendly woman.

And the gunshot? It was the backfiring of a car on the street outside his window. It coughed and backfired once more as Penn crawled out of bed.

He wiped his forehead, swiped at the cockroach scurrying across the nightstand and down the side for safety. He lightly frowned at his failure to hit the crawling insect. It was another thing that crawled. He hated crawling insects. He hated them ever since his days in college biology classes when he had to study worms, and flies, and maggots that crawled over dead bodies. The thought of maggots crawling over his dead body made him shudder. He decided long ago he would end his days sailing the seven seas. He would get eaten by sharks when the end came. Creepy crawly things didn't live in the open seas.

His dreams seemed to him to be over-active lately. That usually meant he had to get back to his creative writing, to writing his novels. He swore he would do that just as soon as he finished this hunt. Maybe he would be able to afford it. Maybe one of his stories would even be published. Maybe he'd find some slow moving publisher who would have sympathy for his plight and publish him just for the fun of it. "That would be nice," he chuckled in wry amusement. He glanced at his watch.

It was nine o'clock. He got to his feet, and headed for the tiny bathroom. He hoped there was running water this morning.

Meanwhile, downstairs, a Belizean bartender wiped glasses behind the counter in the combination cocktail lounge and restaurant. He was listening to Belizean Rap music, bouncing his head and body in rhythm. He looked up and momentarily stopped his glass wiping as a woman entered the lounge.

She was an attractive red head in her mid-thirties, in white pants with a green tank top more revealing than the Belizean hot weather would have dictated. She topped it off with a moderate amount of very expensive gold jewelry that glittered as she scanned the room. With a crisp smile and an experienced gaze, she strode across the room to sit at a table that afforded an unobstructed view of the entrance. "I assume the investigator named Gwinns, I think that's his name, will be coming in here this morning," she said to the bartender. "I need to talk to him, if he does."

The bartender shrugged.

Fifteen minutes later, Penn entered the bar. He wore his usual jeans, and a Hawaiian shirt that saw better days. He was unshaven, because the hot water didn't show up, as he hoped. His hair, what was left of it on the sides, was having a bad hair day. He strolled up to the bar and nodded hello to the bartender.

The bartender smiled broadly in greeting, put down the glass he was drying for the past half hour, retrieved a bottle of Myers's rum from the back bar, put it on the counter beside the glass, and silently nodded in the direction of the red head. "I t'ink she be here fa da talk wid chu," he wwhispered with a sly grin.

Penn peered at the woman as he picked up the rum bottle and glass. "Maybe things are looking up," he said with a smile. He strode across the floor to the woman's table, and boldly sat in one of the three chairs. He poured rum into the glass, and held it casually as he eyed her over the top of it. "The bartender said you want me?" he asked at length, exuding self-confidence.

She smiled, amused by the remark. "That's not quite what I said, so don't get your hopes up." Her response contained an equal amount of self-confidence. "I told him I wanted to talk to you."

"Oh. Well, women don't always say what they mean." He grinned as he took a swallow from his glass. "What's your name, anyway?"

"June. And I presume you're Mr. Gwinns?" she asked.

"Gwinn," he corrected. "No s."

"You're late,' she said, ignoring the correction while glancing at her watch. "I was told you showed up here around nine each morning. It's now nearly ten."

"Yep." He smiled. "My middle name."

"Your middle name?" The remark confused her.

"Late."

"Late?" Was this guy off his rocker, or what, she asked herself. "What's that supposed to mean?"

"My middle name is Late." He took another drink. "I was a month overdue for a July birth date. The name's my old man's idea of a joke."

She peered at him. She wasn't yet sure he wasn't a nut.

"Actually, my full name is Penn Late Gwinn," he explained.

"I see," she said, peering at him, not sure she believed him. "Well, let's get to the point," she added after a thoughtful pause. "I have a proposition for you that..."

"Really?" he interrupted. "I would have thought it a bit early in the day for that sort of thing. I was thinking maybe a little breakfast, spend some time getting acquainted..."

"Don't flatter yourself, Mr. Gwinn," she interrupted him. "It is not that kind of proposition. My employer will be here in a moment or two. Maybe I should let him explain the details."

Penn wondered if he had made a mistake in being so assertive. A woman who wants to control, who apparently needs to control like this one, he thought, usually needs to make the first suggestion.

Just at that moment a man in his late sixties, balding, wearing round frame-less spectacles and impeccably dressed in a white Guayabara shirt with tan khaki pants, strode into the room. With an air of authority, and a sense the he was used to getting what he wanted, or even what he expected, he sat at the table.

Penn eyed him questioningly.

"Penn Gwinn," June said. "This is Mr. Beusch. Thorne Beusch."

Penn peered at the man. "Thorne Beusch?" He smiled in amusement.

"I don't find the name amusing, Mr. Gwinn," Thorne said pointedly.

Penn grinned mischievously. "Pleased to meet you," he said. He wanted to say it was a pointed meeting, but deferred. Besides, he rationalized, the man might have money. "I guess the customary thing to do now is ask what I can do for you," He smiled at the both of them. He wondered if these two were nuts, or what?

"What you can do for me, Mr. Gwinn, is find a certain head that is somewhere in Belize." Thorne got to the point.

"Head?" Penn asked. He was beginning to think these two did have mush for brains. "I think you need someone else. I'm a private investigator, not an undertaker."

"Yes, of course you are," Thorne responded with slight sarcasm. "I am very well aware of your talents, Mr. Gwinn. You are a skilled relic hunter, not merely a run of the mill type private investigator. Not even in your more, ah, shall we say, less fortunate days right after the end of your interlude with a certain one time secretary named Lara, could you have been considered a run of the mill investigator. Not even during your more reckless and tempestuous days after you and your wife separated after your kids were born, when you hit the bottle pretty heavily, did you sustain a reputation of anything but a skilled finder of things."

"Well. I appreciate the compliment," Penn said with a frown, wondering just where the hell this man managed to get all that information. If anything, he was impressed by the man's ability to construct backgrounds, but he wasn't going to show it. "Look," he said at length, with some trepidation. "I'm willing to help find things for people, sometimes, but I'm sure you know removing antiquities from their native surroundings is against the law, even here in Belize."

"I am well aware of the laws of the country, Mr. Gwinn. And I appreciate your point." He reached into his pocket and extracted a checkbook. "However, I think you will be able to see my point. The head I am talking about is a very valuable one, not an ordinary one, and certainly not one of biological structure. It is made of Emerald, carved pure Emerald. It's known as the Emerald Head."

Penn restrained his urge to laugh. I guess, he thought, if it was an Emerald in the shape of a head, that would be a good name for it.

Thorne intently watched Penn's eyes. "Considering its value to me, and to you, I might add, I'm sure the laws won't be too much of a, ah, shall I say, constraint?" He paused for effect. "Besides, I have no intention of taking it out of the country."

Penn took a quick swig from his glass of rum. He noticed their interest in his actions. "Oh. I'm sorry. May I offer you a drink?"

The two shook their heads 'no', in unison.

Penn shrugged, and considered the checkbook. "Just how big is this head?" he asked. He had to admit he was curious. "And just how valuable is it to me?"

"It's the size of an ordinary head..." Thorne began his answer.

"There's never been any Emerald found as large as a man's head," Penn quickly interjected.

"...ordinary for the Maya of several centuries ago, that is," Thorne continued, ignoring the interruption. "It is hollow, though. It's hollow because..."

Penn interrupted again. "Are you sure you don't have this Emerald head confused with the crystal skull found in Labaatun in 1926? The Mitchell-Hedges head?"

"Mr. Gwinn," Thorne quickly retorted with more than a little exasperation. "I've been studying Central American archaeology for thirty five years. Do you think I don't know the difference?"

"Sorry. No offense."

"There were some inequities and confusion surrounding the finding of the crystal skull you name," Thorne said. "The dating of the site didn't correspond to the dating of the debris found inside the skull." He paused to think. "And there was some question about the plaque..."

Again, Penn interrupted him. "I recall reading that." He thoughtfully took another drink. "The man who found the crystal skull claimed his daughter, or was it his granddaughter, found a gold plaque beside it, that has conveniently since disappeared, with an inscription which read that a magic head of clear green stone once fit over the skull."

"It was also written," Thorne said, "that when the Emerald Head is placed over the Crystal Skull, a mysterious vision appears, and..."

"What kind of mysterious vision?" Penn interrupted.

"Were that known, it wouldn't be mysterious, now would it? Anyway, in prehistoric legends the earliest people of South America arrived by sea, landing on the Pacific Coast. The people of the Andes and Central America, the Incas and the Mayas, retain memories of the legend, known as the Naymlap, which concerns the arrival of a great fleet of balsa reed rafts, much like that in which Thor Hyerdahl made his famous ocean crossing of the Pacific Ocean. They were led by a green stone, which could utter the words of the people's God, giving them directions. I believe the Emerald Head is that green stone."

Penn frowned. He didn't want to believe the story. It was too far fetched. "And about the valuable part?" he asked with skepticism.

Thorne opened his checkbook. He tore a check from it, which he handed to June. "I have to presume you are interested," he said at the same time.

Penn shrugged.

June took the check and leaned forward across the table to hand it to Penn.

As he retrieved it he forced himself to glance at it before aiming a discreet look at the woman's ample cleavage. After a second glance, he couldn't keep his eyes off the check. He whistled lightly at the amount, as he carefully set it on the table. He wasn't sure he wanted to put it in his pocket. Not yet. "Sixty six thousand, six hundred dollars is a lot of money," he said, pondering the possible inference to the bad luck symbol of three sixes, which he decided to ignore. That much money can't be all bad. "Just where am I to start looking for this seemingly very valuable Emerald Head?" he asked, at length.

"There is a map," Thorne said. "Or at least, part of one, which will be of some help."

"Great." Penn hoped he wasn't sounding too sarcastic. "Part of a map? What does that mean?"

June reached into her purse and extracted a leather map. She unfolded it and placed it on the table.

Penn peered at the map with interest. "Yes," he said, again hoping he wasn't too sarcastic. "I think you could call this thing a part of a map." He peered at it more intently. "It looks like it might be a map of the Yucatan," he said after some study. "Only it has to have been drawn years ago. Centuries ago, even, maybe before the days of the Spanish rule." He gazed more intently at the map, digesting the symbols. "If it is real," he added as he picked up one side of it, to examine it. "Half of it is missing."

"Very astute," Thorne grinned. "There are two other things about that map that you will find interesting."

"What other two things?" Penn asked without taking his eyes off the map.

"First," Thorne responded. "You're partially right about the date. It predates the Spanish occupation of Belize, and even the Scottish settlements before them." He leaned back with a self satisfying, smug grin.

Penn raised an eyebrow.

"The second is that the missing part, when fitted to this piece, can pinpoint the exact location of the Emerald Head."

Penn considered the remark. He thought about the map, and rethought the situation. His cynicism returned, overpowering his awed curiosity. "Well, that is what a map's supposed to do, isn't it?" He asked with skepticism. "Just how did you come across this map, anyway?"

"I understand your doubts," Thorne responded. "I had even more than you, until I had the leather it is drawn on tested for age. It is authentic, and dates to the mid 900's…"

"Mid 900's?" Penn interrupted him.

"BC," Thorne completed his sentence. "900 years before BC. Or, BCE, Before Common Era, as they say now."

Penn leaned back. Again he whistled. "Remarkable job of tanning the leather, don't you think? To have lasted for two thousand years?"

"Not nearly as remarkable as the powers the skull and head supposedly have when they are combined."

Penn returned his attention to the map. "It is a map of the Yucatan, right?"

"It is. Or, part of the Yucatan."

"Mostly of the Mosquito Coast, what is now Belize," Penn noted.

"Mostly Belize," Thorne confirmed.

"Where's the rest of it? The rest of the map, I mean."

"That, Mr. Gwinn, is where you come in."

"You don't have the rest of it?"

"If I did, would I be needing you?"

"Good point, Thorne," Penn grinned at his quip, which the man apparently didn't appreciate. "So, where do I find the rest of it? I assume that's what you're expecting me to do?"

"What I expect is that you find the rest of the map, follow it to the Emerald Head, and bring the head to me. Or, if you think you can work with just that half, find the head and then bring it to me. It's just that simple."

"Just that simple," Penn repeated the words with more than a little skepticism. "I don't suppose you have any idea where the rest of this map might be?"

"Guatemala," Thorne responded simply.

"Guatemala is a big haystack," Penn commented as he took another drink of his rum.

"Perhaps. But this map is a little larger than a needle, wouldn't you say?"

"It's not larger than the haystack," Penn countered. What the devil is going on, he wondered, Is this guy just playing games? He took a second glance at the check. It's an expensive game, if it is one.

"There is a man in Puerto Barrios, Guatemala. His name is James William Quigley," Thorne said.

"Squiggly, some people call him," June interjected. "For his ability to squirm out of his deals, so to speak."

"Let me guess," Penn said. "Your deal with this Squiggly guy…"

"Quigley," Thorne quickly interjected, having a penchant

for exactness.

"Quigley, whatever. Your deal with him was to buy the other half of the map from him?"

"You might say that."

"So, I have to surmise he took your money and ran, without turning over the map?"

"You might say that, too."

"And that's why you came to me? You think I can get the map from him?"

"And that."

"Without paying him any more," Penn said.

"Precisely."

"And you're thinking I can work this deal without your name being mentioned, because that would, ah, complicate the matter. Right?"

"Right, again," Thorne smiled.

Penn sat back and considered the offer. He picked up the check and pondered it. "Well, let me think about this for just a minute," he said. At length, he made his decision. He tossed the check back across the table to Thorne. "I don't think I like it," he said bluntly.

"You mean the amount isn't enough?" Thorne asked, surprised.

"No. I think the amount is fine," Penn responded.

It was Thorne's turn to ponder the situation. "Oh, I see," he said after a quick thought. "Perhaps, if the payment were in cash? Untraceable, so to speak?"

"That might make it worth while. It would certainly make it more interesting," Penn said. "You understand the complications, I presume?"

"The income tax complications, you mean?" Thorne responded.

Penn grinned and shrugged his shoulders. "As long as we understand each other."

"Very well. I can certainly understand that. All right. My secretary can meet you here in..." He glanced at his watch, "... say, three hours time? With cash. Will that be acceptable?"

"I must say you're a trusting guy," Penn smiled. "What assurances do you have that I won't take the money and run the same way Squiggly did?"

"Quigley," Thorne corrected.

"Quigley. Whatever."

"Do you think I haven't thought of that?"

"And?"

"Your reputation, Mr. Gwinn. Plus a certain group of, ah, people I have at my disposal who would be more than happy to exact revenge, if you were so disposed, that is."

"Pasquale and Luigi?" Penn grinned. "Why haven't you pointed them in Squiggly's direction?"

"Quigley," Thorne again corrected. "Anyway, there's nobody named Pasquale, or Luigi. It is not the Italian Mafia, Mr. Gwinn. I'm Irish." He grinned. "We Irish are often more direct. And considerably more, ah, forceful."

"A point well taken," Penn said. "Why is it that your men haven't exacted their revenge, as you call it, on Squiggly?"

Thorne gave up on the corrections. "Because, I didn't want him to, ah, lose his ability, shall we say, to divulge the map at some later time," he replied. "Besides, they aren't able to pass through Guatemalan immigration. They have certain reputations which bar them.

"You want him kept alive," Penn interjected, noting Thorne's search for the proper words.

It was Thorne's turn to shrug his shoulders in response.

"And this Squiggly character is in Puerto Barrios?"

"Yes."

"Where?"

"His exact location is not known."

"So, he is a bit squiggly." Penn couldn't resist the interjection.

"He does, however, deal in certain antiquities," Thorne said. "Much as you do, I might add. Only his are very often not so antique."

"He sells phony relics?"

"He should be easy to find for that reason," Thorne responded. "As a matter of fact, I've heard he often visits a nightclub on Calle Medellin, where he does most of his dealing."

"And just how did you hear that?"

Thorne shrugged.

"So, let me get this straight," Penn said. "You're willing to pay me a whole bunch of money to get a partial map from someone who is known to deal in phony artifacts?"

"Yes. But don't forget your main assignment is the acquisition of the Emerald Head."

"What makes you think the map part Squiggly has is real?"

"I've seen it, and I've had it tested, as well."

"I don't suppose you're going to tell me how you managed to do that?"

Another shrugged response.

"You're very thorough, aren't you?" Penn grinned.

"Very," Thorne responded with a matching grin.

Penn leaned forward again to study the map. "Okay," he said. "You have a deal. But, I can't get to it for a couple of days. I have some other, ah, business, to tend to first. If that's all right with you?"

"I have no objections to a few days delay, so long as you do perform your job, as well as you say," Thorne said.

"Do you perform as well as you say?" June snickered.

"The information on how to get in touch with me is on the bottom of the copy of the map," Thorne added in the middle of a disdaining glance at June.

Penn raised a curious eyebrow. "Copy?"

"You didn't expect I'd give you the original, did you?" Thorne asked.

"I suppose not," Penn relented.

June reached into her purse again and extracted a copy of the map to hand to him. She retrieved the original map from the table, carefully folded it up, and returned it to her purse.

"Very well," Thorne said as he and June stood. "June will meet you here in three hours," he added, as June also rose from the table. "The next time I see you I expect you to be delivering the Emerald Head. In the meantime, have a good trip, Mr. Gwinn." With that the two turned on their heels and strode out of the bar, leaving the map copy on the table.

Penn stared after them. He refilled his glass and took another drink. "What a goose chase this is going to be," he said to himself as he folded up the map copy and stuck it in his pocket.

CHAPTER 4

Penn didn't actually have anything else to do, of course. He merely told Thorne that so he could spend some time evaluating the case. And, he expected to spend the next three hours or so mulling over it, wondering what he was going to do about it. He decided he could call it a case, since it was a type of investigating work, and he was getting paid for it, or at least he expected he would be paid, as he glanced at his wristwatch.

It was well into an hour past the allotted time before June returned with the money, and Penn was well into too much rum with not enough food. He was pleased to see her. He would have enjoyed seeing her even if she didn't have the money with her.

She strode directly to the table where Penn sat, and smiled at him. Her demeanor was much more seductive than earlier, and her movements displayed a much less formal attitude. "May I?" she asked as she sat.

Penn nearly chuckled. "I suspect you may," he answered. "Whatever it is that you may want, that is," he added.

"How about a drink?" she asked.

"That, too," Penn said as he signaled to the bartender for another glass. "Where's your, ah, employer?"

"Right about now he should be halfway to Houston on Continental Air," she said with a smile.

Penn wondered just how seductive she meant that smile to

be. "Then, you're left here all by yourself?"

"All by myself," she agreed.

The bartender delivered the glass filled with ice.

Penn filled the glass halfway with rum, and sat back in his chair.

"Your earlier suggestion," she said, retrieving the glass, "was a few drinks, maybe something to eat..." She let the sentence drop.

"You're going to make me work for my retainer?"

"Only if you consider it to be work," she countered.

"Speaking of retainers," he said.

June opened her purse and removed an envelope. "All in American money," she said, as she reached across the table and to hand the envelope to him.

Penn decided her cleavage wasn't going to be ignored this time. He made no pretense at being polite.

"I hope it's to your liking," she said.

"It certainly is," Penn responded.

"The money, I mean," she said with a smile.

"That, too." There was something nagging the back of his brain. Why, he asked himself, was this gorgeous woman, who was so cynical and cold three hours ago, now trying to practically seduce him right here in the bar?

"There's something else, isn't there?" he asked, with his cynicism taking control.

She raised an eyebrow. "You mean I'm not making myself understood?"

He laughed at her boldness.

"Maybe if we were somewhere a little more private?" she added.

That was too blunt, he considered. What was she after? Certainly not just a bedtime story; not just a bedding time. He decided he would find out. He stuffed the envelope in his waistband, dropped a Belizean ten-dollar bill on the table, got to his feet, and grabbed her hand. "I think I'm going to enjoy earning this money," he said, leading her from the table. In spite of her bluntness, he was surprised by how willingly she followed.

When they reached the door to his room, she leaned

against him as he unlocked it. Her weight against him forced him through it when it opened.

"Now," she said, after he shut the door. "Let's see if you do perform as well as you say." She pulled off her tank top. It was a tank top with a built in bra. With it gone, her breasts stood out like pinnacles, full, and inviting, swaying gently as she breathed. She enjoyed showing herself to him.

His rising interest in her was unrestrained, and obvious. He wondered if he consumed too much rum to exercise discretion.

Slowly, seductively, she smiled, wetting her lips with her tongue, and unbuttoned her slacks.

Her slacks dropped to the floor much easier than Penn expected, given the snugness of their fit over her well-formed hips and buttocks. But then, he noted, the thong underwear she removed wasn't enough to interfere with the movement. She deftly removed it, as well, and stood completely nude, with her hands loose at her sides, as though waiting for approval. He wasted no time with comments.

"I admit," June purred with contentment, nearly an hour later. "You are as good you claim."

"Perhaps," Penn responded. "But, now," he added. "Why don't you tell me what you're after?"

"Maybe you're better than you claimed," she said with a frown as she sat up. Her breasts swayed invitingly with her movements as she reached over the side of the bed for her purse. Her reach revealed her womanhood, but she was unabashed. She extracted a pack of cigarettes and a lighter from her purse, stuffed a cigarette in her mouth, lit it, and leaned back against the bedstead as she blew out the smoke. "There is something," she said. "Something you might call sticky."

Penn sat up and leaned back against the bedstead. He poured a shot of rum from the bottle on the bedside table into the glass which was there so long it required a good soaking in dish water, not rum. He ignored the stains and thoughtfully took a drink. "Something sticky you don't want Thorne Beusch to find out about?" he asked at length. He grinned with his repeat of subtle humor.

She took the glass from his hand and took a long drink from it without answering.

THE EMERALD HEAD CAPER

"I figured as much," Penn said as he recovered his glass. "There had to be a reason for your change in attitude. This morning you weren't quite as susceptible to suggestion as one would have liked."

"As you would have liked," she corrected him.

"Whatever."

"The Emerald Head could be worth millions," she said. "Unbelievable, countless millions."

"If it exists," Penn cautioned.

"It does. I'm sure of it."

"So is your boss, apparently."

"Yes, but he doesn't see its real value. All he sees is something to be displayed in a museum, something with his name on a brass plaque beside it to give him fame."

"And you see it as something else?"

"As I said, countless millions." She took another puff on her cigarette and blew out the smoke in a long, slow exhale.

From the way she held in the smoke, Penn figured she was used to smoking something a little stronger. "And by screwing my brains out you figured you'd be able to talk me into giving it to you when I find it?"

"You really are quite good at what you do, aren't you?" She took a final puff on her cigarette, and reached across Penn to snuff it out on the ashtray on the bedside table. Her breasts were warm and inviting as they pressed against his chest, but he denied their invitation. "If you mean I'm a cynic as hell private investigator, you're right." He took another drink. Was he really saying that? Was he really turning down a shot at a million or so dollars? Was he being honest with himself, or did he already swallow too much rum to be thinking clearly?

"Maybe I should repeat myself," she said. "The Emerald Head is worth millions."

"You really expect me to take the money from Beusch and deliver the head to you?"

"He can afford it."

Penn frowned. He wasn't sure he liked this woman, after all.

"You're trying to tell me that's a bad idea?" she asked.

"It is for me." He hoped he wouldn't regret his decision.

"Everyone has their price," she said.

"And I'm pretty insulted by your thinking a good romp in bed with you is mine." It must be the rum, he decided.

"Don't be asinine," she retorted. "The romp, as you call it, was for my pleasure. I was thinking, maybe, half the value of the head might be your price."

"There's no price on my integrity," Penn stated flatly. No, he decided. It wasn't the rum.

She studied him. "I see." she said. She got out of bed.

Penn couldn't keep his eyes off her as she reached for her clothes. He watched her as she slipped into them with less effort than it took her to remove them. He wondered how many times she did that to get what she wanted. He wondered if her position with Beusch depended on her ability in that line. "You're leaving so soon?" he asked with sarcasm.

"I think so," she responded as she picked up her purse and turned to glare at him. "It's too bad, too. You're passing up more money than you can even imagine."

"Not to mention a good romp occasionally," he grinned.

She glared at him. "That, too," she angrily responded as she strode to the door. "If you ever change your mind," she added as she held the door open. "You know where to find me."

"Change my mind about the romp?" Penn chided.

She glared again, stomped out of the room and slammed the door behind her.

Penn shook his head. Maybe she's right. Maybe he is being foolish by turning down such a lump of money. Maybe Beusch is wrong. Maybe I'm not a man who can be trusted. After all, there's nothing to keep me from selling the Emerald Head to the highest bidder. If I ever find it, that is. If it even exists, that is.

He hopped out of bed, and was reminded how foolish it is to drink so much rum so early in the afternoon. He was unsteady as he headed for the shower. Maybe the hot water is running by now, he mused, as he turned on the faucets.

The water was hot when he got into the shower, but it only remained hot for several minutes. It was a good thing the cold water was always tepid, otherwise he wouldn't have been able to complete the relatively simple task of shaving without shaving cream, which was a habit he developed as a result of his many jungle treks. He looked at himself in the mirror, and wondered whether or not it was worth the effort, since half the day was wasted, already. But, a clean face made a clean man, he remembered his grandfather saying.

It took less than half an hour to get dressed, grab a taxi, and stop in at the Fort Street Guesthouse for something to eat. It was a little late for breakfast, but the owners of the Guesthouse always went out of their way for their preferred customers. He decided he was going to exercise his privilege as one of those preferred guests this morning.

The owners were two very busty American girls. They purchased the place several years earlier, and Penn was one of their preferred customers because he settled a minor altercation between them and the former owner. They felt so indebted to him for his help that they refused to let him pay for anything when he came in.

This time, though, he would pay them back for the over gracious hospitality. He would pay for his meal, and even give them a large tip. It wouldn't make any difference to them, but it would ease his conscience.

"Penn," Mary Mercale greeted him at the top of the stairs to the landing on the ancient three-story colonial house. "What a pleasant surprise. We ain't seen y'all in near a gator's age." She laughed. Her Alabama accent still pervaded her speech, even after a quantity of years listening to Belizean slang-glish. "What can we do for y'all?"

"Just a little something to eat," Penn replied, bracing himself against the inevitable hug she gave her friends of long standing. The woman's breasts were huge, and her hugs forced them into a person's chest, inhibiting breathing, until she felt satisfied enough to let go. Sometimes the hugs were frightening encounters. "And maybe a little information?" he added after catching his breath.

The girls managed to become a center for the dissemination of information in their tenure as owners of the Guesthouse. They made friends easily, and easily-made friends often easily made remarks about things that would seem unimportant. Most were unimportant, except for those tidbits the girls hung onto with remarkable insight as to their value.

"Well," Mary responded, as she led him to a table in the cooler and more remote end of the porch that served as the dining veranda. "What'll y'all have? Some grits and pone?"

Penn laughed. "I'm thinking more of something in the line of American food."

"Well, how about a nice, juicy hamburger?" she asked, as a waiter sauntered over with his order book.

"For breakfast?"

"Well, now. I always knew you were a Southerner at heart, Honey. I mean, gentlefolk don't always get up with the crack of dawn, I know, but this is Belize, and it is already after noon."

"Okay," he relented. "A hamburger it is."

"I know you'd see it my way, honey child." She nodded to the waiter, who returned the nod and headed for the kitchen.

"Well, that's good for the food," Penn said. "Now, how about a little information? Are you still keeping your ears open?"

"Might be. What y'all got in mind?"

"Puerto Barrios. A guy named Quigley?"

She sat at the table and considered the request while studying the street below the veranda. "I'd normally get a chunk of money for anything I might know about him."

"A hundred dollars?" Penn suggested.

"Honey child," she drawled, turning back to him. "From you? Y'all can't pay for anything here, y'all know that."

"Do you know him?"

"He's a dealer in antiquities. Mostly phony, I hear tell."

"That much I know. Anything else?"

"He's connected."

"With who?"

"Whom, honey child. With whom."

"Whatever."

"South American."

"Are you being reticent? It's not like you to be so secretive."

"I'm thinking, child. At my age, it takes longer for some things, y'know."

"Tell me about it," he grinned.

"And I'm thinking," she continued, "that there's a certain cartel in Columbia..."

"Not the Medellin?" Penn interrupted.

"Not the Medellin," she answered. "Someone who's a lot bigger and a lot stronger. Somebody they call Quad Lateral something or other. You know them?"

"Not the Quad Lateral Council?" Penn asked, surprised. He did know, and what he knew he didn't like. "He's part of them?"

"No, I don't think he's actually a part of them, not really. But, he is connected to them, somehow. At least I heard he is, know what I mean?"

Penn wasn't sure he knew what she meant, even though he said he did. There were times when mere conversation was at least as important as conversational content.

The rest of their conversation turned to more mundane items, mostly about local happenings, rumors, and talk of the strange activities of the local Chief of Police.

The latter topic, of course, was something of more than idle interest to Penn, since he had some experiences with the Chief's daughter, much to the Chief's dislike. But that was something he wasn't about to discuss at the moment. He didn't want to become more of a topic of information for some of Mary's other customers.

One thing he did do to titillate Mary's curiosity was order a plane ticket through her, since she was also a booking agent for one of the local air lines. When he told her he wanted a ticket for Punta Gorda, Belize, on Maya airlines, she couldn't deny her curiosity.

"Punta Gorda, honey child?" she asked. "Catching a boat across the bay to Puerto Barrios, are you?"

Penn shrugged, avoiding an answer.

The waiter returned with Penn's breakfast, and discretely returned inside.

"Well, honey child, y'all be careful, hear?" she said. "I'll get your ticket. You finish your eating. I'll be right back." She rose from the table and entered the main salon.

Twenty minutes later Penn finished his meal, gave Mary

his thanks, and headed for the street where he hailed a taxi. He stopped at his hotel room for his travel case, and forty minutes later he was at the Belize Municipal Airport on board the green, twin engine, eight-passenger high wing plane used by Maya Airlines, the second best airline company in Belize. It's second best because there isn't a third airline.

An hour and a half later, he stepped out of the plane onto the grass field beside the sleepy village of Punta Gorda. He strode into the Coast House Bar next to the boat dock, and ordered a Mayan Temple Belikin Beer, the beer of Belize. It wasn't really his favorite drink, but it was the only drink the bar sold, legally. It was better than nothing to help him pass the time waiting for the boat and the three-hour ride across the bay to Puerto Barrios, Guatemala.

"Another Belikin?" the bartender asked, retrieving Penn's empty bottle.

"Sure. Why not?" Penn responded.

Penn waited for the bartender to set the second bottle of beer in front of him, and reached for it, when someone stuck something round, and hard like metal, in the middle of his back. It was something that felt like the barrel of a gun. He grabbed the beer bottle by the neck, since it was the only weapon of self-defense available.

The bartender grinned.

Penn didn't appreciate the grin. It confused him.

"You no fa da move, Brudda," the person behind him said. "Chu give fa me da Belikin. It no gud fa da lak a chu," the voice added, barely concealing a chuckle.

"I'll be," Penn said. He realized why the bartender was grinning. The person signaled him to be quiet, and the reason was that the person was an old friend of Penn's.

"Lesley!" Penn exclaimed, turning around to greet the portly, dark skinned Belizean who sported a broad smile with two missing front teeth under a shaggy black mustache. "You old pirate!" he added, as he pumped his friend's hand in greeting. The object held at Penn's back was Lesley's ever-present faux-Merchaum pipe.

"What chu do fa da Punta Gorda, Mr. Penn?" Lesley responded with glee, returning his age-old pipe to a shirt pocket that was heavily stained from years of such actions.

"Just a little business to take care of," Penn responded. "Hey. You want a beer?"

"No," Lesley answered. "Chu know me never fa da beer drinkin'. Whisky, now, maybe, fa da frens lak chu, an' maybe one fa da old mans, now, true."

"You old goat. It's got to be Southern Comfort, right?"

"Fa da true," Lesley chuckled.

Penn shot the bartender a quizzical glance. The bar was one of the few in Belize that wasn't licensed for hard liquor. The alcohol taxes were too heavy for the town's population to support. That meant hard alcohol was not readily available. Not readily available meant that sometimes the bartender kept a bottle behind the counter, just for friends.

The bartender shrugged, looked around to assure himself none of the other half dozen or so patrons were from the local constabulary, reached under the bar, moved some things aside, and held up a bottle concealed in a brown paper sack. He quickly opened the bottle, filled a 10-ounce tumbler half full of the brown nectar, and returned the bottle to its hiding place. The amount in the glass was at least three normal drinks.

"How the devil can you drink so much whiskey at one time?" Penn asked his old friend. It was a never-ending surprise to him.

Lesley grinned broadly as he took a seat on the adjacent bar stool. "Be da 'sperience, Mr. Penn," he responded while grabbing the glass. He nearly emptied it of the contraband whisky in his first gulp. "So, now, Mr. Penn," he began, satisfied with the drink. "Wha chu be fa da Punta Gorda?" His question contained serious overtones.

Penn noted the change in demeanor. "Business," he answered with more somberness.

"Business?" He pondered the word. "May be some friens' of old be da bes' help fa da trip fa da biz'nez wid da Guats, true?" Lesley asked, although it was more of a suggestion.

Penn thought about the suggestion. "Well, now, maybe I can use a good interpreter," he said. "If you can keep your hands off the women, that is."

"Ah, Mr. Penn. Some t'ings I not be fa da help, true." He

hung his head in mock shame.

"You old lecher. You must be the father of Belize by now. How many kids are calling you daddy?"

"Oh, Mr. Penn. Every t'ing you hear, most not be fa da true," he chuckled.

"Only half the country?" Penn laughed.

"Fa da true," Lesley laughed.

The whistle blew from the dock.

Both men peered out the window at the boat dock. The Puerto Barrios boat was early. It was just pulling into the berth, and with waiting passengers lined up on the side of the 25 foot outboard boat, nearly tipping it over, waiting for their chance to disembark.

"I be fa da help?" Lesley asked for confirmation.

"You be fa da help, Mon," Penn responded in his poor copy of the local dialect. "Come. Fa da true." He pulled some cash out of his pocket and handed it over. "I think you have about ten minutes to get your ticket, your passport cleared, and onto the boat before it leaves," he said. "Better get moving."

Lesley beamed even more broadly. "I got da ticket, fa true, already," he said.

"Well, you old devil. You knew I was going to need you, didn't you?" He ignored the most obvious question. That of how Lesley knew he was going to Guatemala in the first place. He suspected his recent discussions with Mary at breakfast had something to do with that.

"Hey, Mon. I know chu, fa da true," Lesley smiled as some form of explanation.

"Okay. Let's go." Penn got off his barstool and headed out the door, followed by his old friend, who managed to drink the entire glaass of whisky in three gulps. He was glad he had run into Lesley, for not only was the man an excellent interpreter, but his knowledge of the people of Guatemala, and especially his connections in Puerto Barrios, were of inestimable value.

CHAPTER 5

The boat bounced along the bay for a little more than four hours, instead of the scheduled three. On the return trip to Puerto Barrios it had to fight the choppy seas raised by the late afternoon's head wind blowing in from mainland Guatemala.

"So, here we are in lovely Puerto Barrios, Guatemala, again," Penn remarked when he and Lesley passed through La Oficina De Imagracion De Guatemala. He double-checked his passport and the visa stamp. He didn't want a repeat of one of his prior trips when the visa stamp wasn't imprinted. He had a hard time getting out of the country on that trip. The problem with Guatemala's immigration, from a tourist's point of view, is the way the officers take possession of all the passports. They take them into their office out of view of the holder while they checked the validity of the passports, and kept everyone in a closed room until they stamped the passports and returned them one by one.

There was no problem with Penn's passport, although the Immigration Officer did eye him suspiciously when the document was returned. Few American tourists took this route to his country, and Penn's passport had an unusual quantity of visa stamps though Punta Gorda port of entry.

The first building Penn and Lesley faced when they left Immigration was a brick and broken stucco one that served as a bus station for La Coche De Latinos, the Coach of the Latins bus line.

"I t'ink maybe da bus be fa da better, true," Lesley suggested on seeing Penn studying the bus with a doubtful eye.

Penn was tempted to agree, but the appearance of the worn diesel behemoths parked nearby weren't all that reassuring. Besides, the memory of his last experience with one of the roaring, smoke belching road hogs wasn't reassuring, at all. That was his trip from Pochutla, Mexico, over the ten thousand foot high mountains to Oaxaca one summer when Lara left him on a nude beach in Zipolite for a pharmaceuticals salesman with an appendage that must have been surgically enlarged. But that was another story, one he didn't want to remember, at the moment. Maybe he'd put that one in the Great American Detective Novel he was going to write some day.

Just to the left of the building was the line of taxis. The drivers were leaning patiently on their old Fords and Chevrolets, all of which seemed driven to a state of near shambles. They were unbelievably battered, dented, and rusted to the point of decrepit uselessness. One wondered if they were held together by anything more than the heavy coats of wax and polish that made what splotches of paint that sparingly existed on them shine like a drill sergeant's boots. In the States, the hulks would have been junked years ago. Was this where those junked cars were sent? Were Guatemalan taxi drivers the junk car collectors for the world?

His thoughts were interrupted by the drivers who shouted for attention, hoping to be selected for a fare.

Penn glanced at Lesley. He knew Lesley's disdain for Guatemalan buses.

Lesley relented. "Taxi!" he yelled without waiting for Penn's orders.

Much to Penn's surprise, as loudly as they were calling and as animated as they were in their gesturing, the drivers exhibited an unusual amount of courtesy by deferring to the first driver chosen.

"Si, Senor," the driver mouthed through his crooked tooth smile. He discarded his half-smoked cigarette, jumped in his cab, and hurriedly struggled to get it started. The vehicle, a

THE EMERALD HEAD CAPER

Ford, finally coughed to life and lurched over to confront Penn and Lesley amid a swirling dust cloud thrown up by sliding the near bald tires to a harried stop. The driver nimbly hopped out and opened the rear passenger door, all the while grinning the typically friendly broad grin found on so many Guatemalans.

Penn wondered how these people could be so overtly friendly. Didn't they know what as going on in the interior of their country? Didn't they know that in the jungles the government army was nearly running amok? Half the time the troops had nothing to do but slug down Caribbean Rum and chase the natives in misguided attempts to quell some imagined revolutionary fervor. The other half of the time, the generals got rich by turning their backs on the drug lords.

Or, if they weren't doing that, the troops were plotting some other way to make themselves rich or famous, like trying to retake Belize on their own. The government of Guatemala still wasn't decided on whether or not it should recognize the independence of the upstart country they claimed was originally part of their territory,. Did the dwellers of the urban jungles even care what went on in the back country jungles?

Penn remembered having his share of confrontations and bad experiences in the Guatemalan jungle with the drug smuggling thugs. But that was yet another story he had to cast aside as he stepped into the rear of the cab.

He appraised the vehicle's tattered interior, and was on the verge of getting back out of the taxi, thinking it would be safer to let this cab be taken by someone else, preferably the junk yard tow truck driver.

The driver noticed Penn's reticence, and wasn't going to let this fare slip through his fingers. He knew that a little extra effort in handling Gringos usually paid off with a big tip at the destination. He also knew Gringos were generous tippers even when they were overcharged on the going rate for wherever they wanted to go, even when the overcharge was as much as five or six times the normal rate. After all, the tourists didn't know the normal rates. Besides, he didn't yet have a fare all day, and his wife would have a fit if he returned home empty handed. So, he quickly shut the door behind Penn, ran around the car, slammed the door shut behind Lesley, and scrambled in through the still opened driver's door, all before either of his would be fares had a chance to voice any objections.

The driver's door, though, took a little effort to shut, and that worried the driver. He feared his fares would have enough time to reconsider using him, if he didn't get the taxi moving. He cursed the door, slammed it, pounded it shut, and yanked on it, but still it refused to latch. It repeatedly bounced back open. He used one hand on the windowsill and the other on the door handle. With a mighty tug, he slammed it shut. It still didn't catch, so he gave up. He decided he would keep the door shut by hanging his arm over the windowsill.

He fought the engine to a start by cranking the key in the ignition so hard it was a surprise to Penn that it didn't break.

"Es bueno. Eet ees good, no?" The driver grinned as the engine finally coughed to life, and he reached for the gearshift lever. He crammed the transmission into gear, and with a lurch that seemed endemic to all cars south of Tijuana, headed off to wherever they might be going.

The driver nodded again with great enthusiasm, and with what was apparently the only English phrase he knew, proudly uttered it when he finally coaxed the car into third gear. "Eet ees good, no?"

He accelerated to a frightening speed. He averaged fifty miles per hour on the cramped city streets, and Penn wondered if the speed were necessary to keep the rattletrap running forward if the engine stopped.

The driver, of course, knew if the engine did stop, the taxi would coast at least a few meters further, costing his fares a few Quetzals more. It could be a scene right out of the Keystone Cops.

At least the taxi was getting them where they wanted to go, Penn mused, bracing himself for another reckless turn around a street vendor. The thought raised another question. "By the way," Penn asked Lesley. "Where are we going?" He didn't tell Lesley about his need to visit the Club Medellin.

"I t'ink," Lesley responded. "Da Hotel Berresford be fa da best, fa true, fa da night."

Before they managed to race past the first several blocks, the driver realized he didn't know where they were going, either. With a broad grin, he turned around to speak to his fares, ignoring the traffic ahead of him. "A Donde vamos?" he asked.

"A donde vamos?" Where are we going? Lesley quickly translated for Penn, although he needn't do so. "Vamos al Hotel Berresford," We are going to the Hotel Berresford. "Tu sabes a donde?" Do you know where it is?

The driver smiled and nodded.

The smile was lost on Leslie. "Cuidado!" he shouted. Look out!

The driver turned back around just in time to yank the steering wheel hard to the left to avoid a lumbering donkey cart hogging most of the traffic lane. The taxi veered wildly half way across the barely visible centerline, narrowly missing the poor animal.

The driver eyed his fares through the rear view mirror. "Si. Cuidado," he laughed back, once more turning his head all the way around, again ignoring the road. "Es good? Yes?"

"Well," Penn sighed. "Yes. Si. Es bueno," he replied, relieved the hapless animal was spared. And pleased, too, by the thought that perhaps his command of the Spanish language was at least passable. Maybe things will get off to a good start on this case. After all, he consoled himself as he ignored that nagging feeling in the back of his neck, things could be worse.

After several more near misses and last minute turns, none of which were quite as exciting as the near donkey encounter, the taxi slid to a stop and stirred up another dust cloud.

When the dust cleared, Penn looked out the side window at the three-story stucco building proudly displaying the name Hotel John Berresford across an arched brick entrance.

"Es good," the driver said once more.

"Si, Senor. Esta bueno," Penn confirmed. "Gracias," he added, as he struggled with the door to get out.

"Momentito," the driver uttered. He quickly got out and scurried around to the passenger side, and fought with the door to get it open. He won the struggle, and stood to one side while holding out his other hand with the palm upward to receive payment.

For a second, Penn suffered on1e of those memory lapses many people experience in alien environment. He

Harold R. Miller

couldn't remember how to ask what the fare was. So, instead of stumbling, he silently pulled a twenty Quetzal note from his pocket and handed it to the driver.

The driver politely nodded, and glanced down at the bill to determine its denomination. When he saw how much larger the denomination was than his expected five Quetzal fee, his grin broadened to a very large smile. "Muchas gracias, Senor," he said. "Muchas gracias," he repeated, bowing at the same time to such an extent that it caused his fares to wonder if he might be part Japanese.

"De nada," Penn responded with politeness. Still smiling at the driver, he turned and abruptly ran into a young dark hair girl with shining black eyes who came out to greet the hotel's newest guests. He nearly knocked her over.

"Oh, excuse me," Penn said with a start. "I didn't, ah, perdonme," he quickly restated his apology in Spanish. "I..." But he couldn't go on. Not only was his command of the language too lacking for such an encounter, but, the bright eyed woman was so embarrassed she turned around and strode back to the hotel without performing her assigned greeting duties.

"Que bonita," Leslie uttered, watching the girl. How pretty she is.

"Que bonita," Penn agreed.

The taxi driver had a sudden thought, and he yanked on Penn's shirtsleeve. "Senor," he said. "Es possible que su deseas un taxi por la noche? O, por la manana?" Is it possible that you want a taxi for the night? Or, for the morning?

Penn nodded off handedly. "Si. Es possible," It is possible, he said. "We might need a taxi later."

"Bueno. Es good. Aqui," he said as he pulled a neatly hand printed business card out of his pocket and thrust it at Penn. "Me llamo Esteban." My name is Esteban.

Penn took the card, "Gracias," he said. He stuck the card in his shirt pocket as he faced the hotel.

The driver smiled and scurried back to the taxi.

As Penn and Lesley passed through the hotel doors, they heard the cursing and shouting of the driver trying to get his taxi started.

They sauntered up to the well polished Spanish tile

counter, and found the beauty with the flashing eyes standing behind it.

She smiled at Penn, but not as bashfully as he did when outside. "Buenas dias," she said politely.

Penn wondered if the music in her voice was just for him, or if she sounded that way to everyone. You lecherous old man, he chastised himself. You're beginning to act like Lesley. She's got to be young enough to be your daughter. "Buenas dias, Senorita," he responded.

"How may I help you, Sir?" the girl asked in high British accented English.

"You speak very good English," Penn complimented her as he set his suitcase down.

The girl blushed again, slightly, but this time she stood her ground behind the counter. She obviously felt much more in control from there.

"I hope you have some rooms for rent," Penn said. "With showers?"

"Of course, Sir," the girl replied most politely. She was becoming sure of herself, now that the formality of business began. "For how long, sir?"

"Shoot. I'm not really sure." He shrugged, trying to answer. "Two, three days, maybe."

"Then I will let you have room number 2C. That room is on the second floor on the corner. There are windows in the corners to catch the breeze. That would be our most comfortable room." She reached for a key somewhere under the counter, set it on top of the counter, and opened the guest register. "Let's see, yes, room 2D for your friend. Would you please sign in? Will that be cash or credit card, Sir?"

Penn raised his eyebrow at her as he signed in.

"We usually require advance payment, Sir," she said in apology. "We have found that sometimes, and please realize I'm quite sure this isn't the case with you, that sometimes guests manage to stay longer than they first say, and forget, somehow, to pay their bill before checking out. Sometimes, I hate to admit, that they check out without actually telling us about it."

Penn smiled.

"270 Quetzals," she said politely.

Harold R. Miller

Penn calculated the amount in dollars. "100 dollars? For only two rooms?"

"Exactly, Sir."

"How convenient to have it come out exact. I wonder, is it planned that way?"

She smiled in silent response.

Penn considered her for a moment. Was this the same bright-eyed woman who was so shy a few minutes ago? He found such a possibility hard to believe as he pulled a bunch of bills out of his pockets. He was searching for the right quantity of Guatemalan money when she interrupted his thoughts.

"Ten percent discount is available if payment is made in dollars instead of Quetzals," she said.

At first Penn thought this to be accommodating, then realized that it really was a very practical request. American money on the black market can generate nearly double the official Quetzal per dollar exchange rate. He was beginning to think this woman's original embarrassment was due to something quite different than their little taxi side encounter. However, since he had several one hundred-dollar bills handy, he gave her one. She provided the change in Quetzals almost before he handed her the bill.

He retrieved the keys she handed over, gave one to Lesley, who was at the time contemplating a woman in the nearby restaurant, and idly glanced about the room. It wasn't until some time later that he wished he paid some attention to which key he gave Lesley.

He glanced at the guest register in front of him, and being the nosy investigator he was, scanned through the signatures, those he could read, that is.

Smith, John, Mr. and Mrs. Even in Guatemala, he mussed as he continued scanning the names. He discovered an entry for Thorne Beusch.

"Sir?" The girl looked up, confused, interrupting Penn's thoughts. "Is there something more?"

"Oh. I'm sorry," Penn regained his composure. "This name, here," he pointed. "When did this person stay here?"

The girl read the name, and looked up. "Mr.Beusch did not stay with us, Sir."

"He didn't?" Penn was skeptical. "Why would his name be on the list if she didn't stay here?"

The girl's brown wrinkled with her attempt to remember the circumstances. "Ah, because," she said at length. "He never did arrive. He telephoned his reservation, but never came in."

Penn looked at the signature again.

"That is my writing," the girl explained.

Penn looked up. He was going to ask why the name was in signature form rather than printing, but hesitated. Her answer was a bit evasive for him, but he had no chance to ask the question, because the telephone rang.The girl finished writing the room receipt. She handed it to Penn, and walked into the small alcove off the reception area to answer the phone.

Penn left the reception office still in awe of the interesting coincidence, noted that Lesley was busy with the local woman, and found his way to the outside staircase. He paced down the hallway and tried his key on 2C. It didn't work. He tried it a second time before he realized it was the wrong room, then sauntered to the next room, 2D. The key worked. Two cockroaches the size of Cuban cigars scurried out from underneath the door and across the walkway as he stepped into the" he said, room. The smell of humid, musty air greeted his entrance, as though the room was seldom used. He wondered how long it was since this particular room was occupied. For some reason the question was answered by a tingling sensation down the back of his neck.

He ignored the feeling with a shrugging of his shoulders, turned on the light, and shut the door. He stretched, yawned, and felt the oppression of the still air. He crossed the room to open one of the windows, and went into the well-tiled, but very small, bathroom to turn on the shower.

The barely noticeable dribble of water from the showerhead was more than disappointing, but since there was no other choice, it would have to do.

He undressed at the bed, and returned to step across the six-inch barrier separating the shower area from the rest of the bathroom. He had to chase another hated cockroach out of the drain, but, as much as he hated insects, cockroaches were things a person got used to in the tropics.

Harold R. Miller

Half an hour later he finished his shower, sprinkled himself with Arimas cologne, put on fresh clothes - a pair of jeans and an open short sleeve shirt which he left un-tucked - and got ready for dinner in the hotel restaurant. He hoped the menu offered something other than the typical rice and beans supplemented with corn tortillas. He also wondered how Lesley was making out, but the question wasn't a major concern. Lesley would always make out. That was why the man was called the father of Belize. Most people, who didn't know the man, thought the nickname to be a joke.

The Guatemalan hotel cuisine turned out to be a pleasant surprise. There was an impressive selection of soups, salads, entrees ranging from Bifteca to Camarones, and there were desserts of various types, the least expensive of which was his long time favorite, Flan. He chose the steak. He also substituted Coca Cola for his usual ginger ale to drink with the Caribbean rum, conceding, after all, it was Puerto Barrios on the Caribbean coast, and it was in the Caribbean where Cuba Libres were invented.

After the waiter left with the order, Penn leaned back, gazed out the window, and relaxed while waiting for his meal to arrive.

The day was creeping into twilight, and the cars passing on the street were turning on their headlights. Their drivers were as interesting in their variation as the cars they drove. Some cars were Cadillacs, some Fords, some Jeeps, and then there was a rare selection of smaller, racier Japanese cars. Rice Rockets, he called them.

He was in the middle of his second Rum and Coca Cola by the time Lesley arrived at the table. The man was nervous and fidgety. Penn stared at him for several seconds.

"We be fa da problem, true," Lesley complained as he sat down. He looked about him nervously as he spoke.

"What the devil's bothering you, old friend?" Penn asked.

"A spirit, Mon," Lesley said. "Chu see da spirit some time, Mon?"

"The spirit?" Penn considered the question. "No," he said at length. "I don't think I ever have. Why?"

THE EMERALD HEAD CAPER

"Dis fa da spirit, fa da true!" Lesley nervously said, handing over a note he held clasped in his right hand. "Da spirit be fa da Head."

"What's this?" Penn retrieved the note. He unfolded it and held it up to the light. "Forget the Emerald Head," he read.

He looked up at Lesley. "What does this mean?" he asked.

The message was neatly written in cursive, almost like a woman's handwriting. He surmised the note's author had to have been American. The warning was too much of an Americanism. Was the threat an act of revenge by June? For his not agreeing to her larceny? The idea seemed too bizarre for him.

He turned the note over, and suddenly realized he stepped into something much more complicated than just locating an Emerald Head, something much more complicated than he ever wanted to get involved with. On each of the four corners of the note was printed a large letter 'C', the sign of the Quad Lateral Council. He heard about that organization from another private investigator friend in California. What he heard was not complimentary.

"I t'ink," Lesley said. "I t'ink chu search fa da Head."

"Lesley," Penn responded with slight frown, stuffing the note in his pocket. "You amaze me. What head are you talking about?"

"Da Emeral' Head," he answered. "It mean chu look fa da Emeral' Head. True?"

Penn wasn't going to be lead into explaining his mission quite so easily. "Well. Since you seem to have some idea that I'm in search of this so called Emerald Head, what suggestions, and I'm sure you have some or you wouldn't have brought up the subject, do you have to make?"

Lesley frowned. "Da Emeral' Head," he said at length, with serious caution, looking about as he spoke. "Fa da true da Emeral' Head be real 'nuff, and it be fa da spirits. Fa da true I worry fa da mon, Mon. Fa da true da spirit fa da Head it mak chu lak dead. I t'ink chu no look fa da Head, Mon. Fa true. Chu look fa da Head? Soon chu be lak da head, Mon. Dead. Fa da spirit true."

Penn couldn't deny Lesley's inquisition in the face of his

friend's sincere concern. He slowly nodded. "Okay. Yes. That is what I'm looking for," he admitted.

Lesley's eyes darted about.

"Actually, it isn't the head that I'm looking for here in Guatemala. It's a map. Well, part of a map, actually, that I'm looking for." He was surprised by Lesley's sudden, near overwhelming fear. It wasn't like the man.

Lesley peered at Penn for several minutes in silence.

"I'm supposed to see a man named Squiggly, ah, I mean Quigley," Penn said, hoping to calm Lesley's fears. "I don't suppose you have any idea where I can find him?" he added for diversion.

"Mr. Queegly. He be fa da Club Medellin, true. In Puerto Barrios," Lesley said quietly, all the while peering around the room as though the spirit he was fearing would suddenly pounce on him from out of the shadows.

"Well, for Pete's sake, Lesley. How would you know something like that?"

"I hear a da mon, Mon. He bad, too. Chu wan fa da see da mon fa da head?"

Penn shrugged his shoulders in affirmation.

"Den," Lesley finally said. "I fa da go bak to da Belize, true." He sounded sad. "I no wan be fa da Queegly. I no wan fa da be dead. I no be fa da help. Too bad, Mr. Penn." Again, he nervously peered about him.

Penn was surprised by Lesley's actions, but he didn't try to stop his friend. Lesley had a mind of his own, and once it was made up, it was impossible to stop him. "What the devil is so frightening about this Emerald Head, anyway, Lesley?" he asked. "If it exists, that is?"

"I know da head be fa da spirit. Das all. Strong be da spirit. Chu want be fa da know? Chu ask chu fren' in Belize, da Chief fa da Police. He tell true be fa da spirit, Mon."

Penn finished his drink and ordered his third. "Lesley," he said. "I'll tell you what. Why don't you have a drink or two of good old Southern Comfort, and We'll talk about it. You know I wouldn't ask you to do anything that would be so dangerous." He smiled warmly, the nodded to the waiter.

Lesley was reluctant to stay even long enough to have

his favorite beverage. "You luk fa da map? Not'ing more?" He asked.

"Nothing more."

"Chu no look fa da head?"

"I'm not going to look for the Emerald Head, not here in Guatemala."

Lesley seemed to relax. "Den, maybe I be fa da whisky, true." He smiled at last, although somewhat nervously.

The waiter returned with the whisky, along with Penn's dinner.

Spirit? He thought of Lesley's words. The spirit of the Emerald Head can kill you? That was a puzzler to him, but he wasn't going to bring up the subject again. Not yet.

By the time he finished his dinner, Lesley downed the two whisky's, along with one more, and was looking considerably less dour.

"Now, old friend," Penn began, taking a sip from his own drink. "How do you suppose we get to the Club Medellin?"

"I t'ink," Lesley responded. "Chu tahk wid Mr. Esteban. Da taxi man."

Penn noted the emphasis on the word you, but even so, it was a good suggestion. "Okay. I'll call him," Penn said, "What're you going to do?"

Lesley grinned. "I t'ink, may be da womans I know in Puerto Barrios. I t'ink may be I tahk wid her."

"Well, whatever," Penn said with a shrug.

"Oh, Mr. Penn," Lesley added as Penn got to his feet. "Dat Mr. Esteban?"

"Yeah?"

"He spik wid gud English." He grinned slightly more broadly.

"Well, what the? How would you...? Why...?"

It was Lesley's turn to shrug and grin slyly.

"I'll remember that," Penn said, as he headed for the front desk. He dug up the business card Esteban handed him, and asked the woman at the desk to please telephone him, then, almost as a second thought, he had an interesting idea. He asked her if she could look up a name for him in the telephone book.

He was surprised when the girl found the number for Quigley, and after asking her for another favor, that of dialing the number, he reached the man without difficulty.

CHAPTER 6

At nine that evening Penn stepped out of Esteban's taxi. He hadn't tested Esteban's command of the English language, yet, thinking he might want to save what advantage the little bit of knowledge about Esteban's game might provide at some later time.

He handed Esteban a ten Quetzals bill, and with a few drops of the evening's rain tapping on his semi-bald head, faced the entrance to the Club Medellin. It's an interesting name for a club, he mused, considering the amount of publicity the Medellin drug cartel got of late. He wondered why the owners would select such a name. He hoped it wasn't because of any nefarious connection to the cartel.

The interior of the bar was dimly lit, and the band behind the spotlighted stage blared out some faintly recognizable Latin American melody. It was easily identified as Latin American by the pounding of the conga drum.

He found a table not too close to the stage, in a position that allowed him to watch the lone entrance. James Quigley was supposed to be coming through the entrance sometime before nine thirty, according to the woman behind the counter at the hotel. He didn't question her about her source for that particular tidbit of information, but assumed it was because the man was well known and was a creature of habit.

The waiter quickly arrived, ready to take his order. He

knew Gringos were usually good tippers.

Penn mumbled something about a Cuba Libre in his not too perfect Spanish, and let his thoughts run free as he glanced about the stage, peering through the smoke filled room. The semi-nude girl in the middle of the stage was performing some twisting, turning movements that were supposed to be erotic in cadence with the conga drum.

Burlesque, he mused. That's what they called it in the fifties to keep the dance out of the lewd and lascivious realms of the day's moral standards. In the sixties it was Interpretive Dancing. Recently, the term changed to Topless Dancing, and Adult Entertainment.

The single aspect continuous through the years was the ever present full sized mirror on the back of the stage. It was either for the audience's appreciation of the rear view of the performer, or for the performer's use for self-reassurance. Whatever the age and stage setup, the purpose was the same: to goad the customer into wanting to stay longer and buy more drinks.

The waiter delivered the rum and coke.

Penn tasted the drink, and was pleasantly surprised to find that the bar served Myers's Rum as a well drink. He paid the waiter with a twenty Quetzal bill, made note of the change, as though he actually knew what it should be, and returned to his musing. He took another sip, and killing time, let his thoughts wander. He thought about the name Myers's. It was the only word in the English language he knew which was spelled with an 's' followed by apostrophe 's'.

The band's beating grew louder, and the customers urged the dancer in the second of her three dance routines, into more rhythmic movements. She complied with the demands, though her performance was as trite as Salome's. Her only twist to the art was a serpent tattoo that wrapped around her right leg, which was revealed little by little with each movement.

Penn finished his drink and set the glass on the table. He signaled for another, but the waiter was too far away to notice, and he was forced to be patient.

"Por favor," he said as the water passed in is direction.

The waiter heard him, loud as he was, and so did

several girls leaning against the bar. Some of them nodded enthusiastically in his direction, and he appraised them with a casual glance. He decided there were a few among the half-dozen or so who might make enjoyable acquaintances, but he shook his head against their beguiling smiles. He had work to do.

The waiter returned with the second Cuba Libre, set it down, held up 3 fingers to indicate the charge was 3 Quetzales, and sifted through the pile of Quetzals on the table.

Penn watched the waiter with interest, knowing how quickly an extra bill could be slipped up a shirt cuff without being detected. It was something most any waiter could do, if the waiter had enough larceny in his soul and enough experience in dark clubs, that is. He decided this waiter had the experience, but not the larceny.

The waiter was very careful. He selected a 5 Quetzal note, showed it to Penn for approval, and smiled a thank you for the two Quetzal tip he administered himself.

Penn was halfway through his second drink, and the next girl on stage was halfway through her second dance, when three men entered the lounge. Two of them were dark skinned Latinos, whom he judged to be Guatemalan, or maybe Honduran, with black hair and matching large black mustaches - he wondered if they were brothers. The third man was a Gringo, impressively larger than the Latinos, towering over them by at least a foot. He was massive enough to make two of his Latino associates, and wore his dirty-blonde hair in a crew cut reminiscent of the military. The clean-shaven face was a contradiction in itself, showing a fixed smile under dark, piercing eyes. Probably an ex-Jarhead, Penn guessed. His instincts warned him the man's smile was at least misleading, if not dangerous.

The trio followed the accepted form of protocol for Latin American gangsterism, or so Penn thought, in that the important man, the VIP, was the second person in line, always between his two subordinates. In this case, the second man was the Gringo, and Penn expected the two Latinos to be bodyguards.

The trio stood for half a minute or so just inside the door, looking around. The Gringo pointed to a table near the wall across the room, and they headed for it, keeping the format of their assemblage in its proper structure while weaving around the scattered tables in single file.

When they sat, Penn thought it curious that neither of the smaller men offered a chair for the Gringo, which would have been proper status recognition in a Latin country.

They got immediate service, though, which meant they were known in the lounge, and were used to attention. They felt they were important, and they showed it in their manners.

Penn guessed the Gringo to be Quigley. He didn't like their first impression, so he decided to wait awhile before he let himself be known.

The girl on stage was in the final throes of her version of a carefree Samba dancer, and the red stage lights over her head shimmered in her perspiration. She spent so much of more of her time watching her image in the mirror, that it was questionable whether her efforts were designed for the audience's enjoyment or her own.

The dance ended among a spattering of light clapping from the audience, and Penn decided it was time to get on with his business. He rose, picked up his change, and with purpose, strode through the crowd to the trio's table. He sat in the fourth chair without an invitation.

The still attendant waiter rushed over to take his drink order, nodding nearly apologetically to the trio for his lapse in prompt attention.

Penn ignored the waiter, and played the game of macho self-importance while the three men eyed him with interest. Slowly, he took in their expressions, each in turn, making sure his eyes met theirs for a second of appraisal before going to the next. It was a ploy to make them realize he knew what he was doing, that he dealt with dangerous men before, and wasn't the least bit afraid. Or at least that was the impression he thought he was making.

The Gringo was the last to feel Penn's gaze.

The music from the stage filled the awkward silence while the men returned their confused stares.

At length the Latino on Penn's left uttered the merest grunt.

Penn realized he almost made a mistake. He quietly

turned his stare back to the first Latin, smiled, held out his hand, saying, "Soy Penn Gwinn. Con mucho gusto." I'm Penn Gwinn. Pleased to meet you.

The Latino's frown lessened.

Penn's original assessment of protocol was wrong. The important man of the trio was the little Latin, not the Gringo.

Before anything else could be said, the group's attentions were distracted by the outside night light that suddenly glimmered in through the opening front door, and then blocked by the form of a huge man entering.

The huge man was alone, and was definitely an American, another Gringo. He was a near perfect match to the description Penn was given: immense build, probably 6 feet three or four inches, crew cut hair, and clean shaven. The only thing left out was the potbelly that developed over years of swilling cheap beer in most of the foreign dives of the world. On comparison, he was much more fitting to the description than the Gringo sitting with the Latinos. Two such people in the bar in such and out of the way town at the same time was a coincidence Penn didn't want to consider, other than to note its oddity.

The huge Gringo found a table, then played with one of the B-girls who came over to hustle him. The man was evidently well known in the Club Medellin, as well known as the trio.

Meanwhile, the smaller Latino's frown slowly developed into a formal smile, as Penn's attention returned to the table. "El gusto es mio," the more equal Latino said at length. The pleasure is mine. "¿Pero, que quieres?" But, what do you want? Evidently the man was pleased by the recognition Penn gave him in priority over the Gringo.

Suddenly Penn was at a loss for words. He didn't know what to say to these men, since it became evident neither one of them was the man he was there to find. "Does anyone speak English?" he asked.

The two Latinos smiled. "No. Lo siento," they responded in unison. No. I'm sorry.

Penn forced a smile in face of the non-English response to the question expressed in English. "Senores," he said. "Perdonme. Mi Espanol is mucho malo." Sirs. Excuse me. My Spanish. It is very poor.

THE EMERALD HEAD CAPER

"Okay, Amigo," the main Latino said in clear English. "What do you want with the council?"

The question stunned Penn. The Latino's sudden use of perfect English enunciation wasn't the surprise. It was the question relating to the Council. That was the shocker. "Ah, the Council?" he nearly stammered, stalling for time, trying to think, thinking it was time to get himself out of what could be a most delicate, and dangerous situation. "The Emerald Head," he said.

He wished he had taken more time to think. He wasn't sure he wanted anything from that reprehensible organization.

Both Latinos and the Gringo leaned forward in anticipation. "What about it?" the Gringo demanded.

"I'm sure I know how to find it," Penn responded, realizing he had to follow up on the ploy to extricate himself from this mess. Maybe they would take the bait and let him off the hook, if he played it right, that is.

"And how would that be?" the Latino interjected with utmost politeness.

"Uh, unh, unh," Penn responded evasively. "I need to speak to the top man on this one. When the time comes, I'll talk to him." He grinned sardonically as he rose. "You know where to find me."

The Latino smiled with confidence. "I'm sure we do," he said.

Penn didn't like the sound of that, but he ignored its premonition. "Bueno," he said. "Hasta, Senores," he added. Until later. He got to his feet and returned to his own table to sort out the unexpected turn of events.

Meanwhile, the huge Gringo glanced about the room amid the gestures of his playful companion. He carefully appraised each customer who might be non-Latin, what few of them there were, and he finally came to Penn.

Penn nodded in acknowledgement, and held his drink up to signal recognition. He hoped this was the real Quigley, and not another Q4C operative. They were everywhere, he speculated. Like doggie-do on the streets of Metropolis.

The second Gringo got to his feet, leaving the chair with amazing ease for someone of his bulk, and threaded his way among the tables to squeeze in a chair opposite Penn. "I gather you're the guy who called?" he asked, wasting no time with introductions.

"Penn Gwinn," Penn responded, extending his hand, recovering from his most recent faux pas with the trio.

"Jim Quigley," the man said, as he reached over the table and shook Penn's hand with a grip that might have been better used for strangling sheep. "What is this thing you told me you're looking for that you think I might be able to help you with?"

"I appreciate your coming to meet me, Mr. Quigley. Can I offer you a drink?" Penn parried. He didn't like Quigley's direct approach. It was too affable, too glib and quick witted. Besides, he wasn't going to be specific until he was certain this man wasn't associated with the other three.

One thing, though, was certain. He wasn't as enthusiastic about finding the Emerald Head as he was when romping with June. But then, he argued with himself, the money was as a strong incentive. He frowned inwardly. At one time he would have scoffed at the question of the money, but that was a long time ago. That was another story he didn't want to think about.

Quigley smiled at the ploy, and grabbed at a waitress passing the table. "Hey, Honey," he said, playfully grinning at her. "Bring me a drink, like a good girl, okay?"

The girl laughed and ran her hand over his short cut hair, then hurried over to the bar.

"I represent a certain collector of, ah, older things of value, let's say," Penn began, being careful in taking the initiative, still considering dollar signs. "I hear you can help me with such items."

Quigley shot back a frown. He studied Penn with a gaze that was less than friendly.

Penn smiled casually in defense.

"People get killed in this country for making that kind of insinuations," he growled.

"Hey! I'm not making any insinuations," Penn countered. "First of all, I didn't say you were someone who sold such things. I merely noted that I represent someone who is looking for someone who does, and that perhaps you might know someone like the person I'm looking for." He took a sip of his drink. He was surprised at how calm his hands were. He didn't spill the drink. Maybe it was because what he already consumed had a calming effect on his nerves.

The waitress delivered Quigley's drink, patted him on the head again as she took some of the Quetzals he held out, and laughed again in response to his wink.

Quigley took a sip of his drink in consolation, and returned his attention to Penn. "Yeah?" he said, placing the half-empty glass on the table. "Who?"

"What?" Penn was again surprised.

"Who do you represent?" Quigley shot back. "And what makes you think I know anything about whoever you're looking for? Who told you I might?"

"Actually, the answer to that question is just a bit delicate, you might say." He paused, taking another sip from his drink, playing for time.

"Delicate?"

"Ummh," Penn nodded while savoring his drink. "You see, my client is, well, you most likely know my client." He had trouble getting to the point.

"Who?" Quigley interjected.

"Thorne Beusch." Get right to the point, he decided.

"Cripes."

"You do know him, then?"

"He sent you to look after his wife, didn't he? You're a P.I., right?"

Penn nearly choked. Now what the hell? What did Beusch's wife have to do with anything? "Ah, no. Not exactly," he managed to say without mumbling his surprise. "I am a Private Investigator, true." He paused for thought. "But as to his wife, no. As a matter of fact, his words were..." Penn had to take another sip to think of some effective ruse. "...that he couldn't care what happened to her. He's only interested in the one thing that drew him to Guatemala in the first place. The Emerald Head."

Quigley suddenly laughed uproariously, loudly.

Penn was confused. His expression must have shown it.

Quigley stopped laughing long enough to peer at him, then laughed again.

Penn's frustration over-rode his caution. "What's so darned funny?"

"You."

Penn cocked his eyebrow in question.

"Either you're a damn fool for thinking I'd believe that, or you're a bigger fool for believing Thorne when he told you that."

"Meaning?"

"There's no such thing as the Emerald Head," he said, regaining control of his amusement. He stared at Penn. "Which kind of fool are you?" he asked at length.

"I don't like being called a fool," Penn responded with a frown. He wanted to call the man's bluff, but he didn't want to sound threatening. He didn't relish the idea of fighting a man of Quigley's bulk in such tight quarters, especially after having had so much to drink. "And I don't think you're fool enough to believe your attempt to sidetrack my mission will work."

Quigley became sullen. He stared.

He stared for longer than Penn felt comfortable with, which made Penn slowly and cautiously reset his footing under the table, just in case he had to get to his feet in a hurry.

Quigley had another surprise. He once more busted out laughing.

The waiter serving the next table looked over. He began to chuckle, albeit somewhat nervously. So did the two girls with the two local men at the other table.

Penn was forced to join the laughter, more out of relief than in sympathy with Quigley, but the effect was the same. The laughing relieved the tension, and he hoped that was its purpose, to ease the tension instead of being a subterfuge. Quigley was evidently a man in full control of himself.

"You really do believe that crap about that head?" Quigley asked, when he stopped laughing.

Penn shrugged his shoulders.

"You're sure Beusch didn't concoct that story just to get you down here to check up on his wife?"

"Like I said...."

"Bull bleep."

"Hunh?"

THE EMERALD HEAD CAPER

"Bull bleep. Nora Beusch was, is, the only thing that matters to that man. I know that, and you should know that."

"I don't know that, and frankly, I couldn't care less. Besides, I thought he had more than an unassociated interest in his secretary."

"Secretary? June?"

Penn shrugged again.

"June's his cousin."

That statement added to Penn's confusion. It was a strange family, he concluded, reaching for his drink. "The Emerald Head is the only thing I'm after," he said with emphasis before taking a drink.

It was also Quigley's turn to taste his drink. It was only a sip, but one of his sips was a double sized gulp for Penn, or for any other man. He completed his tasting by downing the drink in one final tossing. "Okay. Well, whatever," he said afterward. He got to his feet. "Whatever," he repeated, chuckled again, and strode out of the bar.

Penn watched his exit, and the dissipation of the only lead for the map, with some consternation. Now what the hell do I do? He asked himself.

He signaled for the waiter, who complied, and seconds later there was a third rum and coke on the table in front of him. Only this time he couldn't pay for it. Someone else had.

"El Senor Queeglee lo pagada," the waiter said. Mr. Quigley paid for it.

"He paid for it?" Penn translated. "Now, why would he have done that?"

His question was sidetracked by a musician thumping conga drums on the stage. The big star of the show discarded her last veil to reveal the entire serpent tattoo on her right thigh, with the serpent's head disappearing in a suggestive location. He decided he wasn't interested in watching any more the show, so he finished his drink, stuffed his money in his pocket, and left.

CHAPTER 7

Charley Pulltrousers sprawled lazily over the bench attached to the rough wood picnic table. It was one of several tables perched under the tall coconut palms on the white sand beach. It was a beach usually filled with tourists during the day, with tourists who hadn't yet learned the dreaded secret of the Caribbean - the tiny, biting, nearly invisible sand flies whose bite caused an itching welt that lasted for weeks.

It was in the early evening, just after sundown, when the tourists had no further need for the outdoors without sunshine, when Charley gazed across the table at his friend stuffing another rock of crack cocaine into the smoking pipe. He lazily, dreamily, smiled. "It be gud stuff, Mon," he said in his typical Belizean Creole accent.

The two friends finished the first pipe-full of the poison, and Charley thought it was a short smoke, too short. It seemed as though his friend didn't put a very big piece into the pipe, because his friend knew the pipe was going to be shared with him. He was disappointed by such a thought. "Gud stuff, Mon?" Charley repeated.

"Yah, Mon," his friend finally answered without looking up.

"Chu gwan gif me da more, Mon?" Charley asked, eyeing his friend.

"Yah, Mon," his friend said, reaching into his pocket for

another rock.

Charley eyed the second piece and wondered at its color. He didn't see the first piece before it was lit, but this second piece wasn't milky clear like it always was before. Was his long time friend up to no good with that colored stuff? "Hey, Mon," he asked. "Wha' chu mak' wid dat stuff, Mon? Dat stuff no good. Dat stuff green, Mon. It lak do color da jungle, Mon. It no gwan be gud."

His friend smiled, crammed the small canvas bag containing the rest of the crack back into his pocket, and struck a match on the table top to light the pipe. "Dis be gud stuff, Mon. Color lak da jewel," his friend said.

"Where chu come wid dat stuff, Mon? Who gwan gif da chu?" He wanted to know where his friend had gotten such funny looking stuff.

"Hey, Mon," his friend defended himself. "I gwan wid a friend, huh? Gud friend, Mon. A Guat, Mon. He say he gwan get fa da friend he gwan be da Colombian, Mon."

"Colombian?" Charley repeated his friend's words. "Chu gwan get wid a Colombian wid dis stuff, Mon?"

"No, Mon. Lak I say. I gwan get wid a friend. He a Guat, Mon. Da Guat, he gwan git wid da Colombian, I t'ink, Mon. He gif fa da me, true."

Charley listened to the story. So his friend's friend was from Guatemala. He wasn't too sure he believed that. He wasn't sure he liked it, even if it were true. The friend from Guatemala was out of reach if the stuff was no good, he thought. But he needed the junk now, so he reached out his hand, palm upward, expecting his friend to let him have the pipe. With some consternation he noted how his friend was hoarding the pipe, not offering it.

He reached over to grab the pipe, but his friend turned aside, taking a long puff on the pipe instead. "Hey, Mon," he complained. "Chu no wan' do dat fa da me, true!"

"Wha chu mean, Mon?"

"I mean, chu go 'way wid da stuff, Mon," Charley iterated his complaint. "What chu fa da do dat, Mon? Chu no wan' wid da share, Mon? What?"

"Share? Hey, Mon. I wan' wid da share, Mon. You gwan

fa da ask, Mon. Tha's all. No fa da ask, no fa da share, Mon."

"Ask?" The thought of having to beg from his friend irked Charley's pride. "Mon, I no gwan da ask. Chu gwan gif fa da me now. I no gwan fa da ask, Mon. I tol chu now, chu gwan gif fa me wid da share."

Charley's friend was angered in response. He changed his mind about sharing his pipe. "Mon. Chu anger me. I don' gif chu dis gud stuff, now. No way. Not now, Mon. True."

Charley eyed his friend suspiciously.

His friend continued the rationalization. "I gwan cotch'm by me own dis stuff. I don' gwan gif wid no ones. I don' haf gif, now, Mon. Chu gwan know dat."

Charley's anger rose. He was having his doubts about his so-called friend. The man was unreasonably obstinate, saying there was no reason why the stuff would have to be shared. Sure, his friend got it himself, but he still should share all of it. "I say da chu now, Mon!" Charley was emphatic. "You gwan mak gif wid haf da stuff wid chu friend, Mon. Right now, Mon!"

"Chu say, Mon?" His friend challenged Charley's demand.

"Mak wid da stuff, Mon," Charley retorted.

His friend nearly sneered to rebuke the demand.

"Now, Mon!" Charley demanded louder. "Chu no gwan gif fa da me now, Mon, I gwan fock chu op!" He expected the threat of a beating to be enough to coerce his friend, even though the man was the taller of the two by at least half a head.

"Hah!" his friend snorted. He took another puff off the pipe, shutting his eyes, feeling the dreamy effect of the smoke.

Charley fumed. In face of his anger, his friend dared to take another puff on the pipe. At that rate, he knew, all the crack for smoking would soon be gone, and he didn't have enough money to buy any of his own.

"Chu gif wid da stuff da me now, Mon!" Charley demanded once more, his anger evident, close to being out of control. "Or..."

"Or wat, Mon?" his friend challenged.

"You no gwan gif da me, Mon, I gwan spik wid da Man, Mon. I gwan say fa da Man you mak wid him wallet, Mon. Day gwan tak chu fa da jail."

THE EMERALD HEAD CAPER

His friend lifted a wallet from some tourist in the Fort George Hotel the night before, and spent all the money from the wallet on several rocks of crack cocaine. His friend promised him half of it when they met, to make sure he wouldn't tell anyone about the theft. But now his friend was backing out on the deal.

"Chu, Mon! Chu selfish, Mon!" Charley nearly shouted. He needed some crack to fill his habit, and now his friend was going to smoke it all without giving him a second shot at it.

His friend took another puff off the pipe.

That pushed Charley over the edge. "I gwan fock chu op, Mon," he said, shifting his eyes around to see if anyone was near. At the same time, he looked for something to use to teach his friend a lesson. He grinned in satisfaction. Near at hand was his weapon, a palm branch that broke off a nearby palm tree. It would be a good and proper weapon, he knew, because the edges were serrated, like a huge knife. When someone was stuck with that, they felt it. He would really make his point if he hit his friend with that. In one last attempt, hoping to avoid a fight at the last minute, he reached for the pipe.

But the friend dodged his reach.

Charley pushed his friend in the chest, hard.

When his friend braced himself to keep from falling back off the bench, Charley jumped up and scrambled over to the base of the tree with surprising speed. He picked up the branch and ran back to stand over his friend. He swung the branch over his friend's head in angered frenzy. "Now I gwan fock chu op!" he shouted, as he swung the branch down hard on top of his friend's head.

His friend raised his arms to fend off the blow, but he was too slow. The palm branch stuck him in the center of the head, splitting it wide open. He slowly crumpled off the bench and sank to the sand, blood spurting from the wound. The pipe bounced off the table and rolled a few feet away across the sand.

Charley stared at his friend. The adrenaline coursed heavily through his veins. "Chu now be focked op, Mon," he said. He looked around, dazed. He didn't expect the blow to be so lethal, but there was nothing he could do about it. He spied the pipe. He dropped the branch and picked up the pipe, stuck it in his mouth, and took a deep draft off it.

The cocaine was nearly gone. With a sly expression of alertness, he remembered the canvas pouch his friend stuck in his pocket. He reached into his former friend's pocket, recovered the bag, and stuck it in his own pocket.

He pulled up his belt, took another long pull off the pipe, sat on the bench, and leaned back, waiting for the tainted smoke to settle in his lungs.

The drug flowed through his blood stream and made his eyes cloud over with its thrill. "Now," he repeated a little softer,

"Now, Mon, I gwan mak me fock op wid dis stuff." With a smile he got to his feet and wandered off down the road, forgetting his dead former friend.

He was no longer concerned the crack was the color of the jungle instead of clear white, like it should be. It still tasted the same, maybe even better.

CHAPTER 8

It was after eight in the morning when the day's mounting heat forced Penn awake. He didn't turn on the air conditioner when he went to bed, because he hated its artificial effect.

He chased away the cockroach when he showered, dressed, and left his room. As he passed 2C, he noted the door was ajar. He poked his head inside the room in hopes of finding Lesley still there. He could use his friend's company, if the man had already kicked out his latest paramour and got out of bed, that is.

Lesley wasn't out of bed, though. He would never get out of bed again. He was sprawled across the sheets, with his eyes fixed in a frozen stare at the ceiling. A pool of blood spoiled the mattress around him, dripping onto the Spanish tile floor.

"Ah, damn it," Penn swore under his breath. He quickly stepped back to look up and down the corridor. For some reason, probably stemming from his former training, he wanted to avoid being seen when he stepped inside the room and quietly shut the door.

He scanned the room for anything that might tell him what happened, grimly noting how the color of the blood didn't match the room's burnt amber decor.

There was nothing that indicated a motive for the murder. It couldn't have been robbery, he reasoned. Lesley didn't look like a tourist; he didn't look like he had any money. Revenge? For what? For seducing someone's wife? He considered that possibility, but discarded it. No, his murderer had to have been someone with a silencer, or he would have heard the gun shots, and jealous husbands don't use silencers, at least not a husband of any woman Lesley would seduce in this part of the world.

The murderer was definitely a professional, he concluded, and he didn't like his conclusion. Who? Quigley? No. Quigley wouldn't have enough time, let alone any motive. The killer needed a motive.

Then it hit him. He was supposed to be in this room, not Lesley. Suddenly he realized the killers definitely were professionals. The Council! The Q4C! But the motive? Of course! He gave them the motive when he mentioned the Emerald Head! Damn it!

"Well, I guess you saw your spirit, after all, old friend," he said at length, as he ran his hand over his dead friend's eyes to close them. He frowned a last good-bye, and quietly exited the room without being seen.

Downstairs, Penn approached the reservations desk. The dark hair girl was gone. He rang the bell on the counter, and an older woman emerged from the small side office. "Buenas dias," Penn greeted the woman with a broad smile.

"Good morning, Sir," the woman answered in near perfect accented English.

"For Pete's sake," Penn said with a frown. He wasn't in any mood for friendly chitchat, but he forced his attitude in order to avoid being too obvious, too questionable, too much of someone other than another tourist. "Doesn't anyone speak Spanish in this country anymore? How can a tourist practice his language if everyone speaks English?"

"Conversely," the woman responded. "How can anyone around here practice their English if we speak nothing but Spanish to all the tourists?"

After a feigned smile, Penn requested his bill. "I'm off to Antigua City," he said in form of explanation, hoping the lie would be believed, and be remembered. "They have a good language school there that I came here to join."

He also hoped the woman wouldn't find it odd that

this tourist arrived from Belize to go to a language school in another part of the country. Antigua was in the northern part of Guatemala. Guatemala City by plane from the U.S., than by bus to Antigua, would have been the more normal routine. He wasn't sure why he wanted such an alibi, but it suddenly seemed wise.

"Very good, Sir," the woman said as she retrieved the check out form. She studied it, smiled at Penn. "It is paid in advance. Don't you remember?"

"Oh, of course," Penn said, suddenly recalling that fact. "I forgot."

"Your friend is checking out of Room 2D?" she asked.

"He should be at the bus station by now," Penn lied. "By the way, he was in Room 2C. I was in Room 2D. See?" He held up the key to show her, and placed it on the counter.

"Si, si," the woman grinned, finding her play on the two C's funnier than Penn could appreciate. "He did not leave his key," she added.

"Oh, well, he probably forgot. You know how those Belizeans are," Penn said.

She laughed at the friendly, joking derogation.

Outside the hotel, he casually flagged down a passing taxi. He was more than surprised when he discovered it was Esteban's. It wasn't the same vehicle, though. It was a much newer one. It was at least a 1970 model, and it was a four-door Chevrolet station wagon. It was more reminiscent of Belize than Guatemala.

He opened the rear passenger door as soon as the vehicle stopped, and climbed inside before Esteban had a chance to get out to run around the vehicle and open the door for him. "Buenas dias, Esteban" Penn greeted. "Compras un otra caro?" You bought another car?

Esteban failed to show any great surprise as he turned around and nodded his greeting. "Buenas dias. Si. Es un nuevo caro. Es good, no?" Yes. It's a new car. It is good, no?

Penn nodded, but he still wondered whether or not it was any good, at all.

"A donde vas?" Esteban asked. Where are you going?

"Pienso," I think, Penn responded in thought. "A la

derecha, por ahora, solamente," Penn continued in his poorly rehearsed Spanish. Go going straight ahead for now, only.

"Bueno. Es good," Esteban expectedly answered.

Several blocks later Penn leaned forward. "Digame," he said. Tell me. "Coneces al Senor Jaime Quigley?" Do you know Mr. Jim Quigley?

"Ah, Senor," Esteban smiled. "Todas las personas en Puerto Barrios conecen El Squeermlee." Every person in Puerto Barrios knows the Senor Queegly.

"Coneces a donde se vives?" Do you know where he lives?

"Si. Quires a ir alla?" Do you want to go there?

"Si, por favor."

"Bueno. Es good." Esteban loved the phrase.

Twenty minutes later, they wound the way up a long curving driveway. At the top of the driveway was a house that more closely resembled a fortress. The gardeners and groomsmen about the house carried Uzis with their rakes and garden hoses. They were probably very good gardeners. They could shoot you, put you six feet under, and cover your grave with roses at the bat of an eye. And they were less than friendly in their stares, as Esteban pulled the taxi to a stop in front of the wrought iron gate that looked like it could stop a tank.

"Que quieres?" the gardener at the gate demanded. What do you want?

"El Senor Quigley," Esteban dutifully responded. "¿Se encuentras?" Is he here?

"No," the gardener responded. "No se encuentra."

Esteban turned around to shoot a questioning glance at Penn.

"I understand," Penn said to Esteban. "Bueno," he said to the gardener. "Cuando se encuentras?" When will he return?

"No se." I don't know.

"Bueno. Dices al Senor Quigley que el Senor Gwinn estaban aqui." Okay. Tell him Penn Gwinn was here. Penn wasn't sure his use of the conjugation was correct, but the meaning was understood, for the gardener nodded.

Esteban turned the taxi around, and began the long slow grind down the steep grade. On his way, to pass the time, he turned on his radio. Penn ignored most of the radio announcer's rhetoric, but he couldn't ignore the references to Hotel Berresford, and to a gringo last seen there who accompanied the man found dead in a room.

Esteban glanced at him in the rear view mirror. "Es de tu." he said. It is about you.

Penn shrugged. "Look. Let's stop the game with the language, Okay? My Spanish is too rusty. Can't you speak any English?"

Esteban was nonplussed. "I can, if you prefer. Anyway, I know your background too well to think you killed your friend."

"You're right about that," Penn responded. After a pause, he continued, "Why the hell haven't you been speaking English all the time?" he asked at length, disgruntled.

"Well, I guess because you started speaking Spanish. I thought that was what you wanted."

"Crap," Penn replied with some disgust. "What do you mean you know my background, anyway?" he added. "What's going on here?" Things were moving a little too fast.

"I was hoping you would tell me," he grinned in the mirror.

"I think I need a drink," Penn said, sidetracking the question. He didn't really know what was going on, anyway.

Esteban reached into the glove compartment and extracted a bottle of White Caribbean rum. He handed it back over the seat, and nearly drove off the side of the mountain for his inattention. "Well," he said, after returning to the road. "I think I need a drink, too, after that one. That was almost an 'Ah, shit', wasn't it? Anyway, I'm sorry, but I'm fresh out of glasses." He made an effort at sympathetic smiling.

Penn retrieved the bottle, popped out the cork, and took a long drink. He savored the taste as he shoved the cork back into the bottle and returned the bottle back to Esteban. He considered he could use a lot more of the stuff at the moment, but he wasn't going to go down that road. Not yet. He was too worried about Lesley, Quigley, and just what kind of problem he managed to get himself into.

Esteban returned the bottle to the glove compartment.

Harold R. Miller

"What did you want with Squiggly, anyway?" he asked.

"I think you have a few answers to give me before I give you any," Penn responded, parrying the question.

Esteban shrugged, fought another sharp turn, braked to a quick stop at the bottom of the hill, and pulled into traffic, heading downtown.

Penn noted the direction of travel. "Where in hell are we going?" he demanded. He wished he were smart enough to take along his PPKs .380 in his ankle holster. Without it, his demands were meaningless.

"Relax," Esteban said with a disarming smile in the rear view mirror. "We're going to make a little stop for a bite to eat, then I'll explain what I'm about."

Esteban wound his taxi through downtown traffic to the edge of the bay, and pulled to a stop in front of a sea food restaurant which sat on a wood plank floor built out over the near wave-less water between the Mangrove trees. "The food in this place is damned good, but more importantly, we can talk without fear of being overheard." He got out of the car, and strode into the restaurant.

Penn followed, but not without some trepidation. He hated being led, anywhere.

The first order, after finding a suitable table near the railing in the back of the platform, was for a bottle of White Caribbean Rum. It was Esteban's favorite, and was passable to Penn's palate, since there didn't seem to be any Korbel brandy on hand. After a quick drink and ordering Belizean Conch for Esteban, with camarones for Penn, they got down to explanations.

"You can expect me to be a little short tempered, right now," Penn began. "Lesley was a friend," he paused to think "Lesley...?" He suddenly realized he didn't know his friend's last name. And it was too late to learn it. I've got to stop drinking so much, he mentally chastised himself.

"I understand," Esteban said. "He was your friend, but there's nothing you can do for him now. And what's more, if you try to do anything, you'll most likely end up in the same condition."

"What are you talking about?"

"The Council."

THE EMERALD HEAD CAPER

"The Council? What cotton picking council?" He knew darn well what council, but he didn't know if Esteban knew anything about the Q4C. "What do you mean, the Council?" He was losing his patience. His frustration level quickly approached.

"I think you know what council I mean. The Quad Lateral Council."

Penn relented, frustrated. "I suppose so. But, why? What would the Quad Lateral Council have to do with Lesley? Why him? He knows nothing, knew nothing, about any international espionage, anything they could possibly be interested in." He avoided mentioning that Lesley's bad luck stemmed from his own mix-up in key distribution.

"The Emerald Head. You told them you know how to find it."

"The what? How do you know anything about that?"

"The third man at the table, the quiet Latino. He is one of our men."

"Now just what do you mean by that? Who is our?"

"You used to be one of us."

"Ah, for Christ's sake. You're with the D.I.A.?"

He shrugged. "I didn't tell you that. You're only making an educated guess."

"I'm not going to play games over Lesley's death. Just what is so damned important about some archaeological relic that the Q4C would commit murder over it?"

Esteban shrugged.

"I want an answer, and I mean to have it!" Penn's anger rose with his frustration.

"If I had it, I'd give it to you."

"Who's your boss?"

"I don't think even the agency has the answer." He paused, then quickly added,

"You mean I'm supposed to let Lesley's murder just pass away without any justification?"

"You've been there before. Remember your last operative partner? What was his name? Bruce?"

"Bull."

Bruce was Penn's partner in field operations with the

agency. Penn was told of Bruce's death in much the same manner, and there wasn't anything he could do about that, either.

"Damn it!" He nearly shouted in anger. He slammed his fist into the table in frustration. He did the same thing when he heard about Bruce. And his hand hurt just as badly when he regained his composure. Damn the spy business. Damn the Q4C and world domination! Damn everything, everyone, all the greedy S.O.B.'s on both sides of the fence! In his mind the words roared. They blotted out reality.

It was the Council who was responsible for Rachel's death in Australia on that chase for the legendary Aqualene opal. But he didn't want to think about her right now. He couldn't think about her. He dared not think about her. His anger would have been uncontrollable.

He peered at the bottle of rum on the table, grabbed it, tore off the cork, and downed three healthy swallows. It nearly eroded his stomach, but it also deadened his senses. He slowly set the bottle back on the table in silence.

"Are you all right, Amigo?" Esteban asked with a frown.

Was he all right? Penn had to think about that one. He was surprised to find blood seeping from his lip. He bit his lower lip so hard in his anger, he split it. He wiped off the blood while answering. "Yeah," he mumbled. "I guess I am."

He wasn't, but he had to fake it. He needed something to get his mind going again, something to take his mind off his bitterness. "How'd your cousin happen to be the taxi we chose when we got here?" he asked, more as a casual remark than in interest.

"It wasn't by accident," Esteban began. "We were told of your coming."

Penn forced himself to concentrate on the answer. The two girls and the 4 Fort Street Guesthouse flashed through his mind, and Esteban's presence was suddenly explained, just as Lesley's was. Of course it wasn't an accident. They told them – 'them' being whoever the 'we' was that Esteban meant - of his coming.

And which of the two girls at 4 Fort Street did the telling? It had to be Mary. She was the only person who knew his travel plans. "Mary Mercale," he said at length.

Esteban shrugged.

"Why?" He began, but let it drop. Suddenly he didn't need to ask that question. "Just what in the devil does the agency want with me?" he asked, instead. "What's so important about a broken down P.I. that they sent someone like you to follow me, especially on this little ridiculous jaunt?"

Esteban dug into his Conch and shoveled a huge chunk of the rubbery meat into his mouth. "Well," he added between chewing. "Why do you want to see Squiggly?"

"The girls at the Guesthouse?" Penn parried. "Are they actually in the agency, or are they just stringers? Contract people?" For some reason he wanted them to be nothing more than stringers, on contract to sell what useful information they might come across in their position. Being agents put them in too much danger.

"You must understand," Esteban said, giving the classic affirmation with a non-answer. "If I had any information on them, I certainly couldn't tell you."

"Not while they're still living, I suppose."

Once more Esteban shrugged his non-committal response.

"Then, you've heard of the Emerald Head?" Penn asked, remembering Esteban's earlier explanation of the justification for Lesley's death.

Esteban again shrugged without commitment.

"Then it's for real?"

"Some people think so."

"People like Thorne Beusch? As well as the Quad Lateral Council, obviously."

Esteban nodded.

"And you?"

"I'm not in the antiquities business. I don't really have an opinion."

"But Squiggly, or Quigley, is. And to answer your earlier question, that's what I wanted to see him about."

"I think you would have been misled if you believed what he told you. He doesn't actually deal in real antiquities."

"I know he deals in phony relics," Penn affirmed. "But

he might be able to provide some clue about the Head's whereabouts." He avoided mentioning the map. Then he had another thought. "How much do you know about the Q4C's operations in this part of the world, anyway?"

It was a question Penn didn't really want answered. He didn't really want to know, because he was well aware that to know meant he was going to have to deal with them once more. He definitely didn't like that possibility.

"To tell the truth, up until now I didn't think they were doing anything in this part of the world's anus. Why?"

Penn took the note out of his pocket and handed it to Esteban. "Lesley gave me this before," he stopped to rephrase his explanation. "Before he left."

"Before he left," Esteban repeated with a nod, approving Penn's choice of words. He took the note, quickly scanned it, carefully folded it, and stuck it in his shirt pocket. "You don't mind if I keep this?" he said. It wasn't really a question.

Penn didn't argue.

"The note sort of proves the existence of the Emerald Head, doesn't it?" Esteban commented.

"I was afraid you would say something like that," Penn agreed with a frown. "I suppose it does."

"Do you think there's anything in Quigley's fortress that would be of some help?"

"I kind of had that idea."

"You don't really want to just talk to him, do you?"

"I think you're beginning to see what I had in mind."

"You might ask for help," Esteban said.

"I might. Know anybody who'd help?"

"You know darn well I do."

"The agency wants to get into his house?"

Esteban simply grinned his response.

"Then, why haven't you?" Penn asked.

"Well, we, I, if there was any agency involved, that is, didn't see any exigent need. Until now, that is," Esteban explained, still being cagey about his involvement. "What're you looking for?" he added.

"What're you looking for?" Penn countered. He wasn't about to mention the half-map he needed. He didn't think

Esteban would believe him, anyway. "I guess we're both looking for the same thing,"

"Anything that might tell someone anything, right?" Esteban said. "And, of course, the Emerald Head, if it's there? Or something that would tell you where it might be?" He grinned again. "Anyway," he continued. "Tonight's as good a time as any to declare an exigent need."

"It's not going to be easy," Penn cautioned. "How do you suppose we accomplish this little caper?"

Esteban smiled. "Ve haf our vays," he said.

Penn hoped Esteban did have his ways, because he had absolutely no ideas at the moment. He wished one of those ways had been to fortify their courage a bit. About one more glass of rum would have handled it, he figured, on top of what he already drank.

* * * *

Esteban awakened Penn from a fitful nap on Esteban's couch at 2:30 in the morning. "It's party time," he said.

"Are you always so cocky?" Penn asked, forcing his eyes open, shading them against the glaring overhead light. "Where's the rum?" he asked, sitting up. "I need some fortification for this expedition."

"No, Senor," Esteban said. "Nothing to cloud your mind on this one. Not if you're going with me." He handed Penn a cup of strong, black coffee.

Penn had no options, so he downed the coffee. He was nearly sober when he joined Esteban in the taxi. It was a condition he wasn't sure he liked, because his nerves were completely jittery by the time they pulled to a stop half a block from the bottom of the hill.

"Now we walk," Esteban said. He got out and opened the trunk. "Here," he said, reaching inside. "Help me with this, will you?" He unloaded some ropes and two small canvas bags. He handed the bags to Penn. "You carry this stuff."

"This stuff?" Penn felt one of the bags. It was soft and pliable. It had a feeling he recognized. "Good grief!" he exclaimed with a loud whisper. "C-4 explosives?"

Harold R. Miller

"Now you're not thinking," Esteban responded. "Why would I want to blow up half the city just to get past those guards of his? No, it's not C-4. It's, well, let's just say they're two very large sleeping pills."

The next things he unloaded were two Walther PPKs .380 auto loader pistols. He handed one of them to Penn. "Know how to use this thing?" he asked in jest.

Penn set the plastic bags on the bumper, and took the pistol. He pulled back the slide, which cocked the hammer, took out the clip and checked it for load, whistled at the hollow points, re-inserted the clip and slammed the slide home, loading the weapon. He carefully set the hammer down to the un-cocked position. "Well, now I feel a little bit better," he said. It was the same weapon he used when he was with the agency. "The first thing I did with the Colt .45 the agency issued me was to sell it, when I had a chance, and buy one of these." He stuck the gun in his waistband, and picked up the two canvas bags while Esteban quietly shut the taxi trunk before they headed up the hill to the wall surrounding Quigley's palace.

It took them half an hour to reach the summit, which was about thirty yards from the side of the lowest part of the wall. They paused there in the brush long enough to survey the situation. The moon was full, and it cast enough light to read a newspaper.

"Where are all the guards?" Penn asked in a whisper that turned out to be louder than it should have been. "They're all gone," he added with a softer tone, mindful of Esteban's chastising glance. That made him chuckle. In years past he would have been doing the chastising for such lapses of self-control. But, then, it had been a long time. And that was another story he didn't want to think about.

Esteban gazed at the scene after a few more seconds of close scrutiny. "It makes you wonder, doesn't it?" he said.

A few minutes later Esteban crawled out of the brush and crept to the side of the wall. He took one of the ropes off his shoulder, formed a loop, and lasso-ed one of the spikes in the wrought iron fence on top of the wall.

"For Pete's sake," Penn chortled in a loud whisper. "Where'd you learn a trick like that?"

THE EMERALD HEAD CAPER

"That's the easy part," Esteban said as he tested the rope. "Climbing up the darn thing is the trick." He started shinnying up the rope as he finished the sentence. "See you at the front gate in five minutes," he added, when he was about six feet off the ground. It took him only three more minutes to climb up and over the ten-foot high barrier.

Penn waited the allotted time for Esteban to scale the wall and get to the front gate, before he crawled from the brush to sneak to the gate. He was overly cautious, with nerves already as jagged as could be without his usual wake up rum. But as it turned out, there was no need for such caution. He didn't see another soul, and by the time he reached the gate he felt confident there weren't any guards left on duty, so he boldly walked out from behind the wall, around the corner, and stood directly in front of the wrought iron bars of the gate.

He studied the handle to the gate latch. There was no padlock, no apparent method of locking it, so he tried the handle. The only thought that came to mind was where the devil was Esteban? He should have been at the gate by then.

The gate swung open easily.

He stepped back, cautiously. The gate shouldn't be so easily opened, considering the number of guards with automatic weapons who surrounded the place earlier in the day. Something was wrong. The hair on the back of his neck rose, and his spine tingled. It was that old feeling he got that saved him from a number of bad situations when he was in the field for the Agency.

He thought about the agency and its situations as a means of subverting his nervousness. Everything was a situation to the agency. He scoffed at how ingrained their training was to be able to remember it so long afterward. It was so long since he had been active; so long since he chucked his entire career because he lost faith in the propaganda the agency fed their field agents. He never lost faith in their stated purpose, but he lost faith in their lies, especially when he realized the truth about the lying ability of the government. He didn't like it then, and he didn't like it now. Funny, he concluded, how such ridiculous memories race through one's mind when the adrenaline is flowing.

Harold R. Miller

He appraised his next move as he carefully stepped through the open gate, and let it shut behind him. He heard the latch click. "Oh, oh," he said under his breath.

"Go no further, Amigo," Esteban whispered from the dark shadow behind the gatepost.

Penn jumped in reaction to the unexpected whispering.

"Quick. Get back here," Esteban added.

Penn located his friend, and scurried into the shadow. "What' going on?" he asked.

"Ssshhhh," Esteban cautioned.

The loud barking of at least two dogs erupted from somewhere in the yard.

"Damn it!" Esteban half shouted. "Open the gate! Quick!"

Penn ran for the wrought iron gate. He grabbed the latch. He tried to lift it up to open the gate, but it wouldn't move. "What?" he asked in rising panic.

The barking got louder.

"Open the gate!" Esteban shouted.

"It won't open!" Penn shouted in response, frantically pushing on the gate.

"Where's the two bags I gave you?" Esteban shouted with more urgency.

"Here!" Penn yelled back as he turned around to hand the two bags to Esteban. He wished he hadn't turned around, for what he saw made him wish he urinated before the night's expedition. If he had, he wouldn't have the near uncontrollable urge to do it now.

Racing towards them were two of the largest and meanest looking Rottweillers he ever saw. They were bounding across the yard in leaps at least six feet long at a time, with their mouths salivating.

Esteban ripped open the two canvas bags, yanked out the smaller bags, and pulled a cord from the tops of each of them.

There was a small explosion, like a 4-10 gauge shotgun firing. Green powder spewed everywhere. It covered them, and it covered the dogs, which suddenly were sliding in a panic to slow down, unsure of the new menace these two delicious looking humans suddenly presented.

THE EMERALD HEAD CAPER

Penn held his breath. The last thing he remembered was the first dog leaping onto his chest, its eyes rolled back, with a menacing low growl emanating from its half opened mouth.

CHAPTER 9

Chuck, Marc and Marcie stood amid clusters of tall cattails and reeds along the river's bank. Several yards in front of them, grounded in the mud, was an old, rundown sail boat about thirty feet long. The mast was broken off, the sails were in tatters, and the paint was peeling off the wood planks of the hull. The name Crystal Skull was printed in cracked and faded black letters on the stern.

"Are you sure we should be doing this?" Marcie asked, doubtfully, staring at the old hulk.

"Why not?" Chuck responded. "The old pirate died a week ago, my dad said. He had no next of kin, no one anyone can find, anyway. Maybe we can find some pictures, or something on it."

Chuck pushed aside the reeds and stepped forward. His foot sunk ankle deep into the river mud. "Dog gone it!" he complained, struggling to pull his foot out of the mud. It made a slurping sound when he got it free. "I guess we better watch where we step or We'll sink to our knees in this muck."

"Yeah," Marcie agreed.

They carefully stepped through the reeds, intent on where they put their feet.

Marc, striving to show his independence, didn't follow in Chuck's footsteps, though, and it wasn't long before he wished he did. His fourth step was in the wrong place, and his right leg went down to his knee. "Hey! I'm stuck!" he yelled in a panic. "I'm sinking! I'm going to drown!" He struggled against the mud, but the more he struggled, the deeper he sank. He became desperate.

Chuck and Marcie sloshed over to help. They grabbed him by the arms and pulled, stretching him nearly prone across the mud.

Slowly his leg came up from the mud.

They were encouraged. "More," Marc yelled. "Pull harder!"

The mud let go with a loud sucking slurp, and Marc's leg was free. Chuck and Marcie fell over backwards, ending up seated in the mud. As they fell, they let go of Marc.

Marc wasn't ready for the sudden release, and fell on his face.

Marcie shook her hands with distasteful gestures. "Uck!" she said. She hated being covered with mud.

Marc managed to recover, and sat up. "Gee. Thanks, guys," he said with sarcasm, wiping off his face. "That really helped."

Chuck, also sitting in the mud, grinned at his friends. "You know what?" he asked. "You both look kinda funny."

"Oh, yeah?" Marcie retorted. She picked up a handful of mud and threw it at Chuck.

He dodged, grabbed a handful of mud and threw it at Marcie.

She ducked, and the mud hit Marc in the face.

"Oh," Marc said. "So that's how it is!" He struggled to his feet with both hands full of mud, which he threw at Chuck.

Half of it hit Chuck, and the rest hit his sister, who also grabbed two handfuls of mud. One she threw at Marc in retaliation, and the other she threw at Chuck, partially in mischief, giggling at the fun of it all.

"Okay! Okay! I give up," Chuck shouted, wiping the mud from his face.

The other two laughed.

But Marcie couldn't resist. She tossed one more glob of mud at Chuck, who by that time, knowing just what she was up to, gathered another handful of the muck.

He held it up, ready to throw.

"Okay!" Marcie ceded. "Truce!"

"Oh, sure," Chuck laughed. "You have to get the last one in before quitting." He raised his hand, threatening.

Marcie shrugged and grinned.

"Not likely!" Chuck shouted, as he lobbed the goo at her. "Now we can have a truce."

Marcie wasn't one to lose a good fight, though. She ducked, grabbed another handful and prepared to throw it.

Chuck was already reloaded in both hands, and was ready for more retaliation, if need be. "Unh, unh, unh!" he cautioned.

"Okay," Marcie relented in face of the greater firepower, or mud power. She dropped the mud. "Truce it is, then." She got to her feet and struggled over to the edge of the water. "I guess we better get this mud off, or it'll dry and we won't be able to walk."

The two boys joined her, washing the mud off their hands and faces.

Marcie glanced at Chuck. A wide, mischievous grin developed across her face, and she splashed a handful of water into his face.

Chuck glared at her. He stuck his hand in the water, but changed his mind in face of her challenging grin.

"Hey! Will you guys cut it out?" Marc interceded. "We came here to see the boat, remember?"

Chuck laughed again, and resumed cleaning the rest of the mud off himself. But he was careful to keep his eye on Marcie.

And she was just as wary, or mindful, of Chuck's actions.

Ten minutes later, and after more careful stepping through the reeds, the three of them reached the foot of the rotting 2" x 12" board that served as a gangplank from the river's edge to the deck of the sailboat.

"What do you think, Chuck?" Marcie asked, eyeing the gangplank. "It looks awfully old. Do you think it'll hold?"

Chuck shrugged in a masculine way, and stepped onto the plank. It sagged with his steps, nearly breaking, but he managed to reach the deck safely.

Marcie gritted her teeth and followed.

Marc, seeing it held his two friends, decided it would be safe enough for him. He warily stepped onto the plank, and scurried up it lest it break while he was in the middle.

On deck, they looked around. Chuck stepped into the cockpit and pushed back the cabin hatch.

It squeaked and groaned, resisting entry, but finally moved.

Chuck peered inside the cabin.

"What's in there?" Marcie asked, joining him in the cockpit, worried about the groaning of the wood planks on the cockpit floor as she stepped on them.

"Guess there's only one way to find out," Chuck responded. He painstakingly stepped through the hatchway into the cabin, warily placing his foot on the top step of the ladder leading to the cabin floor.

The interior of the cabin of the decrepit old sailboat smelled of rotting wood, mildew, and stagnant water caught above the floorboards by the last exceptionally high tide.

The floor was rotting, and the doors to the cabinets fell off their hinges. The curtains on the portholes were tattered, and water sloshed about underneath the floorboards.

Marcie couldn't restrain herself. She had to see what was going on. She carefully stepped onto the ladder, testing it to be sure it would hold her. Even though Chuck just used it, she wanted to be sure he didn't weaken it. She was always the careful one, but once inside the cabin, she felt better, even though she still felt wary of the old hulk. She wondered just how long it would stay upright with their added weight in it. She wondered if the mud would hold it, or if it would suddenly slip off into the river and they would all be drowned, caught like rats in the bottom of a ship. She chuckled at that thought. She couldn't help herself. That's just how they appeared. Like rats inspecting an unknown quantity, carefully, stealthily, and furtively.

"What're you laughing about?" Chuck asked.

"Oh, nothing," she replied. She knew he wouldn't approve of her girlish imaginations. He was just like a man, she concluded, wiping the laughter off her face and trying to become serious. She wasn't entirely successful. Not until she heard the old hulk groan, that is. Then she became suddenly serious, and worried. "Do you think it's going to hold us?" she asked.

"Sure," Chuck responded with as much chauvinism as he could muster under the circumstances.

Marc followed them into the cabin. They made room for him at the bottom of the ladder. "Well?" he asked, "What have you found?"

"Nothing, yet," Marcie answered.

Chuck took the hint and moved forward in the cabin.

The other two silently watched, listening for any sounds that might warn them the boat was moving.

"This place is a mess," Marc said, glancing at the water sloshing around under the broken floorboards, his eyes wide. "And this thing's sinking!" Panic showed in his rising voice. "We ought to get out of here."

"Ah, it can't sink," Chuck calmed Marc's fears, not sure he believed what he said. "It's setting on the mud." He became braver, hearing his own words. "You guys can go, if you want, but I'm going to take a look around." With that, he sauntered forward through the first bulkhead into the forward part of the cabin.

A loud cracking sound emanated from the hull.

Marc and Marcie exchanged nervous glances.

"See! I told you this thing was sinking," Marc said. "It's breaking up," he added, nearly whispering, lest his voice would cause his fears to come true. He hurried for the ladder to climb up on deck.

"It can't sink," Marcie echoed Chuck's words. "It's stuck in the mud, like Chuck said." She hoped that was true.

Another cracking sound came from the bottom of the hull.

"I think it can't, anyway," Marcie warily added, looking around.

"Hey! Wait a minute!" Chuck called from the forward cabin. "Here's something!"

He returned to the main cabin holding a crudely made brass skeleton key. He held it up for inspection. "What do you think of this?" he asked proudly.

Another loud 'crack' came from below the floorboards, followed by a snapping sound. A rushing of water followed the sounds.

The boat settled farther into the mud. Water rushed over the floorboards. The boat rocked to one side.

Chuck and Marcie exchanged glances, and anxiously peered about.

"I think we better go now," Marcie said with forced calmness.

"I think you might be right," Chuck said with equally forced calm.

They rushed for the hatch steps.

Chuck helped Marcie up, and followed hurriedly, nervously looking behind him.

When they came on deck, Marc was already on the riverbank. His eyes focused on the waterline of the old hulk as it slowly rolled to one side. "Hurry!" he shouted. "She's going over!"

The sailboat groaned and lurched.

Chuck and Marcie raced down the gangplank.

The rotting plank added its creaking to the drama. More cracking emanated from the boat. They were louder than the rest. With one final groan, as though it finally gave up the fight, or no longer had an excuse for existing, the hulk rolled over, slid off the bank into deeper water, and sank. Parts of it, broken pieces not attached to the heavy lead keel, drifted away in the river.

The teenagers watched in awe.

"Wow!" Marc said in wonder.

"Yeah," Chuck agreed.

"It's weird, isn't it? That it should all of a sudden roll over like that, after all these years," Marcie pondered, always the romantic.

"What do you mean?" Chuck asked, not sure he wanted to hear her answer.

"Well, it's eerie. It's almost as if it waited for us to come along and find that key before sinking out of sight."

Chuck and Marc peered at her.

"Well, I suppose it's just my imagination," she said. "Anyway, it's time we went home. It's dinner time. Marc and I have a lot of cleaning up to do before our mom will let us in the house, let alone sit at the table."

Marc looked at himself. "Yeah," he agreed as he tried to brush off some of the mud he missed earlier.

"Okay," Chuck relented. "I guess you're right. Let's go. I'll figure out what to do with this later." He shoved the key in his pocket, and struck out to lead the way out of the marshes back to solid land.

Several days later Chuck met Marcie and Marc in the cabin of his father's salmon boat, docked in the harbor. Chuck's father was away for the weekend on business in San Francisco, and it was Chuck's duty to watch the boat when his father was gone.

Chuck sat at the galley table inside the typically small cabin when Marc and Marcie came aboard. The table dominated the cabin, and the one light, slowly swinging back and forth with the boat's movements, matched the brass lamps that hung on the cabin walls. The lamps cast eerie shadows over everything inside. The shadows were particularly weird and grotesque when a person moved about.

"Hey, this is neat, hunh, Marcie? Some trawler!" Marc commented, sitting at the table, looking at everything. He never went inside the boat before. The shadows' shapes on the cabin sides attracted his attention.

"It sure is," Marcie agreed, noting that Marc moved nearer the center of the settee to keep a respectful distance between him and the shadows.

"It's a troller, not a trawler," Chuck corrected. "A trawler fishes with nets. A troller fishes with fishing lines. That's the only way you can fish for Salmon. Anyway, what do you think of this?" He opened the cabinet beside the table and extracted an object wrapped with a towel.

The scene was somewhat too melodramatic, Marcie considered. "This what?"

"This?" Chuck removed the towel to reveal an old seaman's chest about a foot long by eight inches high and six inches wide. It was aged and worn. The hinges were rusted.

"Wow!" Marc commented in awe.

"I found it in the old pirate's cave," Chuck beamed.

"You really found this in the old pirate's cave?" Marcie asked, fascinated. "When did you go there?"

"Yesterday. My curiosity got the best of me." Chuck played his casual role, hoping to appear nonchalant, as he was sure all explorers rightfully should be. "I went to the cave to see if I could find anything. You know, to look around a bit."

"Kind of like why we went to the boat, hunh?" Marc offered, eyeing the chest.

"Yeah. Sort of. Anyway, there wasn't much in that cave. I was about to leave when I stumbled on this thing sticking out of the ground." He moved the chest around, as though to peer at the other side of it, lest he missed something on past inspections. "It was buried near the back of the cave where nobody would go, unless they were really curious."

"We have to open it," Marcie said.

"Yeah!" Marc added enthusiastically. "Maybe it'll have a bunch of gold coins in it. A pirate's treasure!"

"That lock looks awfully strong," Marcie said.

Chuck grinned broadly, as though he possessed some secret.

Marcie eyed him. "What're you grinning about?" she asked. She peered at him, then realized what he knew that she and her brother didn't. "The key! The one you found on the old pirate's boat!"

Chuck nodded with a broad smirk. He retrieved the old brass key from his pants pocket and held it up.

"Wow!" Marc said, impressed.

"Does it work?" Marcie asked, just as impressed.

"Let's try it," Chuck said, carefully inserting the key into the lock on the rusty brass hasp of the chest.

He jiggled the key, forcing it farther into the lock. Some dirt fell out of the keyhole, and he slowly twisted the key. After some effort and some more jiggling, the key finally turned with a click, and the lock fell open.

The three stared in amazement.

"Wow!" Marc was more impressed.

Chuck slowly, carefully raised the lid of the chest, until

his patience ran out. With a masterful flick of this wrist, he threw back the lid, making its hinges creak.

Marcie and Marc immediately craned their heads forward to peer into the opened chest.

Marc was disappointed. "Ah, there's nothing in it but a rolled up piece of old leather," he noted.

"Bound with a green ribbon tied in a bow knot," Marcie added. Her curiosity still aroused.

"That's all?" Marc asked, dejected. "No gold doubloons? No nothing?"

"Interesting, don't you think?" Chuck asked, as he cautiously lifted the rolled piece of leather out of the box and held it up for examination. He turned it over several times to inspect it, and set it on the table to untie the black ribbon. He slowly unrolled the leather on the table.

In the meantime, Marc double-checked the chest to be sure he didn't miss anything, maybe even one gold doubloon. Finally certain there was nothing else inside the chest, he pushed it aside to concentrate on the leather thing that held the other two's attentions so raptly as it was being unrolled.

"It's a map!" Marcie said with excitement.

"A treasure map?" Marc was again getting excited. "It's got to be a treasure map! Maybe it'll lead us to some gold doubloons!"

Chuck carefully flattened out the map on the table, and inspected it closely. "It is a map, all right," he concluded. "Or it could be, but the left side is torn off."

"Yeah," Marc added. "Strange symbols, hunh?" He eyed the drawings on the worn leather.

"Pictoglyphs," Chuck said.

"Pick o what?" Marc asked.

"Picto...glyphs," Marcie patiently repeated the word. "Picture writing. That's what they used before writing was invented." She realized what she said, and leaned over for a closer look. "Pictoglyphs?" she repeated in wonder as she studied the symbols. "But this here, on the bottom. It's something else. The writing looks like Latin. See?"

She pointed to some words scrawled along the bottom of the leather, drawn in red ink. "E..L.. P..A..I..S D..E.. W..A..

THE EMERALD HEAD CAPER

L..L..A..S..," she slowly read the letters. She paused. then pronounced the words. "El Pais de Wallas," she said as she sat up to think about the words. "Why, that's Spanish," she concluded. "It says the Country of Wallas. Wallas Country."

"I've never heard of it," Marc complained.

"Well," Marcie again remarked in her self confident and nonchalant tone. "I see you two never took Latin American History." She grinned at her friends. "The country that's now Belize was called Wallas Land when the Scots settled there to plunder the Spanish Galleons that sailed out from Panama and Central America in the 1600's. In time, the name changed to Vallas, with a V, through common usage, then Valis, with an I-S, with the Spanish pronunciation, then finally became Balis, because the Spanish V is pronounced like a B, and now it's Belize. Or Belice', as the Mexicans call it with their preference for pronouncing the final vowel. Of course, it was officially British Honduras until 1981, when it gained its independence from Britain, and became a sovereign nation on its own. That's when they took on the official name of Belize."

"How do you know that?" Chuck asked.

"Like I said. Latin American history," she responded. "My teacher was a Maya buff, an amateur archaeologist. He always talked about Belize and the ruined temples there."

"Do you think this could really be a map of ancient Belize?" Chuck asked.

"It sure looks like it," she responded, again eyeing the symbols on the leather.

"Wow!" Marc exclaimed.

"Well, it doesn't show all the country of Belize," Chuck interceded, peering closely at the map. "If it is Belize, that is."

Marc pointed to a spot on the map. "There's nothing here but a bunch of wavy lines. What do they mean?" He took a closer look. "And that? That looks like an old fort or something." He pointed to an image where a group of lines came together and would have made a point, except that the top was torn off.

"Hey! That could be a temple," Chuck said. "And the wavy lines, they're probably rivers. There are a lot of rivers in Belize." He pointed to the one odd shaped symbol. It was a skull like the one shown on a pirate's Jolly Roger, the skull and cross bones flag. "That has got to be a drawing of a skull."

"Wow!" Marc said.

"You know what I think?" Chuck continued, as he sat back in his nonchalant manner.

The other two continued peering at the map.

"I think what we have here is a real treasure map," Chuck concluded.

"Wow," Marc said, not losing any of his enthusiasm.

"You really think so?" Marcie asked with her usual skepticism.

"What else could it be?" Chuck responded.

The three resumed their study of the map, now with more intent.

"Listen," Chuck said. "I have an idea."

Marcie quickly smirked, lightly. "Not another one like going out on that bridge, I hope."

Chuck ignored the criticism. "Better," he said, recovering his nonchalance. "We don't have anything else to do this summer, right?"

"You're not thinking...?" Marcie asked, letting the question drop. She knew what he was thinking.

"Why not?" Chuck's nonchalance was overcome by the excitement of his idea. "I can get my dad to put up the money. He wants me to experience life, right? Well, what could be a better experience than going on a treasure hunt! A real, live treasure hunt!"

"Wow!" Marc said. He was no longer worried about the eerie shadows. He just knew there would be real doubloons at the end of this treasure hunt.

CHAPTER 10

Penn fought against the monster dog. He tried to fend off its vicious fangs as it lunged for his throat, and struggled for self-control as the force of the dog's weight slammed him against the iron gate behind him. Then everything faded.

Several seconds later, he found himself on the ground. He shook his head violently. He took several deep breaths. He forced his head away from the green mist from the exploding bags, and slowly the fog cleared. He struggled back to his feet.

He looked around. There were two unconscious dogs on the ground in front of him. To his right, Esteban seemed to be sleeping peacefully, quietly as a babe in a cradle.

He realized what the two exploding bags contained. It was sleeping gas. The greenish tint to the power that blew out of the bags was the telltale sign. He remembering seeing that powder before, when he was in Viet Nam with the agency, although he didn't remember seeing it in such quantities. It was used against an attacker as a safety device, as a means of getting out of tight situations when there was no need for destroying the attacker.

He wondered how long he was out. Normally the powder's effect lasted for about an hour. He hoped he wasn't waking up just in time to see the monstrous dogs come to.

He glanced at his watch. 3:30. No. He wasn't out more than a few minutes. He was lucky. He didn't catch a full breath of the powder, so its effect was weakened. One of the problems with its use, he remembered from his training days, was the defensive, automatic holding of your breath when confronted with it. If you didn't breath it, it didn't work

With a good deal of trepidation, he tiptoed among the fallen dogs and tried lifting the gate latch, again. Suddenly he felt stupid, very stupid. "You idiot," he whispered to himself. "The gate opens the other way." If he had pulled on it, he and Esteban would be in the car, halfway back to town.

He pulled open the gate and stepped outside with a quick glance back at the dogs. He took another deep breath, and went back inside the yard. He knew he had to rescue Esteban, and he also had to get back inside the house, so he left the gate open for Esteban's safety, in case Esteban woke up before he returned, and headed for the house.

Then he had the brilliant idea. The security dogs were out of condition now, but they might wake up at any minute. Since the gate worked, and since it could keep the dogs out as well as keep them in, why not drag them outside and shut the gate? If he did, he could take all the time he needed to search the house. It was obvious that Quigley wasn't about, and neither were his guards, so there wouldn't be anything to interfere. It was a great idea!

He grabbed both dogs by their metal spiked collars, dragged them outside the fence, shut the gate, and made sure the latch was set, just in case. He guessed Esteban would be under for at least an hour, so there would be enough time to find the map, if it were there, which he actually doubted, since Quigley wasn't. And he should have enough time after that to return the still sleeping dogs inside the fence, tote Esteban outside the fence, and get to the car in peace.

He climbed the porch steps, and cautiously waited, alert, listening. There were no unusual sounds, nor was anything visible in the moonlight that was out of the ordinary, so he moved to the front door. Again, he stopped to listen. Nothing, save the early birds chirping in the nearby trees.

He tried the huge brass knob on the massive carved mahogany door. It turned.

He pushed on the door. It opened.

With a half shrug that consigned himself to his plan, he

stepped inside. He hoped there weren't any Rottweilers inside the house.

There weren't any more dogs to worry him, but what he eventually faced could have been just as frightening. Just as frightening, that is, if he believed in ghosts.

The foyer to the mansion was empty. Moonlight streamed in through the windows. The room was void of any furniture, save a Persian rug. He lightly stepped along the rug, barely making out his way in the dark, until he came to the one door leading out of the foyer. He tried the handle. It turned.

He carefully pushed the door open, and was immediately bathed in a bright green light. It was an eerie light that outlined the furniture in the room, throwing grotesque shapes in eerie shades of green. cast shadows along the wall. It formed shadows, and the shadows were moving!

Penn stopped. The hair on the back of his neck raised. He tried locating the source of the green light, hoping it wasn't coming from the Emerald Head. Yet, in a strange way, he hoped it was. That would mean he could grab the thing, get back to Belize, deliver it to Thorne Beusch, and settle down with a full bottle of Korbel brandy. He really needed the brandy at the moment.

But the light wasn't coming from the Emerald Head. It came from a small television screen placed on a shelf across the room. At least he thought it was a television. On closer look, it turned out to be a video monitor, a television without a channel changer.

The presence of the monitor was an interesting question, but the image on the screen was a fascinating subject. It was a strange figure in a flowing robe and bright green eyes. It moved about the screen, addressing an assemblage of natives in the background.

As Penn moved closer to the screen, the green light fluctuated and flashed more vibrantly. The figure bathed in green suddenly stopped, and stared straight at what would have been the camera, as though looking straight at Penn, as though it was aware of Penn's presence. The hair on the back of Penn's neck raised, and his spine tingled.

The image looked like Quigley! He wore a robe with

strange markings painted on its face, but judging by the size and other features, it could only be the squiggly character.

The image's eyes glowed a brighter green, a green so bright it bathed the room in its intensity. Then the picture faded, and the monitor switched off.

Penn saw nothing but green spots for several seconds as he tried to get his eyes accustomed to the sudden darkness. "What the hell was all that about?" He asked himself, as he rubbed his eyes in the darkness.

A sound penetrated the stillness. Something scraped the wall. Someone, or something, was groping along the wall in the darkness.

Another scrape, then a click!

The room blared into brightness.

Someone turned on the lights, only Penn couldn't see who it was. The bright white light was just as hard to see through as the sudden darkness. He dropped into a crouch and drew his PPKs, holding his hand over his eyes to shade them from the blinding light, trying to pierce the brightness. He saw nothing.

"Ah, there you are," someone said from the direction of the doorway.

Penn relaxed. "Esteban," he said as he stood up and stuck his gun back in his waistband. "You scared the hell out of me."

"Sorry," Esteban said, glancing at Penn, and looking about the room, taking a survey. "I was getting a bit worried about you, you know."

"How'd you manage to wake up so soon, anyway?" Penn asked. "I thought that powder would keep you under for at least another hour, or so."

"Simple," he answered with a shrug. "You hold your breath, and it doesn't get to you." He grinned. "Well, not too much, anyway. I gather you're aware of that, too? Otherwise you'd still be back there with your four footed friends." He moved about the room, looking in drawers, behind doors, and behind the books on the bookshelves.

"Your four footed friends, maybe, but not mine," Penn responded, watching Esteban's movements.

"Have you found anything in here?" Esteban asked.

"No," Penn shook his head. "Not really." He didn't want

to try explaining the green video screen. He wasn't sure Esteban would believe him. He wasn't sure he believed it, himself. He watched Esteban, and joined him at the bookshelf. "You know, there just might be something here," he said, as he started searching through the books.

It took about five minutes for Penn to find what he thought might be the object of his search. It was a book of maps, an Atlas. He pulled it off the shelf with some expectation, thinking it would be the perfect place to hide an old map. He thumbed through the pages with obvious interest.

"Hey," Esteban said, watching him. "I know the way out of this place. You won't need a map." He chuckled as he casually walked through a side door to another room.

Penn wouldn't be deterred, and he did need a map, all right. That was why he was more than surprised when he found one. Suddenly, looking through the pages, there it was, folded in half, writing side out, stuck carelessly between some pages in the middle of the book. Just like Hollywood. Just like in the movies. "Well, I'll be damned," he said as he snatched it out and opened it. He peered at it, not believing what he saw.

It was a copy of the map, the same copy as the one he got from Thorne Beusch. He scanned it several times to be sure it was the same. How in hell? He couldn't figure it out. If there were two parts to the map, and he had a copy of one half of it, then wouldn't Quigley have the other half?

He heard Esteban coming into the room, so he quickly folded the copy and crammed it into his shirt pocket, beside the copy given by Thorne Beusch, and slipped the book back on the shelf.

"Well, I guess this is pretty much a wild goose chase," Esteban said, entering the room. "I don't know why Quigley left in such a hurry, but he sure took everything that might have been interesting."

"Yeah," Penn responded. "That's pretty much how I feel, too. I guess we might as well get out of here, right?"

"All right with me," Esteban agreed.

They left the room, made their way to the front door, and opened it.

"Ah, wait a minute," Penn said, as he put his hand out to

stop Esteban. "Do you think your friends are still out cold?"

Esteban frowned. He glanced at his watch. "Well," he said pensively. "It's only been half an hour. They should be."

They cautiously peered out the doorway, ready to slam it shut in case of exigent need.

"Hell, what're we worrying about, anyway," Penn said. "Those monsters are still locked outside the fence, right?" He hoped he was right.

"I think so," was Esteban's weak agreement. It wasn't much of a reassurance.

They glanced at each other.

Penn shrugged, and they tiptoed out of the mansion, across the porch, and down the front steps, half expecting to be attacked at any moment.

At the gate they stopped.

Penn peered through the gates at the dogs, at where he put them, off to one side of the drive. They were still there, and still dead to the world, or so they appeared.

"I think we can get past them without any problems, Amigo," Penn whispered. He quietly unlatched the gate, pulled it open, winced at the creaking of the hinges, and stepped forward.

Esteban followed.

They were ten feet past the dogs when they heard it.

The largest of the two monsters awakened. It struggled to its feet, and was madder than ever over what happened. It wanted to wreak its revenge on the first thing it saw, and the two humans whose strange powder gave it such a pain in the head fit the need.

"Oh, crap!" Esteban yelled as he started running. He never bothered to look around to see which dog was the problem, or what the danger was, or whether or not running was a way to avoid it. He simply started running.

While Penn, the wiser, the more experienced, the more knowledgeable of the two, had to be dumb enough to stop and turn around. He managed to get turned completely around just in time to see the monster lunge at him. It was in mid-air, and snarling, its teeth bared, its jaw opened, salivating.

Penn ducked.

THE EMERALD HEAD CAPER

The monster snapped his jaws shut, and snagged the collar of Penn's shirt in passing over his shoulder. The shirt tore off like the seams were made with Velcro.

"Damn it!" Penn shouted. He lunged for his shirt. "Give me that!" he shouted. He wasn't going to let that monster get his shirt. Both map copies were in the front pocket, and the monster was wildly ripping and tearing the shirt apart.

Penn stepped toward the dog. He realized just what he was doing when the animal stopped long enough to growl at him. He backed up and pulled his PPKs out of his waistband. He took careful aim, and tried to squeeze the trigger.

Only he was too late.

In the intervening time, while he was watching the first dog, the second dog came awake, and lunged, silently, at the metal thing he was trained to tear from an attacker's hand. It wrenched the gun from Penn's hand, shaking its head violently, as though the gun was a living thing to be torn apart.

"Damn it!" Penn again shouted at the top of his lungs.

The dog with the shirt stopped its ripping and tearing long enough to cast a dangerous warning glance at him.

Penn took two steps back.

The dog began munching down, gulping down, the ripped and torn pieces of shirt. The last of the map copies disappeared down its throat.

The other dog was still violently shaking the gun.

Penn wasn't really a coward, but being completely defenseless, with not a chance in the world of ever retrieving his shirt, or the map copies, he decided discretion was the wisest part of valor. He took off running down the hill in pursuit of Esteban, hoping the dogs were too busy in their assault on his shirt and gun to pay him any attention.

When he got to the bottom of the hill, Esteban was already in the taxi with the engine running. He was about to put it in gear and race away when Penn grabbed the rear door and jumped inside, bouncing on the rear seat.

The man in the house across the street from Esteban's car smiled inwardly, amused by the antics of the guard dogs and the intruders into the house he was assigned to watch. He knew the dogs wouldn't actually harm anyone. They were just for show.

He made an entry into his notebook. The incident had to be reported in the morning.

"What took you so long?" Esteban asked with a wry sense of humor, when Penn caught his breath.

"I'd be here a lot sooner if it weren't been for your friends back there," Penn responded between gasps. "Where's your rum?"

"A good idea," Esteban said as he crammed the car into gear and roared off down the road, then opened the glove compartment and grabbed the bottle from inside. "You look like you need it first," he added, uncorking the bottle with his teeth, and handing it across the back of the seat to Penn.

Penn lost no time in gulping down what would probably have been half a glass full, had there been any glasses available. If there were, Penn wouldn't waste time using one, anyway.

He took a second drink, and handed it back to Esteban, who took a suitable swig from it in turn before recapping it and returning it to the glove compartment considerably more empty than it was when he retrieved it.

"Well, what now, Amigo?" Esteban asked, when they approached the inner parts of the city where they felt they were quite safe from any more monsters that might attack them.

Their destination was something Penn didn't take time to consider. They needed a plan, but had none. "What do you suppose happened to Squiggly?" Penn finally asked in service to the question more than in a need for the answer.

Esteban thought for some time. "Well," he said at last. "I know he spends a lot of time in the jungle, searching, or so he says, for the antiquities he claims he gives to the museums in the area." He quieted long enough to negotiate a particularly sharp corner. "I suppose he could be on his way, doing that."

"Is it normal for his guards to leave his place unattended in his absence?" Penn asked. He wanted to sidetrack any further discussion of where Quigley went. He was pretty sure the man went into the jungle, remembering the green picture in the bedroom. Where the man went wasn't the real problem. The problem was what the hell was he was doing, wherever it was that he was doing it?

"I haven't the slightest idea why the house was left

unattended," Esteban responded at length. "It does seem a little odd, though, doesn't it?"

"That's a fact," Penn responded.

"So, what now?" Esteban repeated his question. "I gather you didn't find anything momentous back there?" It was a question that was more a probe of Penn's next move than a curiosity about anything Penn might have found.

Penn responded cautiously. After all, Esteban was a field agent with the CIA, and Penn definitely had his misgivings about that organization. No matter how friendly their agents seemed to be, they still had their prime objective in mind whenever they did anything. He knew that. He wondered if Esteban's question was based on Esteban's prime objective. "I think," he answered at length. "That I might as well get back to Belize."

"You're going to forget about this Emerald Head thing?" Esteban asked. His curiosity was more than casual.

"Might as well," Penn lied. "Squiggly isn't around, and he was my only source of information on the topic."

"Too bad," Esteban said, as though in consolation.

"Yeah," Penn responded. He wasn't going to let Esteban know it, but he did have some other tricks to use in his search for Quigley. Or, at least, he thought he did.

He would have to do a little research, but he was sure he could find his sources, his British military friends who maintained a close watch on the activities in the Belize and Guatemala jungles. The Brits were charged with protecting the sovereignty of Belize, and their reconnaissance groups could tell him if there might be something unusual going on the jungles; if there were any expeditions trekking through the jungles, or any odd happenings.

He hastily made plans to return to Belize and contact his old time friend, British ex-SAS Officer David McGaughy, in San Pedro Town on Ambergris Cay. If anything, David would be a good drinking buddy for a day or two. The Irish were noted for the enormity of their alcohol capacities, and David felt it his responsibility to sustain the reputation.

It was a sense of responsibility Penn sometimes admired, particularly after events as depressing as those he recently experienced. Besides, he rationalized, maybe David would know something about the Emerald Head.

The most important aspect of David's value, though, lay in the fact that he had his finger on just about everything that went on in the various intelligence and police organizations in the entire country of Belize, and often worked as an undercover cop or agent for any one of those agencies, depending on their need.

Penn hoped David wasn't off running around on one of those agency needs at the present.

THE EMERALD HEAD CAPER

CHAPTER 11

The sun blazed down on the small Belizean village perched among two jungle-covered mountain ranges in the northern part of the country. The village was unlucky enough to be perched right on the border of Belize and Guatemala.

Often, due to its proximity, some Guatemalans would stray into the area, claiming it was part of their country. Even the government of Guatemala didn't recognize the area as a separate country until the late 1980's, and most of the citizens of Guatemala still denied the acceptance of their Quintana Roo region as being the independent upstart country of Belize. They resented it, and they wanted it back. Some people in the back corridors of the Guatemalan government cherished the day when they could once again control Belize, thereby nearly doubling their county's size, and gaining their full border with their Northern neighbor, Mexico. The population statistics, alone, with such a return would make it the second largest in the Tesoro, they argued.

The village in the jungle was typically impoverished, with mud brick, tar paper, and unpainted wood shacks roofed with corrugated tin, where roofs were needed. Sticks were used to make the fences that were supposed to keep in the pigs, the goats, the chickens, and whatever else kept penned up for food.

Several curs and an occasional pig were smart enough

to escape the fences, and when they did, they either settled around the mud holes that offered respite from the summer's heat, or in the ditches that channeled the sewers away from the shacks. The pigs snorted, while the dogs scratched their fleas, and occasionally howled at each other, or barked and bit one another in fighting for control of their meager territories.

Occasionally, a grunting pig would fight the dog for the mud wallow. The pigs nearly always won, since they were usually twice the size of the runty dogs.

The children of the village romped around freely, very often lacking clothes, depending on their ages. Anyone under three never wore anything. Diapers were a luxury not known in the less affluent parts of the country.

Everyone fell asleep at night to the chirping, cawing, whooping and calling of the birds and animals of the nearby jungle. Electricity was a modern amenity only dreamed about. There was nothing like television.

On one particular afternoon the burning sun cast its shadow along the wall of one of the shacks just off the central plaza. It was the shack in which Alena lived with her parents. At the time, her parents were working the fields, hoping to sustain their meager lifestyle with the coconuts they could harvest, and with the corn they grew in cooperative effort with the rest of the villagers.

Normally, Alena would have gone with her parents, but on that day she stayed home to tend the smoke pit in the back of their shack where some pork was cooking. It was a major task, but she was fourteen, and she felt herself worthy. Besides, she knew, as long as she didn't work in the fields, she could wear one of her dresses. She particularly enjoyed wearing her native style long white dress with the embroidered neckline.

She felt especially good about herself, as she put another stick on the fire but she was disturbed when a Guatemalan soldier pushed his way through the ramshackle gate, into the yard.

The soldier was in his mid-thirties, with corporal stripes on his sloppy and dirty olive drab army fatigues, with dirty and unpolished black boots. He was badly in need of a shave, and was drunk. His breath smelled of stale alcohol mixed with cigar smoke. He grabbed Alena around the waist and tried to kiss her.

She screamed, but the harder she resisted him, the greater his desire for her became, and the harder it became for her to keep his mouth from hers. Her screams gave him more resolve. He laughed at her shouts, at her calls for help.

"Stop!" a gruff male voice shouted from inside the nearby shack.

The corporal pried his eyes off the girl and peered at the shack.

The man who yelled, stepped from the shack. He wore his uniform with a .45 caliber pistol strapped to his waist, and wore sergeant stripes sewn somewhat crookedly on the sleeves. He, too, needed a shave, but the main difference between the two soldiers was the overweight girth of the sergeant. He was adding even more weight by chewing on a chicken drumstick held in his right hand, and drinking heavily from the bottle of rum he carried in his left hand. He spat out some of the meat. "Melones!" he shouted. "I said stop that!"

The man was Guapito, El Sargente, the leader of the group of five Soldados Del Militario De Guatemala.

Melones gave him an inquisitive look.

Guapito returned a glare in response. He peered in a most threatening way, by leaning his head forward, knitting his brows and squinting his eyes. He did this to insure the corporal would heed his order. A second or two later he took another swallow from the bottle of rum.

Melones heard the order. Although he understood his sergeant's famous 'you better do what I say' expression, he didn't see any reason for it. He continued staring, confused, his eyes forming the question: Why?

"The girl is screaming too much. She is too loud," Guapito explained. "She is interrupting my lunch!"

Melones shrugged his shoulders, and reluctantly let go of the girl.

She spat at him, and ran out of the yard.

"You must remember," Guapito continued with his instructions to Melones, "we are the Army of the Redemption! We are here to liberate this country of Belize, not to destroy it." He paused long enough to shoo some more flies from his chicken leg, and to think of some more rhetoric that would rationalize his presence and that of his renegade soldiers in Belize without official orders. "We must win the hearts of these simple Belizeans," he added at length. Then he laughed, took another bite from the meat, and followed that with another long drink of rum. He wiped his mouth with the back of his sleeve, appraised his chicken leg once more, shooed away yet another black fly, and took another bite as he returned inside the shack.

Melones wiped his face where the girl spat on him. He shook his head, and grinned broadly, as he decided to chase the girl. "I think I will win her heart," he said with a laugh, as he hurried out of the yard, ignoring his sergeant's orders.

Several minutes later, he caught up with her. He laughed again as he grabbed her. The laughter was followed by a yowl of pain.

This fourteen-year-old Belizean girl's heart didn't appreciate the winning Melones had in mind, and she was quite capable of defending herself.

* * * *

At the same time Melones tried to kiss Alena, a pilot of TACA Airlines jet bounced the plane twice on the asphalt runway while landing at the Belize City International Airport. The engines roared as they were put in full reverse to slow the plane, stopping it less than ten feet from the end of the runway. The brightly painted machine turned around on the single lane asphalt strip, and taxied to the single story, cement block terminal building.

Several Belizean airport crewmen rushed out with chocks for the wheels, and a deplaning ramp. They bumped the ramp into the side of the airplane, being less careful than the manuals required of their tasks. But it was too hot for anyone to take notice of such a small mistake. Besides, one more dent in the side of the plane wouldn't be noticed.

Chuck, Marcie and Marc filed down the deplaning ladder from the air-conditioned interior of the metal bird, and like the other passengers, shuddered in defense of the sudden onslaught of the Belizean heat. The cement tarmac burned with the sun's rays, and the walk from the plane to the airport building made Marcie think of the National Geographic documentary she saw about the fire-walkers of Indonesia, and how they must have felt when they pranced across their ritual hot coals.

"If I knew it was going to be this hot," Marc complained. "I would have stayed home."

His remark earned him a glance of disdain from his sister.

"Oh, It's not so bad," Chuck nonchalantly argued, hoping to elevate his friend's mood.

They reached the Immigration and Customs House after a two-minute walk, but even in the shade of the building the heat was oppressive, especially when it accompanied the odor of weary travelers. The smell of the jungle bog less than a hundred yards from the airport added to the overall aroma.

Their passports were checked by a white-shirted Belize Immigration Officer, who was a surprisingly courteous woman, considering the stifling conditions she worked in all day.

Within twenty minutes of their arrival, they were in the Customs area waiting for the bags to be carried in on the conveyor belt from the outside of the building where the baggage handlers worked in the sweltering sun.

Each of the teenagers brought a medium sized backpack for their limited travel gear, since they didn't plan to be in the country for too long. After all, they conceded before their departure, they had a map which showed them the way almost directly to their treasure, didn't they? "It can't take more than a day or two to travel that far," Chuck said in his argument favoring light packs.

"But I have to take more than only one pair of jeans," Marcie had protested. "And at least three tops. What if we get stuck down there for longer than we anticipate?" Her reasoning most always was the final word when it came to logistics, so they all agreed to take at least four day's worth of travel clothes.

With their backpacks held in front of them, the three approached the Customs baggage inspection table. It was one of the three tended by the white-shirted Customs Officers.

Directly in front of them were two Americans, a married

couple in their mid-forties. The Customs Officer, who dutifully checked some, but not all of the baggage presented by arriving passengers, decided to check theirs. "Any t'ing to da'clare?" he politely asked the husband of the couple.

"Oh, hurry up, Harold," the over weight American wife complained to her husband. "Show him the bags and let's get out of this God forsaken place."

"Yes, love," Harold said, timidly placing the first of their four suitcases on the inspection table.

"God," the wife continued her complaint. "This place is so hot. Why can't they put air conditioning in this place?" She glared at the Customs Officer "Why don't you put some air conditioning in this place?" she demanded. "We're American. We're not used to this sort of heat."

Her demeaning remarks changed the attitude of the customs officer, but it wasn't a change she liked.

He frowned. "Put da other bags on da table, too, fa sure," he said in his not quite perfect English. "We be fa da inspect dem, too."

"Yes, sir," the timid Harold said.

"Ah, for Heaven's sake," the woman complained. "Can't you see we're just tourists? We're American. We're not going to try smuggling anything into your country. Who would want to stay in this place long enough to try smuggling anything in the first place?"

"Da firs' bag, please, Mon," the customs officer said, directing the husband to open it.

Harold complied.

The officer gave it a cursory glance, ordered the second bag opened, glanced at it without actually looking into it, did the same with the third, and with the fourth.

Before he finished, the wife was livid.

The other passengers in line were also becoming short tempered.

The officer didn't heed them, though. He was intent on teaching the American woman a lesson in diplomacy. "Patience is a virtue," he said. He practiced that phrase well. It had almost no trace of the typical Creole accent.

"Oh, patience, schmatience," the woman retorted. "We

came here to see your flea pickin' country, not to do any smuggling. Now let's get this thing through with. We want to get to the Fort George Hotel. It's supposed to be air conditioned." She stomped past the table. "Come on, Harold," she ordered. "Let's get going."

"Uh, are we through?" the timid man asked the inspector.

"Chu be da free da go," the inspector responded with a grin.

"Come on," the wife demanded.

"Yes, m'love," Harold said, as he grabbed the last of the four suitcases and lugged it off the table onto the floor. He tried to pick up all four of them at one time, but found them a trifle heavy, and nearly stumbled.

"Come on, Harold," his wife continued in her nagging persistence.

Harold jerkily lifted the last bag, and it came open, spilling the contents all over the floor.

The waiting passengers chuckled and snickered, some in embarrassment, some with glee.

Harold was mortified. He stood there staring at the clothes on the floor.

"Now look what you've done," the wife complained. It was apparently her suitcase, for the entire contents were woman's underwear, most of it unmentionables much larger than average.

Harold quickly dropped the other suitcases, intent on re-packing the opened one.

The smallest suitcase, the one he held under his arm, hit the floor with the crashing of glass. It flew open, and shards from a bottle of bath water spilled out on the floor.

"Good grief," his wife complained as she stared at the mess. "My best bath water."

Harold stared at it.

"Well, pick it up," his wife demanded.

"Yes, m'love," Harold dutifully replied. He got down on his knees, carefully retrieved the broken glass to put back in the small bag, and pushed some of the clothes from the floor into the larger bag.

"For Pete's sake," his wife complained as she shoved him

Harold R. Miller

aside, gathered up the remaining clothes, and forced them into the suitcase. "Can't you do anything right?" She crammed the last garment into the suitcase and slammed it shut.

"Yes, m'love," Harold replied meekly as his wife grabbed the suitcase and stomped out of the customs office with one of her nightgowns trailing from the back of the suitcase.

The waiting passengers broke into more snickers and chuckles.

Even Harold grinned lightly. He stood there, not sure what he should do, wondering whether he should risk his wife's anger by telling her about it, or just ignore it, thereby risking her possible anger later, when she discovered it and wanted to know why he didn't tell her. He finally laughed to relieve his own embarrassment.

The other passengers joined him with uproarious laughter.

"Ah, to the dickens with it," Harold said. He ignored the smaller suitcase with the broken bottle, grabbed the remaining two, and dragged them out of the building.

The other passengers clapped at his sudden show of fortitude.

Chuck and Marc were next in line, and the officer waived them through without a search.

Marcie's dropped her backpack on the table and smiled at the inspector in her most friendly way.

The inspector found her smile suspicious. "Any t'ing to da'clare?" he asked officiously.

"No. Nothing," Marcie sighed. She hoped that she, too, could pass through without the embarrassment of having to have her backpack gone through by some stranger.

"Open da bag, please, Miss," the customs officer said.

"Well, shoot!" she responded. "If you were going to look in my bag anyway, why did you bother to ask me if I had anything to declare?"

The inspector eyed her. "To see maybe chu be tryin' fa da smuggle any t'ing, Mam... uh, Miss." He paused to consider his remark. "Be you?" he added as an afterthought.

"Of course not!" Marcie replied, just a little indignant. "Besides, I'd sure be a fool if I said yes, now, wouldn't I?"

THE EMERALD HEAD CAPER

The inspector never faced this kind of attitude before. Not in such a young lady, anyway. He was perplexed. "I s'pose so, Miss, but rules be da rules. And dis be da Belize, you know, Miss."

Marcie glared at him.

The other passengers again smirked.

The inspector felt uncomfortable with her response, and pushed her bag to the end of the table. "Neva mind," he said hurriedly. "Chu be da go. Next!"

Some of the other passengers in line clapped and cheered for her, but they stopped when the inspector angrily glared at them.

Marcie grabbed her backpack. "Well, thank you for nothing," she responded dryly, as she marched out of the building to meet Chuck and Marc.

"Gosh, it's hot," Marc said when the three of them were together again, outside the building.

"You can say that again," Marcie commented.

"Yeah, it is hot," Chuck agreed. "Welcome to Belize. This is the way It's going to be as long as we're in this country. After all, this is the tropics. Almost, anyway."

"I didn't know the tropics were this hot," Marc continued his complaint.

"You've been in hotter places than this," Marcie said. "Remember the time we went to Death Valley? It was hotter than this."

"Yeah, but that was California," Marc said, as though that might have made some difference in how the heat felt.

There were several taxis parked in front of the airport terminal building. The drivers, some brown skinned and some black skinned Belizeans, were hustling the arriving passengers for fares. Several hopeful drivers swarmed around the trio.

One of them, Ringold, the most aggressive, reached for Marcie's backpack while speaking to her. "Me da best driver in da city," he said. "And da most cheap, too, Mon," he added for surety.

"Hey! Give that back!" Marcie retorted, yanking her backpack out of Ringold's grasp.

"Jes' fa da help, Miss," Ringold said, looking abashed as

he ushered them to his taxi. "I jes be fa help chu, Miss," he assured her. "Da mos' cheap in da city," he added, as he opened the passenger side door of his four door, 1970 Ford station wagon with one mismatched front fender.

Marcie glanced at her friends in a questioning way.

Chuck shrugged his shoulders. "He's as good as anyone, I guess," he said.

Ringold grinned broadly. "Now chu leave t'ings to me. Brudda Ringold, he treat chu okay, true."

He guided Marcie into the front seat of the station wagon taxi. He shut the door, but it didn't stay shut. He slammed it shut, and it bounced open again. He slammed it harder, finally getting it to stay shut.

Satisfied with his success, he opened the rear door for Chuck and Marc, had no trouble getting that door to shut properly, and grinned triumphantly as he put their backpacks into the rear of the station wagon. The trunk lid had no trouble staying shut because it lifted upwards, and gravity was its lock. He bounded around the car, scrambled into the driver's seat, ignored the fact that his door didn't quite shut all the way, and twisted the key in the ignition to get the car started.

The car backfired, coughed, and with a puff of black smoke from the exhaust pipe, came to life. Ringold put it in gear, and with a jerk the clutch caught, finally getting them underway.

"Where to, Mon, uh, Mon's?" Ringold cheerfully asked, ignoring frequent chuckholes in the road. He deftly maneuvered the station wagon taxi around many of them, but hit some, evidenced by the sudden bouncing and occasional jostling of the vehicle.

"Ah, what's the best hotel in Belize City?" Chuck asked after a few minutes of bouncing.

"The best, Mon? Well, Mon, dat be da Fort George," Ringold answered with deep consideration. "But you don' wan' da be fa dat place, Mon," he added, trying to speak with clearer English, with less Creole accent. "She be fa da rich peoples. Da be fa da tourists. Chu, I t'ink, be fa da Four Fort Street Guesthouse. Dat be fa da likes a chu, true."

"What'd he say?" Marc asked Chuck.

"I thought you spoke English here," Chuck commented in

a sideways response to Marc's question.

"Dat is de English, Mon," Ringold answered in defense. "Dat be da good betta English. I speak da Creole, like fa da mos' people, ya no fa da know I be fa da say."

"Oh," Chuck said, not sure he understood even the best of Creole.

"Can you tell us where to buy camping gear?" Marcie interceded.

"You go fa da jungles, Mon?" Ringold asked.

"Maybe," Chuck answered for her. He was evasive. He wasn't sure it would be a good idea to let anyone know they were headed for the jungle. Especially if they guessed they were on a treasure hunt.

"Well," Ringold answered after some thought. "Da bes' store, she be da Queen's Outfitters on da Queen Street. True."

"Can you take us there after we unload our stuff at the Guest house?" Marcie asked.

"Oh, I t'ink," Ringold smiled. "Maybe I first tak chu fa da Guest House, den maybe chu cotch anudda taxi later. Dat be betta, I t'ink. No charge fa da wait, dat way."

The three rode in silence for the remaining twenty minutes it took to get from the airport road, through town, and to the 4 Fort Street Guesthouse. It was located on the jetty formed by the juncture of the Belize River and the Caribbean. The Fort George Hotel was only around the corner, so the location was just as good, in terms of the cooling afternoon sea breeze, and its rates were cheaper.

Not that it mattered, as it turned out.

CHAPTER 12

Penn spent the remainder of the early morning at Esteban's apartment, and talked Esteban into taking him to the docks for the mid-morning boat ride back to Punta Gorda, Belize. By noon, he was on a Maya Airline flight to Belize City Municipal airport, and by 3:00 p.m. he settled into the rear seat of the six passenger Cessna 307 that Tropic Air flew from Belize Municipal to San Pedro Town.

It was near 3:30 p.m. when he strolled in under the large palapa covering Charley's Grill to order a Korbel brandy in a snifter over ice, with a squeeze of lime. It was the only bar in Belize where he could get away with such an order. Since that was the way he liked his drink, that was the way it was going to be served to him in his favorite haunts.

The afternoon sea breeze blew in from the southern Caribbean, forcing waves across the reef barely a hundred yards from the shore. A vivid white line of foam separated the deep blue sea from the clear water inside the lagoon.

The view never ceased to impress Penn, and the breeze was welcome relief from the sweltering heat, even under the shaded, thatch covered, wood floored veranda.

"David McGaughy, Mon?" the bartender in Charley's Grill responded to Penn's inquiry. "He no be da here mos' tree, four days, true." He smiled as he sat half a glass full of Penn's favorite brandy on the bamboo bar.

THE EMERALD HEAD CAPER

"Oh?" Penn commented, disappointed his friend wasn't around. After all, David's wife operated the local Chinese restaurant. She and Penn didn't get along, which was why he avoided looking for David there. Even David avoided spending any of his free time there, if he could get away with it. However, for David to be gone for three or four days meant involvement with something major. "Did the Brits ask for his help again? Is that why he's been gone for so long?" he asked.

"No, Mon," the bartender said. "The Mon and Mister Richy, they be fa da jungle. Some say some t'ing 'bout dey be fa da Emerald Head. Chu know fa da Emerald Head, Mon?"

Penn was too surprised to answer the question. What the devil was going on? Did everybody know about that damned Emerald Head? Was everyone in the whole darned world looking for the Emerald Head? "Ah, no, I guess I don't," he responded at length, lying. "Well, if you happen to see him, tell him I'm looking for him, will you?" He tossed a Belizean five-dollar dollar bill on the counter, which included a sizeable tip to accent his request.

"Mister Richy?? Penn muttered. Mister Richy was Richard Gunter, the local, and only native, University of San Francisco graduate, marine biologist.

"Right, Mon," the bartender grinned as he retrieved his tip. "An' where be fa chu?"

"I think," Penn answered after some thought, "I'll be at Mom's Triangle Cafe in the city every morning for the next few days. Tell David he can catch up with me there. Tell him I'd like to see him about something important, okay?"

"Okay, Mon. For true. I tell him."

Penn gulped down his drink and headed back to the sandy street leading to the small local airstrip. Spending any more time on the cay would be a waste, since there were some things to get his hands on before he could consider looking for the Emerald Head himself. One of those things happened to flash through his mind. Perhaps the daughter of the Chief of Police was still around. He would make it a point to call her at the first opportunity.

When he returned to Belize City, he went straight to the Four Fort Street Guesthouse. He didn't need a room, but he

115

Harold R. Miller

needed a telephone. It had to be a land line, not a cell phone which anyone could intercept, and a private telephone where he could make his calls without the interference of someone standing next to him, urging him to hurry up and get off the damned thing so they could use it, as was the problem with using public telephones in Belize. By five p.m. he climbed the front stairs to the Guesthouse.

"Well," Mary Mercale said, greeting him at the doorway. "I never expected y'all'd be back so soon, Honey Child."

Penn eyed her. That, he considered, was a fact. He wondered just how much she knew of his chase into Puerto Barrios after Quigley. After all, she told Esteban he was going to Guatemala. He wondered why Esteban didn't tell her he was returning? Or did he?

"Well," he said with a wide grin. "You know how things are. Sometimes you win. Sometimes you lose." He recalled the lost, or eaten, map copy, but he didn't want to recall the loss of his friend. He didn't want to even think about that. There would be other times. He would visit Lesley's grave, and say a few prayers.

"And sometimes y'all don't get what y'all went after," she responded pointedly.

That took Penn back, but he never answered, never said anything witty and pointed, like he should have. "Can I use your phone?" he asked, instead. He needed to call Thorne Beusch and get another copy of that map, or half map. If he could only remember the telephone number written on the bottom of the map part he lost. He, at least, remembered the town, so he decided he would try long distance information, not an easy task in that part of the Caribbean.

The phone system in Belize was the worst in the world, save possibly Ghana, or Guinea. Or was it Guyana he was trying to recall? There were so many. But that was another story. It was hard to remember. He had to stop drinking so much, he chastised himself. It fogs the memory. Or maybe I ought to start drinking more, to erase the memories.

Mary made the phone available, and he tried to make his call, but he never got anywhere. He did manage to get the number for Thorne's office, but no one answered his call, so he hung up after the twentieth ring.

He glanced at the pencil and pad beside the phone. There was some doodling on the pad, a lot of lines like those made by people talking to other people on the phone. He didn't try to make any sense of the lines, but the notebook suddenly made a great deal of sense. The memory of the map flashed through his mind. "I wonder," he thought. "Can I remember enough of that map to sketch it?" He grabbed the pencil and began sketching.

After half an hour and half an eraser later, he decided he remembered about as much as he was going to remember of that map. He picked up the sketch, peered at it once more to try to shake loose any other detail he might have missed, grinned as he folded it up and stuck it in the pocket of the shirt Esteban gave him in Puerto Barrios. He left the Mary's office and returned to the bar.

"Well," Mary Mercale greeted him in the bar. "I was beginning to think you died in there. Did you get your call through?"

He considered she knew darn well whether or not he did. "No such luck," he said in appeasement of her over-worked curiosity. "You know how it is."

"Don't I, though?" she laughed as she walked away from the bar to talk to some other guests; a rich Frenchman and a woman companion half his age. They were complaining about the lack of personal service.

It was after his third Rum and Coke when Penn decided he didn't want to stay in the 4 Fort Street Guesthouse, even though he could afford it after depositing Thorne Beusche's check. He wanted to stay somewhere nice and out of the way, like Bellevue Hotel, instead. At least he could be alone with his thoughts, outside the reach of Mary Mercale's persistent curiosity. He paid his bill and left without explanation, and headed for the Bellecue for a goods night's sleep.

The following morning, Penn strolled out of the Belleview Hotel in Belize City, just across the river's mouth from the Fort George Hotel. He walked to the usual waiting line of taxis, and hoped to find one that didn't look too much like it would fail to get him where he wanted to go; something that was also fairly usual in Belize.

Harold R. Miller

Ringold's taxi was in the waiting line. He wasn't first in line, so the drivers in front of him were perturbed when he got out of his taxi to waive to the fare prospect, but they found other things to occupy their minds when they realized Penn knew Ringold.

Ringold greeted Penn like an old friend, extending his hand. "Mon. I don' believe t'is," he said with a wide grin. "For True! Why chu fa da stay here in Belize, my friend? I t'ink maybe you go see da Guats for biz'ness."

Penn laughed. "Good to see you too, old friend," he said. "I did go to Guatemala, but I came back." What the hell? He asked himself. Did everyone know he went to Guatemala?

"More business," Ringold said, pondering his friend's presence. "Dat not so good, true! Da las' time chu end up in da city jail, Mon. Chu got da take wid da care, Mon, dis time."

Penn laughed again.

"Chu leave da Chief of Police daughter alone now?" He grinned mischievously. "Da Chief, he still mad."

Penn laughed again as he climbed into the passenger seat of the station wagon and slammed the front door as hard as he could to make it stay shut.

Ringold got into the driver's seat, started the car, and amid a puff of black exhaust, roared away from the hotel.

A Belizean in a white Guayabara shirt stepped from the shade of the hotel overhang and lit a cigarette. He eyed the departing station wagon.

In his usual rush, Ringold tried to miss the ever-present potholes in the Belizean road. Again, he wasn't too successful.

"Hey!" Penn reprimanded his friend. "You almost missed that one."

"I maybe miss one or two, true, but mos' I can get, Mon," Ringold laughed. "Where fa chu go, Mon?"

"The Queen's Outfitters, I guess. Is Madam Cheap Sell still running the place?"

"She be running dat place from now 'til Belize be returned to da Guats, Mon." He twisted the wheel to try to miss another pothole. The taxi bounced. He didn't succeed. "And dat be fa da never, Mon!"

"For Pete's sake. The Guatemalans are still trying to claim

THE EMERALD HEAD CAPER

Belize?"

"Yah, Mon. Right now, big talk a da 'vasion, Mon."

"Invasion? Hell, the Brits would stop them in a hurry if they tried that." Penn glanced out the window. He had a thought. "You better stop and let me get a bottle or two of rum before we get to Cheap Sell's."

"Goin' to make fa da discount, hunh, Mon?" Ringold smirked. Four minutes later, he pulled the taxi to a stop in front of convenient liquor store, one of many on the streets of Belize City.

Penn went into the store and returned several minutes later with two bottles of Myers's dark Jamaican rum. He held them up while he got into the taxi. "These will get me a good discount, don't you think?" he joked.

Ringold eyed the two bottles of expensive rum, the most expensive available in the country. "Maybe," he chuckled.

Ten minutes later the taxi pulled to a stop in front of an old two-story building with corrugated sides and a wood with glass pane front door. The building was a left over from pre-Hurricane Hattie days, and the flood left its marks on the walls nearly eight feet above the sidewalk. No one painted the building since that time, which wasn't unusual for things in Belize City. Paint was not one of the most common commodities in the city.

Penn got out of the taxi carrying one of the bottles of rum behind his back. The other bottle he stuck in his belt under his shirt behind his back, out of view. He appraised the building with a smile of familiarity, reading the writing on the glass pane. "QUEEN'S OUTFITTERS," he read. "Mdme. Chee Sell, Prop." He smiled as he opened the door and stepped inside.

He was greeted by the warming odor of rope, beeswax, and Teakwood used in ship's stores. It was a smell he relished. It reminded him of his good days aboard his yacht, the Flyin' Penguin; of the days before he got mixed up with Lara; before she found love at first sight and ran off with that pharmaceutical salesman on the nude beach in Mexico, whose over-sized appendage over-awed her. He often wondered what she was doing now. Spawning babies in Mexico, probably, but he didn't want to think about that.

The interior of the general merchandise store was cluttered

with articles of clothing, house-wares, camping gear, lamps, wire, rope, and innumerable miscellaneous gear, all stacked and piled on shelves and counters throughout, in no particular order.

Standing behind the sales counter, beside an ancient cash register in the one clear spot on the counter, sat the person most people called Cheap Sell.

The name was an Americanized bastardization of Madame Chee Sell. She was a seemingly ancient Oriental woman of small physical stature, a wizened face with wispy gray hair, and clear, piercing black eyes. When Penn entered the store, she was chewing on a sugar cane stalk which protruded from her mouth like an overgrown cigar. She was engrossed in reading a receipt that looked as though it might be as old as she is.

Penn quietly shut the door, trying to avoid ringing the old-fashioned cowbell hanging from the doorframe to alert the owner of patrons, and quietly sneaked over to the counter, sidling up to Chee Sel on her right side. He knew she couldn't see clearly out of her right eye. That was why she always kept squinting out of it, somewhat reminiscent of Popeye, with the sugar cane looking all the while like the corn cob pipe of the cartoon character.

He kept the rum bottle behind his back, and came within two feet of the counter when Chee Sel grinned broadly. He didn't take her by surprise.

She slowly turned to peer at Penn, keeping the sugar cane between her aged teeth. "So," she said, nearly cackling with glee. "You think Madam Chee Sell no see you? All a time, you think maybe you sneak up on Madam Chee Sell? You no can do. I see you!" She laughed loud, heartily and friendly. "So, Penn! You back in town now?"

"Damn!" Penn said, feigning disappointment. "Some time, Cheap Sell. Some time I'll make it." He stepped up to the counter. "Hi, Cheap Sell," he added.

"My name, Chee Sel," she indignantly corrected him. "Not Cheap Sell. All a time you call me Cheap Sell. Chee Sel! My name Chee Sel!"

Penn grinned mischievously. "Okay. C h e e S e l." He drew the name out for emphasis. "I'll be sure to remember that."

The old woman grinned with satisfaction, having made her point. "That good, you 'member." She took the cane out of her mouth, inspected it, twisted it around and stuck it back in her mouth, to again clamp down on it with her aged teeth. "Now. Why you back Belize?" she asked. "You likee Belize, hunh? You no come here long time. "

He decided not to tell her he didn't go to the states, that he simply was too busy to drop in on an old friend. "Yes," he answered, instead, wondering how she managed to speak over the sugar cane. "I like Belize. I came back because I have more business to tend to." He glanced around the store. "Yeah. I like Belize," he repeated thoughtfully.

"That good. You betta' off here. States no good. I no likee states. Too much many peoples. Not so much here." She chewed thoughtfully on her sugar cane while eyeing her friend. "You bring rum? Good rum? I likee Myer rum. You bring Myer rum?"

Penn laughed. "You don't ever waste time with formalities, do you, Cheap Sell?"

She glared at him again for the mispronunciation of her name. She opened her mouth to object again, but she stopped when Penn brought his hand from behind his back.

"Here," he said. "Myers's rum."

She grinned broadly. She was delighted. "We drinkee now," she cackled. "I get glass." She grabbed the bottle from Penn's hand and began searching about the stacks of merchandise on the counter, tossing items around in her efforts. "Where glass?" she complained. "No ding gum glass!" At length, she straightened up. "No matter," she said as she broke the seal on the bottle and opened it. She took the sugar cane from her mouth and carefully placed it on the counter, tipped the bottle to her lips and took a long swallow.

Penn watched her in amazement. Not even he, with all his recent experience, could drink rum in that quantity.

Chee Sel finished her drink and held the bottle out.

"You betta off take one drink. Makee you betta. Little drink, though. You not drink all up."

"No. Thanks, I don't think so, Cheap, I mean, Chee Sel.

I got some buying to do." He didn't want to get drunk at this point. There was too much at stake. In reconsideration, he wondered if he was getting over his need for booze. Sometimes it wasn't so important as it was in the past.

Chee Sel shrugged her shoulders. "Okay," she said as she waived her hand at the store. "You lookee. You buyee. Plenty discount. Good rum. You lookee." She lifted the bottle to her lips for another drink as Penn began rummaging through the aisles of merchandise.

It took thirty minutes for Penn to find all the merchandise he needed, carry it to the counter, and stack it in a manner which safeguarded it from being knocked off the counter by Chee Sel in her curious studying of it all.

That was also how long it took for Chee Sel to polish off the first bottle of Myers's rum while inspecting the merchandise.

Whenever Penn paused in his moving up and down the counters, Chee Sel would grab a pile of the merchandise of the stack, ring it up on the cash register, and stuff it into a gunnysack. When she was certain Penn wasn't looking, she would ring up an item twice. If it were a small item, maybe she would ring it up three times, grinning slyly all the time.

Penn finished his searching, and brought all the things he wanted to the counter, plus quite a number of small items he really didn't want, but which he quickly dropped into the gunnysack when Chee Sel was concentrating on the cash register, and wouldn't see his actions. He enjoyed playing the game. Sometimes it was a challenge to see who could outsmart the other. It was an inconsequential game, in terms of money, for they both realized the other person knew, even expected, it was going on. All in all, the price would work out to be just about the same as if nothing were toyed with, register-wise.

Finally, Penn glanced at the pile of hats on the end of the counter. He selected the one 'Indiana Jones' style hat, tried it on, and glanced in the cracked mirror behind the counter.

Chee Sel nodded approvingly. "That good hat," she said as she added its sale to the register. "I likee on you. Ever'body archee-logist and big artee-fact hunter man wear same hat. Need whip, too."

"Always trying to make a bigger sale, hunh, Cheap Sell?"

THE EMERALD HEAD CAPER

Penn kidded as he reached into his pocket and extracted a wad of Belizean money. "No. I don't think I need a whip, thanks. I'd just end up wrapping it around my neck, or something."

Chee Sel shrugged and rang up the total for the merchandise.

An overweight Belizean male in his mid forties entered the store. He carelessly slammed the door behind him, and casually glanced at the counter, before moving about to scrutinize various items of merchandise, then abruptly exited the store without making a purchase, without saying anything.

Chee Sel peered at the man's exit, then returned to her task of stuffing the rest of the merchandise into the nearly full gunnysack. "This plenney stuff," she said at length, finished with her stuffing. She studied the cash register total. "One hunna' fi'hee dolla'. Maybe 'nough stuff, maybe not 'nough. Maybe you betta off get more." She peered at him slyly. "What you got behind you in shirt? Maybe you likee something you no likee pay for?"

Penn laughed. He knew she would eventually bring that up. He reached under his shirt and extracted the second bottle of Myers's rum. "This is what I have behind my back," he said as he handed the bottle to her. "It's for you, too. I didn't want you to have it earlier, you'd drink it all by now. Better you save some of it for later, don't you think?"

Chee Sel grinned. "You one plentee smart fella," she said as she took the bottle. "Okay. One huhna' dolla'. No less." She placed the bottle under the counter.

Penn peeled five Belizean twenty-dollar bills from his roll and handed them to her. "Here you are, Cheap Sell. You drive a hard bargain."

"Bargain? You drive plentee hard bargain! Me, I feel plentee good. Rum too good, maybe. I give all store away today. Maybe, I think you do alla this for reason. You get me plenty feel good, take alla t'ing discount. Maybe all store discount. Maybe."

"Maybe," Penn replied. "So maybe you better not drink the rest of that today." He picked up the gunnysack and slung it over his shoulder. "Anyway, I'll have that drink with you when I get back."

Harold R. Miller

Chee Sel reached for the new bottle. She quickly uncapped it and took a drink. "One for road," she grinned. "Alla time need one for road."

Penn laughed and strode to the door. He reached for the door handle, but just as he was about to grab it, the door opened.

In stepped Chuck, followed by Marc and Marcie.

Penn stepped back and curiously glanced at them as they filed past.

Marcie shot a glance at Penn, and did a double take. She didn't know why, but the man looked vaguely familiar to her.

Penn politely nodded to her and exited the store, shutting the door behind him.

Chuck noticed Marcie's curious expression. "What's wrong?" he asked her.

"Oh, nothing, really," she replied, turning her attention to the store. "I just had the funniest feeling I've seen that man before, that's all"

Chee Sel was still behind the counter. She eyed the children with suspicion. "You got plentee money?" she asked. "This store alla same cost plentee."

Chuck frowned. "Oh, I think we can pay for what we want." He began searching the aisles, followed by Marcie and Marc.

Half an hour later they managed to carry all their purchase to the counter, and Chee Sel rang it up.

"How much do you want?" Chuck asked when Chee Sel finished.

"Plentee money," she answered. She glanced at the stuff she put in the sack as she rang it up. "You got everyt'ing?"

"Come to think of it," Marcie answered as she glanced at a coil of rope at the end of the counter. "We better take some rope, too." She uncoiled some of the quarter inch diameter Nylon line from the display, and wound nearly fifty feet of it around her elbow and the base of her thumb. She wrapped the end of the rope around the coil to keep it from uncoiling, and dropped the coil on the counter.

"Plentee more money," Chee Sel said, adding the cost of the rope to the sale. "Two hunha dolla'," she said.

THE EMERALD HEAD CAPER

Chuck winced, as he removed a book of Wells Fargo Traveler's checks from his pocket. He signed two of them and handed them over.

Chee Sel glanced at the checks, stuck them in her cash drawer, added the coil of rope to the gunny sack, and placed the sack on the counter. "Plentee good sale," she said. "You come more plentee soon."

Chuck grabbed the gunnysack, tossed it over his shoulder in his nonchalant way, and lead the way out of the store.

As they reached the door, the same heavy set Belizean man returned and rudely pushed past them.

Chee Sel was in the middle of another drink when the man slammed the door shut. She jumped, and spilled some of her rum on the floor. "Alla same damn!" she swore in her fashion while the man strode over to face her. "Ding gum you!" she swore at the man. "You makee me spill good rum. What you want? You betta be plentee important. You makee spill rum."

"What did the gringo want?" the man asked gruffly. "He bought a lot of camping gear. Did he say where he was going?"

Chee Sel put her rum bottle under the counter for safe keeping, placed both hands on the counter, and glared at the man in a defiant manner. "You no nice. I no likee you. Maybe I no tell you."

"Did those kids get the same stuff?" he asked, ignoring her response.

Chee Sel glared at him without answering.

The man studied her for a minute, reached into his pocket and pulled out his wallet to present his Belizean Police identification card and a star badge.

She eyed the badge, and forced a wide grin. "I no know you policemans," she said. "Solly. Plentee solly."

"Yeah, sure," he said with a disgusted expression. "Now tell me. Did that gringo say where he was going?"

"No. He no say. But I know. He buy plentee stuff. He go jungle. South, maybe. I think, maybe lotta jungle, lotta time outside. Plentee stuff."

"South?" the man asked.

"I say maybe so. I t'ink so. Plentee jungle stuff. Only

125

jungle south."

"Those teenagers," he asked. "They bought a lot of stuff, too?"

"I t'ink maybe they go plentee jungle, too," she responded.

"Are they with him?"

"I no t'ink so. I t'ink maybe all a same no."

The man shoved his wallet back into his pocket and headed for the door.

Chee Sel watched him leave. After he slammed the door behind his exit, she lifted her rum bottle. "Ding gum cop!" she said before taking another drink.

CHAPTER 13

It was the middle of the afternoon. The heat was again oppressive, although it didn't bother the Chief of Police of Belize City as he sat in the middle of his old and weary office in his old and weary wood office chair at his old and weary wood desk. The only fixture in the office that didn't stem from before the colonial days was an electric overhead fan churning its three-foot wooden blades in constant battle against the multitude of flies.

An old wood door closed the one entrance to the office. There were two windows, both covered by wood jalousies which were stuck halfway open, left in that position for too many years to be movable. Even if the jalousies were closed, they wouldn't keep out the afternoon's heat, because half the slats were missing, or broken. Of course, there wasn't any glass in the windows, a normal condition for Belize government buildings, because air conditioning was a luxury not to be wasted on civil servants.

An ancient file cabinet set along one wall beside a stand-up cabinet with doors locked by a padlock, and a bare light bulb hung on a wire from the chipped plaster ceiling.

The low watt bulb cast a soft shine on the forehead of the Belizean cop who recently visited Chee Sel's store. He held his hat in his hands as he stood in the center of the room, facing the police chief.

Harold R. Miller

"You are sure they are all going to the southern jungle?" the chief asked.

"Yes, Sir," the cop said. "They bought gear and provisions for the jungle, and they told the owner of the store they're going south into the country."

"Did they mention why?"

"They didn't say, according to the owner."

The Police Chief looked at his watch. He frowned. It was getting late, and he had important things to tend to. "I see," he added, almost as an afterthought. "Very well. Thank you." He picked up a pencil and began scratching some notes on a well-doodled piece of paper on his desk. He looked pensive, then noted the cop was still standing before him. "I think you did a good job," he added.

The cop beamed, got the point, nodded, and left the room, trying to quietly shut the creaky old door behind him.

As soon as the cop left, the Police Chief put down his pencil and got out of his chair. He locked the office door with the old fashioned skeleton key, and turned off the overhead light. He extracted another key from his pocket, and unlocked the wood doors on the old wood cabinet.

He retrieved an eye shaped crystal from an ornately carved small wood chest on a shelf in the cabinet, and with care, as if it were a priceless heirloom, placed it on an electronic base built into a wood altar on another shelf of the cabinet. He stepped back, closed his eyes for deep concentration, and slowly opened his eyes to peer at the crystal.

The crystal started glowing. It shone opalescent, dimmed, and glowed anew with brighter colors. It glowed bright orange, and turned to vivid green. Its eerie luminescence flooded the room, creating an alien ambiance, one a person would imagine the Venusian landscape to be; pallid green, the color of impending death.

The Police Chief's eyes glowed in matching green, blazing with an inner fire, as he concentrated on the crystal. The crystal's intensity fluctuated, and the variations were reflected in the Police Chief's eyes.

The electronic speaker below the altar vibrated.

The Police Chief slowly grinned. He received the message,

a word from beyond. He nodded, and shut his eyes.

The crystal's eerie glow faded.

The Police Chief opened his eyes. He was satisfied with the message received through the crystal.

He replaced the crystal in the wood chest, shut the cabinet and locked it, returned to his desk, where he grabbed the telephone and dialed a single digit. "Send in the Captain of Patrol," he ordered when his office secretary responded to his call. "I want him to find some gringos for me."

* * * *

Chuck, Marc and Marcie finished stowing their gear into the rented Suzuki Samarai in the front parking lot of their hotel.

"Well," Chuck said, as he climbed into the driver's seat. "I guess that makes us just about ready. Right?" He looked at his friends for their confirmation. "I'll drive, unless anyone has any arguments?" He opened the passenger's side door and began to climb into the front seat.

"Marc," Marcie said to her brother. "You can get into the back. I'm going to be doing the navigating, and I need the front."

"You're gonna do the navigating?" Marc responded with concern. "I thought I was." He frowned.

Marcie gave him her warning glance.

"I ought to do the navigating," Marc persisted. "Since that's man's work."

Marcie lowered her eyebrows and glared.

"Okay," Marc quickly relented. "Okay. I guess you can navigate just as good as a man can, anyway." He quickly climbed past the front seat into the tightly packed, cramped rear seat of the two-door vehicle.

Marcie got into her passenger's seat, and Chuck put the vehicle in gear. His first experience with the quick clutch of the Japanese four-wheel machine ended up in a lurching start, and his shifting into second gear was an exaggeration of letting out the clutch too slowly. It wasn't until he wrestled the machine into third gear, the one suitable for the city traffic, that he gained control of it, much to the relief of his passengers.

Marcie studied her free tourist map of downtown Belize City, and directed their route through the narrow streets leaving the hotel. They traveled along Queen's Street and up to the Swinging Bridge near the center of the normally bustling town, where all traffic inexplicably stopped.

"What do you suppose is going on here?" Marcie asked, glancing at the line of stopped cars.

Not only were the cars stopped, but the lines of bustling pedestrians were also stopped.

. "They seem to be waiting for something to happen, don't they?" Marcie commented, catching the smiling glances of one tall, dark skinned local man leaning against the nearby railing on the bridge's approach. She glanced at him, but quickly turned her head in embarrassment.

He laughed, confident, cocky, sure of himself in his role of the native in his land frequented by gawking tourists. He placed the young people in the Samarai in the same category of tourists.

"Hey! Look at that!" Marc said, distracting her chagrin. "The bridge's swinging open."

The three craned their necks to look around the line of cars in front of them, but they needn't have bothered, for the end of the bridge came into view as it swung around.

"Well, for Pete's sake," Marcie said impatiently, trying to hide her embarrassment over her interest in the attractive native who was still eyeing her with a confident grin. "You'd think this country could at least put in a permanent bridge." She avoided the persistent stare of the Belizean native less than five feet from her side of the car.

"Da bridge, Miss," the native offered in explanation, without being asked. "It be da swing bridge fa da boats dey fa da Haul Over Creek can go fa da ocean, Miss."

Marcie turned to him. She smiled, caught herself, and blushed.

"It so da boats go fa da sea," he repeated, as if more of an explanation was needed.

"Oh," she responded, carefully avoiding the man's flashing black eyes.

THE EMERALD HEAD CAPER

"She be open 'nudda twenty minutes, fa true," he added. "Evy'day, dis time, noon, she be fa da open for twenty minutes. True." He grinned. "Chu got not'ing fa da do but fa da wait. Maybe tahk wid da natives?" He lightly laughed in his confidence. "May be, in dat time, for true, you find some body wid fa da tahk?"

The suggestion was too bold for Marcie's acceptance. She wasn't about to be that friendly with anyone she didn't formally meet, even if he seemed nice, and was striking, in an interesting way. She was told about meeting men in such a manner. "I don't think so," she responded, trying to be cool in a friendly way. The more she thought of his suggestion, the more nervous she became "No," she added. "I don't need anyone else to talk to, thank you." She was careful to make her tone less than friendly, as a means of defense.

The native shrugged, and grinned. "Jes be fa da help, Miss," he said, before striding back into the crowd behind them. He reached into his pocket and pulled out his pipe. He retrieved another green rock from his other trousers, and stuffed it into the pipe. A few minutes later he walked around the corner to Mom's Triangle Café, smoking his crack, wondering why everyone was so unfriendly. Was he the only one in all of Belize City who felt good?

"You shouldn't be so friendly with the local populace," Chuck cautioned. "You never know what they have in mind."

"He seemed friendly enough," Marc offered.

"Chuck's right," Marcie responded. She was sure of herself, now that she made the right decision in turning down the man's offer of friendliness, which she was certain would lead to more complicated things. She didn't need anything like that so far away from home.

Chuck was the first to note the bridge's change in direction after about twenty minutes of silent, not too patient, fidgety waiting in the noon time heat. "Well, at least the bridge is swinging back in the other direction now," he said. "Maybe they're closing it."

"About time," Marc said.

The clouds gathered over the city, and the typical afternoon rain began, as the line of cars began moving. It moved slowly at first, then with the customary recklessness and abandon that characterized driving in Belize City, even during the rain.

When the teenagers crossed the center of the bridge, they saw the three bridge attendants who operated the human powered cranking pin used to wind the bridge around on its axis. The men carried the four-foot long crank handles over their shoulders as they strode off the bridge.

"Good grief," Marcie remarked, watching the men. "Can't they afford machinery to do that sort of thing in this country?"

"Human power is much more reliable," Chuck said, while he maneuvered the Samarai through the heavy pedestrian traffic flooding into the street at the end of the bridge.

"Good grief!" Marcie remarked again, when they threaded their way through the crowd on the busiest two-lane street in the city. Pedestrians darted across in front of the cars, and the drivers honked fruitlessly, angrily, some of them shouting rude phrases at the non-caring pedestrians. Most of the comments were in heavy Creole accents unintelligible to the three in the Samarai, even though it was a form of English.

Marcie was amazed by the scene. "This is worse than New York," she said.

"At least as bad," Marc added.

Chuck laughed. "When have either of you ever been to New York?"

"Hey! I read about it," Marcie quipped in defense.

"Yeah," Marc added.

"Sure," Chuck laughed.

"Look out!" Marcie suddenly shouted.

A taxi darted out from a side street, passing dangerously close in front of them.

Chuck slammed on the brakes, nearly sliding.

The taxi driver's timing was accurate. He missed the Samarai by at least several feet, as his 1970 model Chevrolet station wagon belched exhaust smoke across the road.

"Good Grief!" Marcie exclaimed for a third time. She tended to repeat herself when amazed, or surprised, by anything. "He nearly hit us!"

"Not to worry," Chuck said, putting the vehicle in gear again, carefully glancing up and down the cross street before continuing. "I missed him by a mile."

Past the intersection he accelerated in response to the persistent honking of horns. The drivers behind him were impatient. He noted the police cruiser parked at the curb, and hoped they didn't notice the incident.

The police in the cruiser did notice the Samarai, though. They pulled out from the side street and butted their way into the line of cars directly behind the Suzuki, with their red and blue top lights flashing.

"Now what?" Chuck complained, stopping at the side of the street. The cruiser stopped close to his rear bumper.

"Well, good grief," Marcie came forth with her favorite phrase once more as she turned around to see the two policemen get out of the police cruiser.

"Oh, oh," Marc added his most common phrase.

One policeman approached the driver's side window of the Suzuki as the other stood slightly behind and to the right side of vehicle.

"Good afternoon, Officer," Chuck said to the policeman in his most courteous tone. "Is something wrong?"

"Yah, Mon," the officer responded in his most officious tone. "I t'ink so. Chu license, please, Mon?"

"Ah, driver's license?" Chuck responded, reaching for his wallet. "I have a California license. It's good here, isn't it?" He searched through his wallet for his license. "Anyway, what did I do wrong?"

"Chu no stop fa da stop sign at da corner," the policeman said, accepting the license held out for him.

"But..." Chuck began. He glanced back at the intersection. "There isn't any stop sign there."

"Ah, but dat be only fa da moment. Der be da stop sign der mos' day," the policeman said. "Today it be fa da broke," he added, cursorily glancing at Chuck's license. "Fa da broke don' mean no fa da stop. Da law be da same, no matta."

"Hunh?" Chuck asked.

"For Pete's sakes," Marcie complained. "That's absurd!"

"Yah? Chu t'ink so?"

"I do think so!" Marcie repeated indignantly.

Chuck shot a reprimanding glance at Marcie, trying to tell

her to be less rude.

She ignored him.

"I don' t'ink so. Da law be da law." He seemed to grin, having made his point. "I t'ink, too, chu betta come wid me fa da police headquarters. True!"

"What?" Marcie complained in spite of Chuck's attempts to signal her to keep quiet. He visited some foreign countries, and knew the power the police had in them. They weren't anything like the police in the United States.

"Now. Chu fa da come now, fa true!" the officer asserted, opening the driver's door.

The second officer opened the passenger side door.

"Chu come wid us, now, I say," the policeman repeated his order.

Marcie glanced at Chuck. She wished she heeded his reprimand.

"Oh, oh," Marc said.

Chuck shrugged and got out of the car.

The second policeman reached in to help Marcie out of the passenger side of the vehicle.

"I don't need any help," Marcie said, yanking her arm free. "I'm coming."

Her sudden rebuff surprised the policeman.

"Oh, oh," Marc repeated.

"Chu, too, Mon," the policeman said to Marc.

Marc quietly got out of the vehicle and joined the others as they headed for the police cruiser.

CHAPTER 14

Penn was sleeping in the double bed beneath a slowly revolving wood blade ceiling fan in another second rate motel room. It was again hot and humid. That was why he was covered by a threadbare linen sheet up to his waist.

A blonde of attractive and busty proportions was lying beside him; her ample form outlined by the sheet.

A steel jail cell door slammed shut in the distance.

Penn jumped at the sound. He sat up. He looked around. The bed, a well-worn jail cell cot, was empty beside him. He rubbed his hand over his forehead in realization he was dreaming, again.

He looked around and re-appraised his surroundings. Much to his dislike, he recognized the inside of the very dirty jail cell which held him captive.

Light entered through the one window with rusted bars in the wall. It shined across one of the four cots hanging off the another cement wall, one covered with graffiti scrawled between the broken and chipped plaster. He was wearing off the affects of the prior night's over indulgence in White Caribbean rum. At the moment he wished it were Korbel. It didn't leave such a terrible reminder of the prior night's foolishness.

He also wished he could remember what he did with all the gear he bought from Chee Sel. Where'd he put it? Trying to remember made his head hurt. "Damn cheap rum!" he complained aloud. The noise of his complaint only made his head hurt more.

He decided to stand. Slowly, he placed his feet on the floor. He looked at the cell window, and shook his head to clear some of the cobwebs. It didn't work. Immediately his head hurt some more. "Got to have something to get over this," he groaned. He reached inside his half-unbuttoned shirt. "Ah," he grinned. "Here it is."

He retrieved a nearly empty half-pint of the same Caribbean White rum, deciding a little hair of the dog was in order. He uncapped the bottle and lifted it to his lips. He was in the middle of a quick swallow when he heard the jailer coming down the corridor, plodding along with all the noisy pomp and circumstance of an important person, of someone acting as though expecting an audience with the queen.

The jailer stopped in front of the cell, and with a noise that sounded to Penn like a sledgehammer, pounded the rusty skeleton key into the cell gate lock. With a twisting flick of his wrist that revealed many years experience in dealing with the very same door with the same old fashioned skeleton key, he unlocked it and slammed it open. There were no rubber doorstops in the jail, and the door banged against the ancient cement block wall, resounding like an explosion of a bursting balloon, sending chipped plaster flying.

"Here be da 'commodations fa da nite," the jailer said with a laugh, motioning for his charges, the three teenagers ushered along behind him, to make their way inside the cell.

Chuck and Marc were the first to enter the cell.

A reluctant and very vocal Marcie followed them. "What do you think you're doing?" she shouted at the jailer as she stopped at the cell door. "You don't have any right to put us in jail!"

The jailer shrugged, grabbed her by the arm, and shoved her through the door.

"Let go of me, you... you ape!" she complained, as she shook off the jailer's grip.

The jailer laughed as he let go of her, and slammed the door shut with a clank loud enough to wake the dead from the cemetery half a mile away. He twisted the oversize skeleton key in the lock, yanked on the door several times to make sure it was locked, and chuckled again as he strolled back to the office out of view. A second door slammed shut with enough force to awaken those from the cemetery who missed the first wake up call.

Through it all, Penn sat with one hand against his ear, fighting the sound. The other hand held the rum bottle next to his lips. After the jailer left, he decided to finish his drink, which was also the last of the bottle's contents. He studied the emptied bottle with some disappointment, screwed the cap back on, and tossed it on the bunk before turning his attention to the three teenagers. "Well, well. Company's come," he remarked with a forced grin. "Darn it," he complained, reminded by his hangover that sudden outbursts weren't enjoyable.

The teenagers stood in a single line abreast, facing him. "Hey. Aren't you the man we saw at the outfitters?" Marcie asked.

"You're the girl who stared at me for so long," he answered. He wiped off his brow. "Well, you can get a good look at me now. Do I look any better?" He meant to sound sarcastic, but he was afraid he sounded a little too disparaging.

"You might, if you bothered to get a shave and maybe clean clothes," Marcie replied, glaring at him.

"Hey! Maybe I don't like shaving. And I like my clothes. They're... comfortable."

"Comfortable! Hah! If you washed them, they'd probably fall apart." She frowned and looked around the jail cell. "I can't believe we're in this place," she added as she returned her gaze to Penn, giving him a look of disdain. "And with some drunk, too."

"Look, young lady," Penn defended himself, although he wasn't sure he knew why he had to. "I don't need your temper tantrum, all right? It's not my fault you got yourself thrown in here, so don't try to take it out on me." He wiped his brow again, regretting his sudden outburst and the effect it had on his head. "I need another drink," he added.

"It looks to me like you've had enough, already," Marcie criticized. "Is that why you're here? For drinking?"

"No, it isn't, as a matter of fact." He defended himself again. "I was stone sober when they picked me up." He retrieved the bottle from the bunk and studied it. There might be a sip left in it, he decided.

"Hah! Stone drunk is more like it," Marcie continued.

"Sheez! You sound like my ex-wife. She always had a fit when I took a drink." He uncapped the bottle and tipped it up to his lips, forgetting it was already empty. "That's why I left her in the first place," he continued his argument with Marcie through the bottle, "and now you come to start where she left off? That's all I need." He was silent for a few seconds. "Or, was it why she left me?" He sucked on the bottle to get the last drops, then tossed it on the bunk. He followed it with the cap, not bothering to return it to the empty bottle.

"Listen," Chuck interceded. "We're all more than a little upset about this thing, so let's take time to calm down. Okay? They can't hold us in jail just because we ran a stop sign that wasn't even there."

"Oh," Penn said. "So that's why they threw you in here?"

"Yeah," Chuck answered, as he turned around the try the lower bunk in the opposite wall.

"They can't do that, even in this country, can they?" Marcie asked, as she sat on the bunk beside Chuck.

"They can if they want to," Penn chuckled, then hiccuped. "Making it stick in front of a judge is another thing, though. Of course, it may be a month of two before they get around to taking you to a judge." He peered at Marcie, then glanced at Chuck and Marc. "It's funny, isn't it?" he said. "That you three were arrested for the same thing I was? Quite a coink..." he hiccuped in the middle of the word... "kadink, ah, coincidink, coincidence, I'd say." He paused for a few seconds to think. "And there's 'nother coinca..." He paused long enough to stifle another hiccup. "...ah..dence, too. Why were you there?"

"There where?" Marcie demanded.

"In Cheap Sell's store?"

"Why were you?" Marcie countered with some suspicion.

"I was getting..." hiccup... "some gear for a trip to the southern jungle," he answered, peering at her, curious about the coincidence.

Marcie studied him for several minutes before her curiosity got the best of her. "The southern jungles?" she asked in a tone rife with suspicion. "Why?"

"What is this, an inka.. quition?" he demanded. "I was hired to find something, that's why," he responded. Although the last of the rum settled his hangover problem, it made him slur his speech a little. Funny, he mused, how such a little amount of rum would do that. The thought led to others, and made him chuckle.

"Some goose chase," he snickered, trying to return to the subject at hand. "I'm beginning to think it's not worth it. Even if I do have an old map." He wiped his brow and wistfully glanced at the empty bottle. "Or what I can 'member of it," he added with a frown. He rethought what he said. Damn it! I got to watch my words.

"Map?" the surprised trio exclaimed in unison.

"Even if it might be only a copy," Penn continued, carefully watching his words.

"A copy?" Chuck asked.

He peered at them. "Yeah. So what?" he asked. "A copy of a leather map." He paused. "Leather map? Hah! Probably made last year of old goat skin." He shook his head, trying to clear his thoughts of the rum induced cobweb. "A map of some magical, crystal, emera... a green ol' map," he added. He had to rephrase in mid-sentence. He wasn't sure he wanted them to know what he was talking about.

"Where's your map?" Marcie asked.

"Why?" Penn responded, truly suspicious. At least as suspicious as he could be under the circumstances. "You don't want to steal it, do you?" He waived his arm around in the air as though warding off any such attempts.

"Is it leather?" Marcie continued.

"I said it was a copy, din' I?" Penn responded, staring at her, wondering if his speech was still full of slurring. "It's a copy of a leather one."

"Oh," Marcie responded, evidently disappointed.

"Is it... was the original torn in half?" Chuck asked.

Marcie and Marc exchanged glances, then stared at Penn with anticipation.

Penn returned their stares. He took some time before answering. He wasn't sure if the time was needed to form some strategy, or if it was needed just to think. At least his rum numbed mind was clearing, some. "So what if it is?" He replied. "It's just an old copy... of half a map." He leaned back against the wall. "And how did you know it is, might be...maybe...if I had it, or could remember it, that is, why?" He took a deep breath. Got to clear my mind, he said to himself.

"Oh, my gosh!" the trio commented in unison.

"This is unbelievable!" said Chuck, the first to regain composure.

"It's incredible!" Marcie said.

"Wow!" Marc added.

They stared at Penn. Even though they didn't see his copy, they were sure it was the other half of theirs.

Their amazement was short lived, though. It was interrupted by a grappling hook fastened to a large manila rope, tossed through the jail cell window. It clanked down the inside of the wall, and tension was applied to the rope. The hook dragged up the wall to snag the window bars.

"What on earth?" Marcie asked.

Penn grinned with confidence. "That'll be Ringold, I bet," he said. His pulse rate increased, getting excited about getting out of jail. Good, he thought. Maybe it'll help clear my mind. There's something about these kids that requires concentration.

A car engine roared outside the window. Tires squealed on pavement, and the hook jerked. The window and half the cell wall crumbled away. Dust flew everywhere.

Penn got to his feet and wobbled to the opening. He stepped over some of the rubble, stumbled, caught himself, and motioned to the teenagers. "Are you going to stand here like donkeys all day? Or are you getting out of here with me?" The excitement of the jailbreak helped clear his mental cobwebs. Funny, he thought, how rum affects a person.

The teenagers exchanged glances.

"We can't escape!" Marc said.

"That's against the law!" Marcie said, as she peered at Penn. She recalled his earlier remark. "A month or two before we even get to see a judge?" she said. "No way! Come on!" She grabbed Marc's hand and raced through the rubble of the fallen wall, hot on the Penn's heels.

Chuck lost no time in keeping up.

Just outside the wall, Ringold bent over the badly bent rear bumper of a 4 wheel drive Land Rover, untying the rope to the grappling hook.

"Hey, Ringold, old buddy!" Penn shouted at him. "How did I know it would be you?" He shook his head in defense to the ache the rush of activity caused.

"Hey, Mon! Chu my friend, fa true!" Ringold responded with laughter as he cast aside the rope. "Chu come, now, hurry, true!" he added, rushing to get into the Land Rover. "Dey be da come soon, I t'ink." He hopped in behind the steering wheel. "We betta go quick lak!" He put the vehicle in gear.

"All right, Ringold," Penn laughed as he signaled for the teenagers to get into the vehicle, holding the passenger side door open for them, ignoring the continuing pounding in his head.

Marcie, followed by Marc and Chuck, wasted no time in scrambling into the rear seat, followed by Penn getting into the front seat. Penn didn't get the door completely shut before Ringold roared off down the street with a squealing of tires.

At the same time, three Belizean policemen stumbled out through the rubble of the fallen wall. They took out their pistols and began firing at the fleeing Land Rover.

Their aim was bad, though. They had to shoot while climbing over the rubble of the wall. But then, pistol shooting wasn't a strong point in the Belize Police Academy.

As a matter of fact, their academy training didn't consist of much more than several days of drilling, listening to the pertinent laws being read to them by someone appointed as their instructor, and a day or two getting fitted with a uniform. It wasn't surprising they couldn't hit the broad side of a barn, or even the side of the ramshackle, dilapidated, vacant government building that was their firing range during training.

The Assistant Chief of Police, hearing the shooting, ran around the corner of the building. He took a minute to assess the situation, watched the Land Rover tearing away down the street, then ran for the police cruiser parked nearby, realizing what was about to take place was something he only dreamed of, a high speed chase after fugitives from the law. He considered himself lucky as he scrambled into the cruiser. It took several minutes of struggling against a nearly dead battery to get the cruiser going, as was typical of most vehicles in Belize, before he could start the chase.

Several minutes later, Ringold's Land Rover raced through the city streets, splashing through mud puddles from the afternoon tropical rain, swerving wildly to miss some hapless native trying to cross the street, and another native trying to ride a bicycle with one flat tire and the other only half full of air.

The police cruiser was hot on the tail of the Land Rover, closing in on it.

Ringold glanced into his rear view mirror during one straight stretch of street. "Mon!" he exclaimed. "Dey on us now, true!" He was fast approaching an intersection. Without a second thought, he slammed on the brakes, although they didn't slow the vehicle down nearly enough, and cranked the wheel hard over.

The Land Rover raced around the corner, tipping up on two wheels.

"Whoa, Mon!" Ringold said in grinning confidence as the vehicle returned all four wheels to the pavement, barely missing a street vender's cart loaded with mangos.

The vender shouted at him to slow down, and signaled him with the universal single digit sign.

Marcie barely noted the vender, as she grabbed for something to hold on. The only thing available was Chuck's neck. "We'll all be killed!" She shouted.

Chuck considered his neck might get broken before he had a chance to get killed in any auto accident.

The Land Rover bounced as it rebounded, and tipped in the opposite direction.

Ringold fought for control, and he nearly regained it, only he didn't count on the streets being so slippery from the earlier rain. The vehicle skidded. He fought the slide. When it recovered, so did he, only to find himself struggling even more as the vehicle slid in the opposite direction due to his over controlling. It hit a deep mud puddle, hydroplaned, lost traction completely, and entered a spinning slide.

Ringold grasped the wheel in surprise at his lack of

control, and almost wrenched it from steering column.

Marcie squeezed tighter around Chuck's neck. She screamed again.

Chuck would have shouted something, too, were he able to breathe.

"Oh, oh, oh!" Marc exclaimed.

"I t'ink we be fa da stop, now," Ringold said, feigning self control when the vehicle came to a complete stop, after rolling backward for twenty feet or so.

The assistant chief of police in the police cruiser had to make a panic stop to avoid hitting the Land Rover head on. With hands drained of blood from clenching the steering wheel in preparation for the crash, he took a moment to regain his self-control before opening the door. As he stepped out, he felt his nerves responding. He got angry, and drew his pistol. He almost hoped the jail breakers in the Land Rover would try to make a run for it. "Chu!" he shouted as he crouched down behind the opened car door with his gun pointed at the Land Rover. "Chu get out fa da car! Now! I say!"

The occupants of the Land Rover remained inside.

The assistant chief did not like someone ignoring his power. He fired a shot at the Land Rover, but luckily he was nervous. His bullet careened off the pavement and hit the globe on the nearest lamp post, smashing it to smithereens. The pieces barely landed on the street by the time the occupants scrambled out of the Land Rover with their hands in the air.

Ringold was first out of the vehicle. He stood to one side, peering at the policeman.

The assistant chief, now certain everything went the way he wanted it, certain he was once more in control, approached his prisoners. He cocked his gun just in case he would need a second shot at the lawbreakers.

"Manuel!" Ringold shouted at the policeman.

The assistant chief hesitated, his gun held at the ready. He perked up as Ringold shouted his name a second time. He lost some of his nervousness. "Ringold?" he called back. "Dat be chu, Mon?" he asked, regaining his calm.

Ringold dropped his hands and strode over to greet the policeman. "Manuel!" he said in greeting to his cousin. "Hey!

Harold R. Miller

What chu do, Mon? You be scarin' the bejesus out of us, dat for true! Put down da pistol, Mon."

"Ringold?" the assistant chief laughed when he recognized his cousin. "Ringold!" he repeated. "I for true never knowed fa da be chu!" He put his pistol back in his holster, forgetting to uncock it. "What chu fa da be doin' here, Mon?" He peered at Penn and the trio, who still had their hands in the air. "Chu an dem, all breakin' outta jail, Mon?"

"Hey, Mon," Ringold responded. "Dem be me friens'. Dey ain't 'sposed to be fa da jail! No way!" He grinned in response to his cousin's doubtful expression. "Das why I break dem out. An' now you cotch us?" He laughed, as though it was all a big joke. "Maybe," he resumed in speculation. "Maybe, as I be da cousin da chu, chu fa da let us go, Mon? Maybe?"

The assistant chief scratched his head in thought. "Well, I don' know, Mon. Chu be fa da jailbreak. Dat be illegal, Mon." He paused to think. "For true, Mon?" he began anew. "Dey no belong dere?"

"For true, Mon," Ringold beamed.

The assistant chief thought for at least a minute. "Well. Okay," he finaly said. "Chu say for true? Den fa da true. I never cotched chu." He glanced at the others. "But chu no tell no mon no t'ing, Mon! Da chief? He hear? I no longer da 'sistant."

"No t'ing, Mon. Don' worry. Be happy." Ringold assured him.

"Well, okay, den. Chu betta get now, den. I tell da chief chu no got cotched. Doan' nohow knowed who broke da jail down."

Ringold raced back to the Land Rover. He motioned for the others to join him as he got inside. They climbed in as he started the engine, barely getting in again as he put the vehicle into gear, popped the clutch, and with a lurching start, squealed into a U-turn, racing down the street, once more taking the nearest corner on two wheels.

This time Marcie grabbed Marc's neck for safety since Chuck put him beside Marcie for his own safety. "We're going to get killed!" she shouted.

"Auuuggghhhh," Marc tried to shout an alarm against being choked.

THE EMERALD HEAD CAPER

The officer climbed into his vehicle. He reached over to start the engine, putting his weight against his cocked pistol. He jumped as his pistol fired. The bullet blew a hole in the floorboards, ricocheted, and blew out the left front tire.

That made him really mad. He decided he would catch his cousin again and put them all back in jail for causing his problems. But, when he put his car in gear and stomped on the gas pedal, the flat tire made him lose control. He ran into the same lamp post he hit with his first shot.

The crash completed the attack on the lamp post, and the result was total destruction.

He sat there, the front end of the car was under the bent over pole, with steam pouring out of the hood. He wondered if he should just walk away and never go back to headquarters, or go back and suffer through his chief's anger.

"We better pick up our gear and get out of town, fast," Penn said. "Before the police chief gets word of our escape and sends every cop in the country out looking for us."

CHAPTER 15

An ancient, faded green, battered military Land Rover without a top, rumbled along a muddy road through the Belizean jungle. It splashed through the mud puddles left by a recent afternoon's tropical downpour, and bounced over ruts, rocks and rotting logs that were partially cleared from the road.

The vehicle was an example of what served the Guatemalan Army as a scout vehicle, and Melones was driving. He was steering with one hand while trying to take a drink from his bottle of Caribbean White Rum held in the other.

Guapito, the sergeant, rode in the passenger seat. He looked disgruntled as the poorly maintained Land Rover bounced over yet another mud puddle.

There were three other Guatemalan soldiers crammed into the back, and one of them sat precariously on the edge of the vehicle. Everyone was soaked by the recent rain.

Melones, responsible for checking the vehicle out of the Guatemalan Army's motor pool the week before, didn't consider a need for a canvas top. He didn't expect rain to be so profuse in the jungle, and everyone, particularly Guapito, took every opportunity to criticize him for his gross lack of forethought,

Guapito hated being wet. Being wet made him feel like a water soaked cat. The fact that he actually resembled one that afternoon was something he ignored. His jungle hat, once the pride and joy of his uniform, sagged from the soaking, and his always present cigar jammed into the side of his mouth was so soaked he couldn't light it if he tried. And he didn't try, for the rain continued from sunrise, when they left the Belizean village. That latter fact didn't help his disposition, either.

At last the rain stopped, and Guapito pulled the cigar from his lips. He studied it. Could he at last get it lit? He wondered. Realizing the futility of even thinking of it, he angrily threw it into the jungle. Looking around, he spotted the bottle Melones held, and grabbed it out of the coporal's hand.

Melones shot an angry look at his sergeant, but he dared not argue. Not with a sergeant as ruthless, and at the same time as courageous, as Guapito. After all, wasn't Sargente Guapito Gonzales Gamorra y Sadoma, the only non-commissioned officer in their brigade who had the initiative, and the fortitude, to make them heroes by taking charge of their invasion and organizing their march to overthrow - no, liberate - the Belizeans? How could he argue with such greatness? He returned his eyes to the muddy track through the jungle and concentrated on keeping the Land Rover out of as many mud holes as he could.

There was one particularly large mud hole, though, he couldn't avoid. He hit it squarely, making the Land Rover sail into the air.

Guapito chose that unpropitious minute to take a long swig from the bottle of rum. His hand flew up from his mouth, the rum poured out of the upturned bottle, adding to his water soaked fatigue uniform, not that any addition to the wetness could be ascertained, as messy as he was.

The soldier sitting on the edge of the back of the vehicle bounced high into the air. He let out a yell of surprise, splashed into the puddle, and slid a dozen yards. When he got to his feet, the Land Rover was half a block ahead of him. "Oiga!" he shouted

It took half a mile before the other two soldiers in the rear managed to get their point across to their sergeant that their comrade was running as fast as he could through the mud and puddles, trying to catch up to them.

Melones looked back, and slammed on the brakes, fearful Guapito might do something terrible to him if he lost one of the squad.

In the meantime, Guapito, thinking he regained control

of the rum bottle, tried to take another swallow. The sudden stop, as sudden as could be while sliding through the thick mud, threw him forward. He yanked the bottle down just in time, before it was rammed into his mouth when the bottle hit the windshield, for it could have caused removal of the last of his two front teeth in a most unceremonious manner, if he had any front teeth left after the last cantina brawl he tried to interrupt in Guatemala City. As it was, he was going to have a bump on his forehead for several days.

That was the last straw for him. He turned in his seat and glared at his corporal. He was so mad he couldn't utter his thoughts. In frustration, he took off his hat and swatted Melones across the head half a dozen times.

Although no pain was delivered in the blows, the smashing of the hat did manage to wring some water out of it. Guapito shook his head and sat back in his seat, lifted the bottle once more, and held it to his lips.

Of course, that was the moment the soldier caught up to the vehicle and jumped onto the back railing.

The vehicle bounced up and down. The bottle slipped from Guapito's mouth, and again he suffered a dousing of the light brown fluid, only there wasn't enough left in the bottle to make much of a mess. Out of sheer anger, he threw the bottle as far as he could into the jungle.

He tried to say something to his soldiers, but being their leader, and realizing he needed the devotion of every last one of them if he were to be successful in his overthrow campaign, he moderated his anger, shook his head and sat back in his seat. However, still needing to release his anger in some way, he took enough time to again swat Melones across the head half a dozen times with his hat.

Finally, his anger spent, he sat back. "Okay, Corporal Melones," he said. "Let's get on with our journey. And from now on take it easy. I want to be sure to get to our destination with my entire squad." He carefully fit his hat back on his head. "If I said it once, Melones," he added, "I say it again. You must be more careful. Where will we be if I lose the men before we get to Belize City to liberate this country?"

Melones carefully put the vehicle in gear. "Si, mi

sargente," he said, letting the clutch out as slowly as he could, careful lest it grab and make the Land Rover jerk to a start, as it usually did.

Guapito reached into his knapsack resting on the soaking floorboard in front of him, and retrieved another bottle of Caribbean White Rum. The alcohol was his favorite, and he believed he brought enough of it along. There were three bottles left, he noted, carefully folding over the top of the knapsack before leaning back. Since the last bottle Melones brought was empty, he would have to rely on his own supply.

He unscrewed the cap, and made sure there would be no problems with the Land Rover before taking a swallow from it.

There were no problems with the road, and Melones, still wanting the drink he was after when the entire fracas started, eyed his sergeant wistfully, licking his lips.

* * * *

The name of Mario's Burgers was scrawled in faded white letters on a strip of weather beaten board tacked to the post in front of the thatched roof palapa. It identified the palapa as a Belizean version of a fast food hamburger stand, if one could imagine such a thing stuck in the middle of nowhere on the edge of the southern jungles. The palapa stood on the crest of a low hill next to the jungle, on the muddy road leading south from San Ignacio, Belize.

Under the roof were half a dozen wood tables, a wood counter, an old, cast iron propane stove with four burners, and a large grill. The old fashioned Coca Cola machine precariously perched on a rotting wood pallet behind the counter saw better days, but a new refrigerator and several restaurant type glass display cases were set near the end of the counter.

A generator behind the palapa roared, coughed, backfired, and spewed black exhaust every so often. It provided the electricity for sixteen of the twenty four hours in the day. But that was only during the days the place was in operation, which wasn't too often, since the proprietor was prone to enjoying extended fishing trips somewhere along the Rio On River back in the jungles.

The proprietor was in, though, when Ringold pulled into the parking area amid several dogs barking their welcome.

"Time fa da food, I t'ink," Ringold explained, as he got out of the Land Rover.

"Well, I'd say so," Marcie said. "I am hungry."

"Yeah, me too," Marc agreed, as he followed Chuck and Marcie out of the vehicle.

Penn was badly in need of something to get his head back in working order. He agreed heartily.

The two dogs immediately ran up to Ringold to reassure themselves he was to be welcomed, and after a cursory sniff or two, returned to their places in the shade under one of the four poorly painted white picnic tables which served for seating arrangements. It was too hot to bite anyone, anyway.

Wickstraw, the proprietor, a Brit in his mid forties, was short, with balding blonde hair. He was also quite rotund, which indicated the food was good. He strolled out of the nearby shack while wiping his hands on his pants, eager to serve his customers. They were the only customers in three days.

"Welcome," he shouted boisterously. "Please sit. What'll you have? Beer, I bet. On a day like this, every one wants a good, cold Belikin, don't they? How many? Five?" He re-appraised the teenagers. "Three maybe? How about cokes for the two kids?" He eyed Marcie and Marc as he said that.

Chuck grinned. Marcie frowned, and Marc was a bit confused.

"Wickstraw, you old goat," Penn greeted as soon as the man stopped talking, which never seemed to be soon enough. The man was likeable, but the only problem was he tried too hard to please. "I'll have some rum."

"Ah, my dear old friend, Penn. I'm so sorry. I am fresh out of rum." He grinned broadly. "Are you sure you don't want a belly ache...I mean, Belikin, beer?"

"I'll have a coke," Marcie interceded.

"Me, too," said Marc.

"And me," Chuck added.

"Yeah. Me fa da Coke," Ringold said.

"All right," Penn said. "Cokes for everybody, I guess."

He led the way into the palapa and sat at the shadiest table. He shooed away several large flies and one huge cockroach trying to make a meal of something on the end of the table. The something, Penn surmised, was probably left over from the last customers.

"Ugh," Marcie winced as she sat down, eyeing the cockroach scurrying off the table.

"You might as well get used to them," Penn said. "That's nothing compared to what you're going to see deeper in that jungle out there." He nodded in the direction of the dense foliage that ran up to the back of the clearing.

"I hate bugs," Marc offered.

"Well, so do I," Penn countered.

Wickstraw returned and placed five opened Cokes on the table. "Cold ones, for a change," he commented. "My Coke machine is a bit worn, but my new refrigerator's a dandy."

"Now. Hamburgers?" Wickstraw suggested. "And french fries? I make some darned good french fries, for an Englishman, that is," He laughed. "The cheeseburgers are even better." He shot a friendly wink at Marcie, meaning she should accept his suggestion.

Marcie smiled in return. "Okay," she said. "I'll have a cheeseburger."

"Me, too," Marc said.

Ringold and Chuck agreed.

"For everybody, I guess," Penn added. "I'd rather have a little rum with it, though."

"You don't need any of that," Marcie chastised.

Penn glared at her. He was about to say something, but changed his mind. "You say you got your half of the map off an old pirate who owned a boat named The Crystal Skull?" he asked, changing the subject.

"Yeah," Chuck responded. "The old pirate was a Belizean."

"I can imagine," Penn said. "The crystal skull was a carving found in Labaatun in 1926, in case you didn't know."

"We know," Marcie said.

"Do you have your half of the map with you?" Penn asked.

Chuck glanced at Marcie, who nodded her head and reached into her knapsack. She retrieved the part of the map, unrolled it, and spread it out on the table, pushing aside the plates. "There," she said, after placing a coke bottle on each of the opposite corners to keep the map from rolling up again. "One genuine Belizean treasure map," she smiled. "I think," she added, not quite so certain.

Penn retrieved his hand drawn copy of the map from his back pants pocket, and unfolded it. He moved it around, orienting it over the leather map, and placed it down in alignment with Marcie's map. "I'll be," he said. "Look at that."

"It fits!" Chuck exclaimed.

"Kind of weird, isn't it?" Marcie proffered.

"Wow!" Marc said.

Penn carefully scanned the symbols on the assembled map, tracing the lines, studying it. "This is a rough outline of the Yucatan Peninsula," he explained, outlining the shape formed by the mating of the two map halves. "And these symbols..." He paused to study them. "The ones in Latin indicate the sea, the mountains, the jungles, and several rivers. And look," he pointed to each corner of the assembled map. "In each corner there's a sketch of an emerald, with rays and an arrow emanating from it."

He moved his hand across the map, from corner to corner. "If we draw lines from each of the four arrows in the direction they point, they'll cross about here." He pointed to the spot where the lines would intersect. He hoped his hand drawn map version didn't miss anything important, like any dangers to watch for on the way to wherever it was supposed to lead the observer, but he put that thought aside as his interest focused on the map.

"Yeah," Chuck said.

"That's about forty miles Southwest of the Rio On Cave, near Big Mountain and the Thousand Foot Falls," Penn said pensively. "That's close to the Guatemalan border, near the Southern Peten Region," he added, as he sat back and took a drink from one of the bottles of Coke. "That's a dangerous area. There's some ruins there still waiting to be uncovered," he added, as he put a Coke a bottle on the corner of the leather map half, which was slowly re-curling itself.

"Do you really think those ruins could be what this map leads to?" Marcie hopefully asked.

"The lines sure cross there, don't they?" Penn responded. He remembered the words of Thorne Beusch.

"Are their still parts of this country nobody's ever seen?" Chuck asked.

"I've been there," Penn said. "I've seen those ruins."

"What?" the three teenagers responded in unison.

"Several years ago," Penn began explaining. "I saw some ruins there. Darn near got done in by a bunch of Lancandons, though, and I nearly got munched on by a crocodile, too."

"Lancon whats?" Marc asked.

"Lancandons," Penn replied. "Natives."

"Dem be fa da natives dat come fa da jungles dere," Ringold hastily explained, not wanting to be left out of the conversation entirely. "Most be tame, but some? Dey don' lak civ'lization."

"Oh," Marc said, satisfied with the explanation, but not sure he understood every word of Ringold's Creole pronounciations.

"Then you know how to get there?" Chuck asked, his excitement building.

Penn nodded. "Yeah," he said. "But, it's pretty rough country. Crocodiles, and Fer De Lance snakes. Tarantulas as big as your hand, all kinds of creepy crawlies."

"Good grief," Marcie interrupted. "Don't tell me a grown man like you is afraid of bugs?"

Penn eyed Marcie. He was about to reply when he was interrupted by the arrival of the cheeseburgers and fries.

Wickstraw glanced at the map, standing beside the table, holding the plates in both hands. "Now where do you expect me to put these?" he asked.

"Oh," Marcie responded, quickly removing the Cokes from the map and rolling up both maps. "Put them here, please," she said, while she stuffed the maps into her knapsack.

Wickstraw obliged, and stood back as his customers ate.

"Well, Wickstraw," Penn said, after taking several bites. "For an old British goat, you can still cook up a good burger."

"English," the man corrected. "I'm English, not just British. A small point, but important just the same, to any one from the U.K., you know."

Penn grinned. "Okay. You old English goat."

"Isn't great to have such good friends?" Wickstraw winked at the teenagers.

One of the dogs jumped to its feet, growled, and ran into the nearby jungle.

"Darn it," Wickstraw complained. "Now what the bloody devil do you suppose he's after?" He stared after the dog. "I suppose I'll to have to go after him, or he'll get lost again." He strode after the dog. "Darn fool Australian Shepherd. You'd think the Aussies would teach a dog how to not get lost, wouldn't you?" He stalked into the jungle.

Fifteen minutes passed in near silence, as silent as it could be, that is, considering the noise from the generator, the coke machine, and a myriad of birds in the nearby jungle.

"So. You're afraid of bugs," Marcie joked, returning her attention to Penn.

"Not the bugs, so much," Penn replied thoughtfully. "But..."

"But, what?" Marcie pressed her point.

"Well. There's rumors, too, about the things that go on in that part of the country. Lots of strange noises in the night."

"Da peoples," Ringold interceded. "Dey say dey have da bumbly-bees along da river at night. Dey be big fa da carry away da baby. For true! Dey fly along da river!" He gulped down some of his cheeseburger after finishing his explanation.

"Wow!" Marc said, astonished by such a possibility.

"Surely you don't believe that?" Marcie jibed.

"For true, Mon, ah, Miss," Ringold defended himself between swallows.

"Well," Penn said with a shrug. "You don't have to take his word for it. You can ask some of the natives. I've talked to some who have seen and heard those bees."

"I will ask them," Marcie challenged. "When we get there."

Penn eyed her, and took the last swallow from his Coke to disguise his frown.

"At any rate," Chuck said. "I suppose we ought to be going on, don't you?"

"Sure," Penn agreed with a shrug. He dug a Belizean twenty-dollar bill out of his pocket, put it under one of the dishes, and got to his feet.

"Do you think that's enough?" Marcie asked, eyeing the bill. "We have money, too. We could pay part of the bill."

"Nah. Keep your money. You may need it," Penn said with a sardonic laugh. "Anyway, that's more than he's made all week," he added, heading for the Land Rover.

The others joined him, and soon Ringold had the Land Rover splashing down the road, which was beginning to show signs of drying out, thanks to the Belizean mid-day sun.

CHAPTER 16

Late in the afternoon, Ringold's Land Rover struggled through the jungle on the muddy track, and ground to a halt as the track faded into the jungle.

Ringold got out and peered at the disappearing trail. He walked a dozen paces or so through the overhanging brush. "Dis road," he said perplexed. "I t'ink she no be fa da go, true."

"What happened, old buddy? You think the jungle overgrew it, or did you take a wrong turn somewhere?" Penn asked, joining him.

"Wrong turn?" Ringold said, perturbed by the insinuaation. "No way, Mon. I come here maybe two years ago. Da road, she be fine, den." He slogged his way twenty feet or so farther along the disappearing track, followed by Penn. "Now? I doan' know, true. She be most gone."

Penn peered down the disappearing trail, all that was left of the broad track they started out on twenty miles back. "Well," he said. "I guess there's enough here to follow on foot."

They returned to the land Rover to talk with the teenagers, who were outside the vehicle, looking around.

"What happened to the road?" Marcie was the first to ask the question.

"She gone, Mon, ah, Miss," Ringold explained.

"What now?" Chuck asked.

"Now?" Penn responded. "Now we walk. I told you it wasn't going to be easy."

"Okay, Mon," Ringold said. "You walk in da jungle, true!

Me? I take da Rover. I back fa da city."

"Well, suit yourself, Ringold," Penn said as he turned to the teenagers. "Let's get the gear out of the rover and start walking. We have some trekking to do before we get to where we're going, or, to where I think it is we want to go. We can take a shortcut, now, without the Rover, without too much of a chance of getting lost."

"Oh, that sounds positive," Marcie chided.

Penn shrugged his shoulders, and unloaded their knapsacks.

Five minutes later, they said their good-byes to Ringold and headed off alongthe trail.

"Good grief," Marcie complained after several hours of trekking. "I never knew a jungle could get so hot and steamy."

"Yeah," Marc agreed.

"That's why it's called a jungle," Penn said. "It's going to get hotter than this. Especially around mid-day tomorrow. You'd better get used to it. You're lucky we spent the first part of today riding in the Land Rover."

"Oh, Great," Marcie said with sarcasm. "That's a relief to know."

"I don't mind the heat," Chuck interceded, slapping at a mosquito. "It's these mosquitoes that bother me. And the flies."

"Yeah," Marc agreed.

"That's another thing you'd better get used to," Penn explained. "You recall I said I didn't like the jungle because of the bugs? That's just some of them."

"Oh, great," Marcie added, slapping at a mosquito that had the misfortune to land on the back of her neck.

"Anyway," Penn continued. "The mosquitoes are bad now because It's getting close to sunset. They're not so bad during the day."

Ten minutes later, they came to a small clearing. With more swatting, sweating, and something close to swearing, they assembled places to sit. Marcie, though, being a proper lady, maintained her decorum throughout and avoided the swearing part.

Penn stopped and peered about, casting a glance at the sky.

"The sun is going down," he said, dropping his knapsack. "This is a pretty good place to spend the night, I think. We better make camp and get a fire going before it gets dark, and that happens darn fast once the sun does drop. The fire will help keep away the mosquitos, if we put enough coconut husks in it. They act as a natural Citronella."

Marcie let out a sigh as she peered around. She picked a spot near the center of the clearing, and let her knapsack down. "Speaking of sleeping outdoors, I don't suppose you thought of bringing a tent, did you?"

"A tent?" Penn smiled. "You don't want a tent in the jungle. Everything gets in it and nothing gets out. Pretty soon it gets too cramped to sleep, and you have to get outside, which makes the darn thing useless, as far as I can see."

"You have an answer for everything, don't you?" she chided him again.

"Answers enough," he chuckled. "Anyway, no, I didn't bring a tent, but I brought something better."

"A trailer house?" Chuck joked.

"Nope. Tarps. As a matter of fact, four of them, one for each of us. And mosquito netting."

"We sleep on the ground with tarps?" Chuck asked.

"No, we don't sleep on the ground, period. Unless you want the company of a tarantula, or maybe a Fer De Lance, in the middle of the night. They like nothing better than drawing close to a nice warm body during the coolness of the early morning hours."

"What?" Marcie asked, looking about nervously. She was more than concerned about that possibility.

"Not to worry," Penn went on. "That's why we sling the tarps from some trees to sleep in. Fer De Lances won't climb trees unless they see something to eat in them. We're to big for them, in that sense."

"Hammocks," Marc commented happily, getting the point.

"Right, and this is how we sling them." Penn took out one of the tarps and strode over to the nearby tree. He wrapped the rope on the end of the tarp around one tree, stretched the rope on the other end of the tarp to the adjacent tree, and tied it, leaving about half the tarp hanging down, with the other part being the hammock. He sat on the hammock to test it. "See? Nothing to it," he said. "Now, of course, there's the other part."

He strung a rope from tree to tree above the hammock, and retrieved some mosquito netting from his bag, which he draped over the rope down both sides of the hammock. He folded the hanging part of the tarp up over the mosquito net.

"In case it rains, just pull this tarp all the way over to keep off the water. Now, I suggest you three find suitable trees and do the same." He returned to his feet and pointed out several trees. "Stay close together. That way there won't be any curious Belizean Leopards cruising around between us during the night."

"Leopards?" Marcie asked. "They have leopards in Belize?"

"One of the prettiest cats in the New World," Penn explained, as he began hunting firewood and coconut husks. "When you get through slinging your hammocks, help gather some firewood. Make sure it's dry, or we'll never get it lit."

"Dry?" Chuck asked. "How are we going to find anything dry after the rain?"

"Yeah." Marc supported the question. It seemed like a good one to him.

"I don't mean dry, like without water on it. I mean dry, like it's been dead for a while. Nothing green, or still growing." Penn explained.

"Oh," Marc learned something else on this trip, which, so far, was more than simply interesting. He was completely engrossed in the experience. He wondered why his sister didn't find things as interesting.

It took less than ten minutes to gather enough firewood, and another five minutes for Penn to get the fire started with the help of his Zippo lighter. He stepped back after the blaze flared, and rummaged around in his knapsack. "Dinner time, don't you think?" he asked as he extracted two cans of chili beans.

"Well, good," Chuck said with some enthusiasm. "I'm sure hungry."

"Me, too," Marc chimed in.

Marcie rummaged through her knapsack, extracted a can

Harold R. Miller

of fruit cocktail, and held it up. "For dessert," she said.

Half an hour later, with their ravenous appetites satisfied, although it took another can of chili to do that, they sprawled out around the campfire, leaning on the knapsacks. The moon was bright, but the light was mostly blocked by the jungle overgrowth. Night noises emanated from the jungle, consisting largely of bird and monkey calls. Every once in a while the roar of a leopard came from farther away.

Penn grabbed a bottle of Belikin beer, one of the four he brought, from his knapsack, fumbled in his pocket to retrieve his jackknife, unfolded the bottle-opener blade, and flipped off the bottle cap. He took a long drink from the bottle as he put the knife back in his pocket.

Marcie eyed him. "I thought you didn't like Belikin Beer?" she asked cynically.

Penn shrugged, and took another drink. He finished the bottle, and tossed it back into his knapsack. Since bottles were scarce in Belize, they carried a high deposit and refund value. Beside, he rationalized, he hated cluttering up the purity of the jungle with man made junk. He retrieved a second bottle, and was in the middle of opening it when Marcie glared at him.

"Don't you think you've had enough of that stuff?" she challenged.

Penn held the bottle in his lips, as he thoughtfully peered at her. Several minutes passed in silence before he answered. "There you go again, sounding just like my ex-wife." He pointedly took a drink from the bottle. "What'd you say your last name was?"

"I didn't, and it's no wonder she left you, drinking like that."

"It wasn't the drinking, so much," he responded in defense. "It was more like, well, I always had to see what was on the other side of the mountain, so to speak. She got pregnant, and I got this job hunting for a certain artifact in Peru. She didn't want me to go. I felt I had to. Well, one thing led to another. We just split, that's all."

"Where are you from, anyway?" Chuck asked.

"California," Penn answered after taking another sip from the warm Belikin.

"No kidding? So are we," Chuck said.

Penn was about to say something more when the night noises of the jungle stopped. Everything was eerily quiet. He put down his bottle and looked around at the jungle. He held his hand up for silence as he listened.

Buzzing sounds came from far off, carrying through the night air, over the jungle.

"What's that?" Marc asked, peering around at the jungle with eyes wide.

"It almost sounds like..." Chuck tried to identify the sound, letting his sentence drop.

"Bees!" Marcie uttered, also peering around, trying to identify the direction of the sound.

"And large ones!" Chuck added.

"Oh, oh," Marc said, wide eyed, looking around nervously.

The buzzing faded, and within seconds the normal jungle night sounds returned.

Penn shrugged and took another sip from his Belikin beer. "Well, Ringold told you about them," he said at length. "Now do you believe him?"

Marcie was skeptical. "How could there be bees large enough to make that much noise?"

Penn shrugged again, emptied the beer, returned the empty bottle to his knapsack, and got to his feet. "Well, who knows?" he asked, as he climbed into his hammock. "Anything can happen. This is Belize, remember." He swatted another mosquito, and shut his eyes. "I guess we'll find out soon enough," he added. "Right now we better hit the sack. I have a feeling we're going to need our rest before we get through this little adventure."

* * * *

Not too far away, a lone Lancandon Indian paddled his log canoe down a slow moving muddy river. He came to a stop near the steep bank where the jungle growth hung from a ledge that was part of a covered mound. He nudged the front of the canoe into the overhanging growth, and pulled the canoe around the overhanging growth into the entrance of an ancient stone lined canal.

The canal led into a low cavern, also made of stone. The river water filled part of the floor, and burning oil lamps stuck into holders in the walls every ten feet provided light.

The water ended at a low landing about fifty feet in from the entrance, where there was an ancient archway leading from the landing through the stone wall. A second opening through the wall was recently blocked off at water's edge. The earlier river channel was diverted.

The Lancandon nosed his canoe up on the landing, got out, and pulled the bow of the canoe up onto the landing. He grabbed a gunnysack from the canoe and hurried off through the archway in the stone wall.

CHAPTER 17

The self styled Liberators of Belize bounced along the muddy jungle road in their open Land Rover. They came to a fork in the road, and Melones suddenly slammed on the brakes, sliding the vehicle to a stop.

The solder riding in the rear was, again, thrown off the vehicle, in a forward direction. He bounced off Guapito's back, and rolled into a mud puddle. The others stared at him in surprise. Their surprise quickly turned into chuckles of amusement. The muddied soldier got up and headed back to the vehicle, not too much the worse for wear.

Guapito gave Melones another of his disparaging glares. "Melones!" he said. "Where are your brains? Why did you stop like that?"

"The road, mi sargente," Melones despondently answered. "Which way do we go?"

Guapito darkened his glowering at his corporal. "Which way do we go?" he asked at length. "You mean you do not know which way we are to go?"

Melones shook his head in embarrassment.

"But how can that be? You told me you knew which is the way to Belize City." Guapito was too amazed to be angered.

Melones frowned, embarrassed.

Guapito removed his hat and slapped Melones across the head with it.

The others in the back of the Land Rover roared in amusement. They quickly quieted as Guapito turned around and glared at them.

Guapito returned his hat to his head, shook his head in frustration, and reached into his bag for another bottle of White Caribbean Rum. He lost even more of his temper in the struggle with the seal around the bottle cap, but he finally bested it. He took a long drink from of the liquid, screwed the cap back on the bottle, and returned it to his knapsack in exchange for a folded map.

Struggling to unfold the reluctant map created even more frustration, and by the time he unfolded it, sticking one corner of it in Melones' face, he was nearly too impatient to get it flattened out enough to read. Finally, after much swatting at the paper, at the mosquitoes, at the map again, which seemed to be defying his orders by trying to return to its folded condition, he managed to focus on it.

He looked at the fork in the road, looked around at the jungle, turned the map around, thinking he might have it upside down, realized he didn't really know which way was North, and turned it sideways, which didn't help, either. He let go of it to scratch his head in thought. After several seconds, having no desire to let his subordinates conclude he might be lost, he pointed at the right fork with strong assertion.

Melones put the worn out vehicle in gear, and with a jerking start, drove off down the left fork as Guapito hastily folded the map and stuffed it back into his knapsack, not realizing Melones didn't follow his direction.

"I hope we do not have the bad fortune to meet any of the Army of this backward country of Belize while we are trying to find out which way we are to go," Guapito said, grabbing onto the side of the vehicle for support. "How would that look to the people of Belize when we liberate them?"

* * * *

The following day was just as hot and humid as before. Penn and the teenagers felt the mounting heat in their jungle trekking, andwhen they unexpectedly broke out of the jungle at the edge of a river, their single thought was to cool off with a quick dip.

THE EMERALD HEAD CAPER

Marc was the first to suggest the swim.

"Not a good idea," Penn cautioned.

Marc was confused, but his confusion cleared when a nearby crocodile scurried off the riverbank into the water. "Oh, oh," he said, quickly taking several more steps backwards.

"Crocodiles," Chuck commented in awe. He and Marcie retreated from the water's edge to the safety of the jungle.

"That's all we need," Marcie dryly commented, watching the beast slither away through the water.

"Don't worry," Penn calmed them. "They won't hurt you, as long as you keep out of their way." He remembered his last encounter with the hostile Lancandons and crocodiles. He was worried about the natives more than the crocodiles.

"Some consolation," Marcie said, as she forced herself to look away from the river. "Well, what now? The trail ends here."

Penn set down his knapsack. He held out his hand towards Marcie. "I think its time to recheck the maps," he said.

Marcie sighed, sat on a nearby log, retrieved the maps from her knapsack and handed them to him.

He kneeled on the ground, placed the map pieces in front of him, and studied them. He glanced at the river, at the sun, and back at the maps with thoughtful intent. "From here we go down river," he said. "At least that's the easy direction." He paused to study the terrain. "And it would be a good idea to keep a sharp eye out in this area for Lancandons, too," he added. He peered up and down the river. "Ah, I thought so," he said at length, getting to his feet. He pushed his way into the jungle, heading up-river.

"Where're you going?" Marcie asked. She didn't want to follow, lest she meet some crocodiles she didn't want to know.

"To get some rides," Penn responded, disappearing in the brush. "I'll be back in a second. You wait here."

"Rides?" Marcie shot a glance at Chuck.

Chuck shrugged his shoulders in response.

Several minutes later Penn returned, floating down the river in a canoe. He beached it near the teenagers, and grinned at them. "Nice of the natives to leave us some transportation."

Marc was aghast. "You're going to steal a canoe?" he

asked.

"It isn't stealing," Penn explained. "The canoes are for anyone needing them. That's tradition in this part of the country. Find them, use them, and leave them for someone else." He stepped out of the canoe and grabbed his knapsack. He tossed it into the canoe, retrieved one the three paddles, returned to the rear of the canoe, and sat, holding onto some jungle overgrowth, waiting patiently. "Well, are you coming, or not?" he asked.

The teenagers exchanged glances, and lost no time joining him.

Chuck grabbed the second paddle, taking the front seat, and behind him sat Marc, then Marcie. They tossed knapsacks in the middle of the craft.

"Okay, Chuck. Shove off," Penn directed.

Chuck pushed against the riverbank with the end of his paddle, and with a struggle, managed to get the bow off the mud. They floated, although not by much. The canoe showed barely more than three inches of freeboard by the time they settled in on their way down river.

"I'm not so sure about this," Marcie said warily, studying the edge of the canoe. "It looks like we'll sink at any moment."

"Relax," Penn calmed her. "The river's all flat. We won't have any trouble."

Marcie shot a skeptical glance at him.

A second crocodile slithered off the bank on the other side of the river, and slowly headed towards the canoe.

Penn loudly slapped his paddle on the surface.

The beast slowly turned around and headed back to the riverbank, much to Marcie and Marc's relief.

Chuck was too busy paddling in the front of the canoe to pay any attention.

Soon they were gliding down the river and away from the crocodile's territory, which was more to Marcie's liking.

Also to her liking was the fact she had nothing to do but watch the scenery float by as they passed between overhanging trees and an occasional rock cliff. She took the time to gaze at the passing jungle foliage, and decided it was beautiful, all green in as many variations of the color as could be imagined.

Once in a while, she spotted groups of flowers of the brightest red, yellow, and orange colors, splashing their petals across the many hues of green. In her reverie, she imagined herself on an African safari, forging down the Zambezi River, or maybe the Zaire.

Her reverie didn't last, though. The river narrowed, and the speed of the water increased. She was the first to notice the change. "The river's getting narrower," she half shouted to Penn, surprised by the sudden loudness of her voice amid the silence of the jungle. "And it looks like it's moving faster," she added in more controlled tones.

"River's do that," Penn replied with feigned nonchalance. Actually, he really had no idea what rivers did, except run down hill.

They rounded a bend in the river and came upon a large rock sticking up in the middle of the water. The river moved much faster around it, splashing and roiling around the rock.

A dull roaring emanated from down river.

Again, it was Marcie who noted another change. "I think I hear rapids," she shouted at Penn.

This time her voice couldn't override the river's noise so easily. The distant roar got louder with each second, and the water moved faster. But, that wasn't the immediate problem, the rock directly in front of them was.

"Better put some effort into it!" Penn shouted to Chuck and Marc. "Get away from that rock!"

He didn't have to give them directions, though. They were already paddling with all their might.

The canoe rocked back and forth as they struggled to steer it around the river rock. The sides dipped below the water line. Water flooded into it in great gushes with each rocking movement.

"You're getting water in the canoe!" Marcie shouted with alarm.

"Oh, oh!" Marc responded to no one in particular.

They increased their efforts, managing to barely miss the rock. They continued down the river, but the canoe sat dangerously low in the water from the extra weight of the water it took on.

Marcie began bailing with both hands.

The river's flow increased, requiring more effort from the two paddlers, which made the canoe rock more widely. More water rushed in.

"Head for the shore!" Penn shouted. "There's too much water in the canoe. It's going under!"

Chuck paddled with an effort he didn't know he could muster.

Marc added to his effort.

Marcie decided to ignore the intake of water caused by each side to side lunge of the canoe, and used her hands as paddles.

Finally, they forced the nose of the canoe onto the muddy riverbank. With the rise of the front of the canoe, the rear of it sank. Water rushed in, flooding it completely.

Penn grabbed knapsacks and tossed them onto the riverbank as the teenagers scrambled off the canoe. He followed, and as he ran forward, the rear of the canoe, rid of weight, bobbed up. As he stepped onto the bank, the front of the canoe slid off the riverbank, and it floated down stream.

"The canoe!" Marcie shouted, stretching out over the water to grab it. She missed it by several feet.

"Well, there goes our ride," Penn complained.

"Great," Chuck commented, glancing at the jungle. "Now we have to walk through this stuff, again?"

"It looks that way," Penn agreed, as he checked his watch. "But not 'til tomorrow. It'll be dark in another half an hour. We better make camp for the night."

"Make camp? Here?" Marcie asked, glancing warily around. "How about the crocodiles?"

Penn retrieved his knapsack. "There won't be any crocodiles along here. The river's too swift. But, just to be safe, one of us can keep a look out. I'll take the first watch, right after we eat something. Who's going to be second, in about four hours?" He began collecting dead branches and coconut husks to make a fire.

Marcie selected several tin cans of food from the knapsacks for their meal.

Soon the campfire was blazing on the river bank. The

moonlight illuminated the campsite, and reflected off the lids of the emptied tin cans. The reflections joined the beams of light cast by the flames, and danced around the foliage.

In about half an hour, with their stomachs filled with pan fried beans and canned hot dogs, the weary hikers relaxed. That's when a low buzzing developed in the distance.

Marcie was the first to hear it. She bent an ear towards the river. "What's that?" she asked in a hushed voice, straining to listen.

"What?" Marc asked nervously, looking around.

Chuck pointed his ear at the river, and raised his hand for silence. "Listen. I think I hear it, too."

"What?" Marc repeated, more nervously.

The buzzing increased. It drew closer.

"The bees," Marcie said, almost whispering.

"What?" Marc said a third time. That was all he could say, wary as he was.

Penn got to his feet. He began kicking dirt into the fire to put it out. "Quick! Help me put out the fire!"

The others complied. Marcie ran to the river with her mess kit and scooped up some water to pour on the fire. Not so much as even an ember glowed when she finished.

The buzzing grew louder.

"Hurry! Get out of sight!" Penn said, leading the way into the jungle.

The buzzing flooded the camp.

Penn and the teenagers peeked out from behind the cover of the jungle brush. They couldn't believe their eyes.

Seven single place hovercraft, each covered with black and yellow fiberglass bodies with plastic wings meant to resemble huge bumblebees, roared into view along the river. Their exhausts were modified to sound like the buzzing of a bee as their plastic bodies glistened, reflecting the moonlight. They sped over the surface, moving up the river and around the bend out of view.

Penn was the first to step out of hiding after the hovercraft passed, and the teenagers slowly wandered back to the side of their former campfire, confused by what they saw.

"They were hovercraft painted like bees," Chuck said,

still peering up the river after the mechanical bees.

"Yeah. Wow," Marc said, impressed.

"I knew they couldn't really be giant bees," Marcie said.

"Now, if that isn't some puzzle," Penn said. "What the devil was that all about? Why are they trying to imitate giant bees way out here?"

"To scare the natives?" Marcie conjectured, not entirely sure of her conclusion. "To scare them away from something?"

Penn considered her explanation. "That's a good probability. But, why? What is going on here that requires the natives to be frightened away?" He shook his head as he unrolled his tarp and looked for a suitable pair of trees. "Well, that gives us something to work on tomorrow. Right now, we better get some sleep. I'll wake up Chuck in time for the second watch. Tomorrow we get to go hiking, and with any luck, we'll find a trail back in the jungle, somewhere, that follows this river."

CHAPTER 18

The next morning's dew hung low over the river and flooded the jungles with steam.

Penn, followed by Marcie and Chuck, with Marc nervously bringing up the rear, began their hike along a barely discernible trail in the dense jungle brush. He found the trail during a short search after breakfast - another batch of canned hot dogs - and decided at the time that it would be a good route to follow, since it ran in the general direction of the river.

After some contemplation, he wondered whether it wouldn't have been easier to take a boat up from the Caribbean into the mouth of the river, than to try the jungle route they followed. However, he mused, while stepping over yet another dead log, I guess it's a little late for that.

After an hour or two, they broke through the jungle overgrowth and emerged beside the river, again, among some rocks, beside a large mound overgrown with jungle vines and brush.

Chuck eyed the river. "I think we've seen this before," he said.

"Yeah," Marc said, hurrying forward to leave the last position in line.

"We've been following this river for the last few miles," Penn added to the observations. "Well," he said, as he slung his knapsack off his back. "It's time for a lunch break."

The others agreed, and hunted for comfortable places to sit.

"I wonder what happened to the rapids?" Marcie asked.

"There's probably a fork in the river," Penn responded. "I don't think those hovercraft could make it over any rapids."

"You know," Marcie said, peering about. "That looks like a bunch of old ruins over there." She nodded in the direction of some more mounds protruding out of the jungle farther down the river.

Chuck followed her glance. "Yeah. That's kind of interesting, isn't it?"

Marcie's curiosity was piqued by Chuck's comment, and she set off to investigate the mounds.

"Hey! Don't get out of earshot," Penn cautioned. "You can get lost in there."

"Don't worry," Marcie replied. "I'm only going around the corner for a minute. Besides, there's another path here."

She strode along the path for a few yards. She saw some mounds. She studied them. After some considerable thought, she concluded they must be ruins. "Hey!" she yelled. "This must be some kind of temple, or something!" She pushed her way through some overhanging tree branches. "Hey, everybody. Look here!" she added.

"What now?" Chuck asked, as he and the others hastily jogged into the jungle to locate Marcie.

They found her standing in a small clearing, staring at the jungle-covered mounds. At the edge of the tallest mound stood a stone stele nearly covered with jungle vines, and on top of the stele was a carved skull. "Look! On top of that stele!" Marcie pointed at the stele. "It's a skull carving!"

"This has to be the Mayan ruins noted on the map!" He said, looking around. "We made it!" he added with growing excitement.

"Well, not entirely," Penn cautioned. "We made it this far, that's true. But, now comes the hard part." He eyed the stele. "If we are at the right ruins, that is." He strode over to inspect the edge of the jungle-covered mound. He walked along the base of the mound for a few yards, and pushed aside some vines to peer into the void behind them.

The others joined him as he cautiously pushed aside some more growth to reveal a dark opening in the mound. It was made of stone blocks, crumpling from the intrusion of roots and growth over the centuries.

"A tunnel!" Chuck was getting enthusiastic about their find. "It looks like it leads beneath the ruins."

"Yeah. A tunnel," Penn agreed without quite so much enthusiasm. "Interesting," he added. "Remember that inverted 'U' shaped line near the center of the map? It could have meant a tunnel entrance." He wasn't sure he liked his conclusion. "Tunnels have the biggest collection of creepy crawlies you've ever seen," he unhappily added.

"I still can't believe you're afraid of insects," Marcie said in disbelief as she pushed past Penn and peered into the overgrown entrance.

"What's wrong with that?" Penn again found himself on the defensive against this girl's logic.

"That's funny, that's all," Marcie mused, glancing at him.

"How do you know it's full of bugs?" Chuck interrupted, returning everyone's attention to the tunnel entrance.

"Because they all are," Penn responded. "I've been in some of them. Actually, in lots of them."

"Well, we came this far," Chuck proffered.

"Yes, we have," Marcie agreed. "I think we should find out where it leads."

Penn looked around at the jungle, and at the sky. "It's almost sundown, again. Maybe we should wait until morning to go inside."

But Marcie was impatient. "Well, shoot!" she said. "It won't be any lighter in there in the morning, will it?" She retrieved her flashlight hanging from her belt - as it should be for all experienced Girl Scouts, which was something she learned while she was still in high school - and boldly stepped into the tunnel. Her flashlight made a collection of cockroaches and various insects scurry for the cover of the roots entwined and protruding through the tunnel walls.

"I told you it was full of creepy crawlies," Penn declared. "I'm not sure I like this," he added, as he followed her. Lacking a flashlight, he hurried to secure a position just behind Marcie so he could see.

Chuck and Marc exchanged glances. "Let's go," Chuck

suggested.

"Okay," Marc agreed, but not as enthusiastically.

They grabbed their jungle flashlights from their backpacks, and followed Marcie.

The group pushed their way deep into the dark, musty stone block tunnel. Spider webs, an occasional tarantula, centipedes and other crawling insects that frequented the tunnel walls were exposed by the glow of the flashlights.

Penn struggled to not let it be known he even noticed them.

"How far does this thing go? Now it's going uphill." Marcie commented after several minutes into the tunnel.

"How should I know?" Penn responded, warily glancing at the spider web over his head. He hoped the tunnel didn't go too far. He also hoped it would dead end soon, so they would have to turn around and go back to open territory, leaving the bugs behind.

"I thought you said you've been in this tunnel before," Marcie commented.

"I said in some tunnels, not this one," Penn replied.

"You mean you don't have any idea where this tunnel leads?" Chuck asked.

"Nope."

"Then why are you taking us into it?" Marcie asked, a little perturbed.

"Me? Hey! This was your idea, remember? You're leading."

A buzzing sound suddenly penetrated the tunnel. The group froze.

"Oh, oh. That sound's like those bee things again!" Marc said.

"Don't be silly, Marc," Marcie responded. "They can't be in this tunnel." She shined her flashlight deeper into the tunnel. "Come on," she said, cautiously stepping forward again.

The buzzing sound grew louder. It increased, and rapidly decreased, as though someone was revving up the two-cycle engines that drove the vehicles.

The group came to a sharp bend in the tunnel, and light emanated from the other side of the bend.

THE EMERALD HEAD CAPER

"Hey! There's light up there," Marcie said. "And those noises are coming from there."

"Well, that seems like a good observation," Chuck commented with some sarcastic humor. "After all, where else could it come from?"

"Don't get smart," Marcie cautioned him with the same sarcasm.

They slowly crept around the bend. Ahead of them was the end of the tunnel. It was lit, and was less than fifty feet away.

"I don't believe this," Penn said, pushing his way past Marcie to take the lead, and crept forward. "Turn off your flashlights," he directed said. "I don't think we want anyone to know we're here."

"Why?" Marcie asked, innocently curious.

"Because. That's why," Penn couldn't think of any rational reason, other than his sense of foreboding.

"Oh, oh." Marc said, again bringing up the rear of the line.

"You said it," Chuck added in a loud whisper.

Halfway to the end of the tunnel, they came to another tunnel that branched off to their right. The end of it was lit, as well.

Penn stopped and cautiously peered into the other tunnel, then into the main tunnel.

"Now which way?" Chuck asked.

"What difference does it make?" Marcie replied. She boldly crept past Penn to take the lead. She peered into the side tunnel, and pushed forward in that direction.

Several minutes later the group gathered at the end of the side tunnel, to discover it exited high in the wall of a room deep inside the ruins.

The room was lit by a string of bare electric light bulbs hanging from the ceiling on bare wires, and the river flowed along one side of the room. A channel where the river once flowed was blocked by a recently constructed block wall, which diverted the water back out of the ruins through a long, larger tunnel. On the bank of the river were parked six of the mechanized bumblebees like those they saw on the river outside.

Harold R. Miller

One man idly sat in the cockpit of one of the machines, and the engine covers on two others were open, with their drivers revving up the engines, testing them.

"See! I told you they couldn't be any bees in the tunnel," Marcie whispered loudly, eyeing the hovercraft. "That's the river down there. It has to be part of the one we just left."

"I'll be damned," Penn remarked. "What is going on here, anyway?"

"Look there," Marcie added, pointing to an opening in the far wall of the room, back from the water.

Three men in army fatigues carried several clear plastic bags containing small green rocks. They carried the bags to the men in the hovercraft, handing one bag each to the men, then got into the remaining machines. They started the machines, and all six machines slowly moved out onto the water, exiting the room through the large opening where the river flowed.

Marcie pointed to the other side of the room after the hovercraft left. "Emeralds," Marcie whispered. "What they were carrying in those plastic bags had to be Emeralds!"

Penn wasn't sure he agreed.

"Come on," Marcie said, turning around in the tunnel. "We have to see what's at the end of the other part of the tunnel." She led the way back to the fork, and down the other part of the tunnel.

At the end of the second tunnel they furtively peered over the edge and faced another large room much more impressive. It was a huge cavern, lit by lights strung on poles set among several large steaming vats perched over gas burners in the middle of the room. Several drying trays lined the back wall, with a green substance spread on them for drying. A platform of stone was built into the wall at the far end of the room, and a green skull as high as a man, perched on the platform.

Twenty or more Lancandon Indians busily worked about the room, the vats and the drying trays. Three of them used an overhead crane rig to lift one vat off the fire. They moved the vat over to a drying tray, tilted the vat, and poured the green viscous contents of the vat into the tray. As two of the natives returned the vat to the fire, the third used a wood rake and spread the liquid out across the drying tray.

THE EMERALD HEAD CAPER

The lights dimmed. The workers stopped their activities and faced the platform with the huge green skull.

The skull glowed. An eerie green light emanated from all around it and inside it. The light brightened, as an image wearing a hooded cape seemed to emerge from its interior. The image stepped forward onto the platform, and steadily gazed at the workers.

The workers knelt. They focused on the image. They watched it with reverence, staring in awe. A quiet mumbling stirred among them.

The image raised its right arm as it spoke to the workers. "Are you my subjects?" the image asked in a deep monotone, augmented in volume by hidden speakers, and electronically altered.

The workers mumbled their ascent.

"But not all of you," the image said with rising volume. "There are some among you who are not."

Louder mumbling rose from the workers as they rejected the complaint.

"There are some among you who are not loyal. There are some among you who would reveal the secrets of the Emerald Head to outsiders. They would dare to risk my anger. They would dare to risk losing all that I have given you."

The mumbling of disbelief among the workers rose to near shouting.

"You will seek and find those among you who are such traitors," the image demanded. "You will bring them to my altar, to me. You will bring them to me, or you will suffer the wrath of the Emerald Head!"

Fire erupted from the mouth of the green skull. The workers rumbled in fear and awe. The image suddenly dissipated. It faded like the morning dew in the heat of the rising sun.

The workers cowered in fear of their idol, like Dorothy in front of the Wizard.

The lights went up, and the workers hesitantly returned to their tasks, some glancing back at the skull.

The teen-agers peered into the cavern, spellbound by what they saw.

Penn paid close attention to the show. He remembered the

video monitor at Quigley's.

A Latino man in army fatigues stepped into the entrance of the tunnel in front of them. He carried an Uzi sub-machine gun. "Alto!" he barked. "Que pasa aqui? Quien estan?" Stop! What's going on here? Who are you?

"Oh, oh!" Marc uttered.

CHAPTER 19

The room was made of stone blocks, and was about twenty feet by twenty feet square. It was lit by more bare light bulbs hanging from electrical wires strung across the stone ceiling, held there by spikes driven into the mortar between the stones.

A large wood plank door, mounted on rusty iron hinges, penetrated one wall. A large wood table occupied the center of the room.

An electronic console was placed against one wall, with a radio transmitter and a video monitor attached. Headphones hung on a counter in front of the console. A television camera was mounted on a tripod near the console, and the lights on the console glowed in dim colors, indicating the electronics system was on.

A green cape with a hood hung over the back of one of the chairs by the table, and a mask with green glass eyes sat on the table.

Two guards, Latino men dressed in sloppy army fatigues and carrying Uzi automatic rifles over their shoulders, stood at the door.

General Omegas, a Latino male in his mid fifties, dressed in surplus American army fatigues, sat at the table. With him sat Quigley, in jungle camouflage fatigues and smoking a cigar. He sat at the end of the table with a bottle of rum in front of him, with a glass of rum in his hand.

"The chief of police wants more money for his part,"

the general said. "He said, that without more money, he won't reveal the intruders."

"The chief of police is no worry to me," Quigley replied. "You continue supplying the material, and I'll make sure the shipments are made on schedule." He took a sip from his glass. "The chief of police will not get more money," he added. "He gets too much now, as it is. I'll take care of these intruders myself."

"But…" the general tried to object.

"There are no buts!" Quigley interrupted. "If you don't like it, well, there are other generals in the Belizean Army. They'd love to be in your boots."

The general glared at Quigley. He relented, took a swallow from his glass, and grimaced as the liquid went down his throat. "It won't be necessary to consider such a thing," he said. "I do my part, and I will continue to do it as we agreed." He put down the glass, got to his feet, and strode to the door.

The guards stood in front of the door and refused to let him pass.

Quigley casually finished his drink, and with a sinister grin, nodded to the guards.

They stepped aside. The general angrily opened the huge door, and exited, slamming the door behind him.

Quigley stared at the door. He contemplated the recent discussion with his minion, wondering about replacing the man.

His concentration was interrupted when the door was re-opened. A guard roughly escorted Penn and the teenagers inside.

Quigley calmly studied the group. "So," he said at length. "I didn't think it would take you long to make your way to my little operation," he greeted the group, speaking directly to Penn.

"Squiggly," Penn said without enthusiasm. "I should have known."

"Oh?" Quigley responded. "What makes you think that?"

"It was your image I saw on the screen in your place."

Quigley studied Penn for several seconds, mulling over Penn's admission, before he turned his gaze on the teenagers.

THE EMERALD HEAD CAPER

"Just what are you doing here?" he added, sternly.

"That's none of your business," Marcie replied. She was indignant, surprised by Penn's recognition of the man.

"Ah, a fiery one, for such a young lady," Quigley grinned. "You made the purchase of all the jungle gear from Madame Chee Sel, aren't you?" he asked with a change of tone, more serious.

"How'd you find that out?" Marcie retorted.

"That, to quote your words, is none of your business." He grinned and drained the rum from his glass. He got to his feet and approached the group. He walked around them, and stopped to face them. "Well, never mind. I must know, though, just how much of our operation you have seen."

"What operation?" Penn defied the question.

"Are you trying to make me believe you didn't come here to destroy my processing plant?" Quigley asked, dryly.

"Processing plant? I don't know what you're talking about," Penn said. "We're searching for the Emerald Head, nothing else."

"Don't tell him that!" Marcie tried to intercede, but she was too late.

"The Emerald Head?" Quigley smirked. "You're kidding me. You really are searching for the Emerald Head." He studied the group, and laughed "No. You are sincere, aren't you? You have no idea what the Emerald Head really is?"

A red light blinked on the console. An electronic bell chimed, drawing Quigley's attention.

Quigley studied the light. With a slight frown of annoyance, he retrieved his cape and mask. He put them on, raised the hood over his head, strode to the console, and flipped on a control switch.

Bright green lights flooded the area, and he stepped in front of the television camera. At the same time, the television screen on the console came into focus with the face of the chief of police.

"You want something?" Quigley asked, facing the camera.

The chief's image turned an eerie green. His eyes shone green as he replied. "Yes. Have you been alerted to the possible

Harold R. Miller

presence of the gringos in your area? They are escapees from my jail. I want them if you see them. I want them back in my jail to prove no one can escape me!"

"I know all. I see all," Quigley said in his monotone. "And I have them in my power as we speak. I will send them to you to do with as you desire." The lights changed intensity for effect. "You have done well to warn me," Quigley continued. "You will be rewarded. You may go now."

The bright green light faded, and the image disappeared from the screen.

Quigley turned off the control switch, took off the mask and cloak. He returned to his chair to sit and face his captives.

"What was that all about?" Penn asked with a sarcastic grin.

"It amuses you?" Quigley replied. "It's just a bit of electronic wizardry. It helps keep my work crews in line. The back jungle natives are such terribly superstitious people, you know." He poured some more rum into his glass and sipped from it before continuing. "Now, where was I? Oh, yes. I was about to show you the Emerald Head, wasn't I?"

"You have it?" Chuck asked.

"Really?" Marcie asked, doubtful.

"Wow!" Marc added, just as doubtful.

Quigley laughed as he got to his feet. He strode for the door while motioning for the group to follow.

The guards ushered the group along. They fell in behind Quigley and followed him out of the room.

Quigley lead the group down a line of corridors that was more recently carved in stone, blocked here and there with imitation stone masonry. The corridor lead to the main processing room the group observed from the tunnel. The entrance was through a door in a side wall near one of the processing vats.

Quigley stopped when they reached the center of the room, and pointed to the green skull on the platform. "There!" he said with glee. "You see before you the Emerald Head."

"What're you talking about? That's nothing but a stone carving," Penn argued.

"But that, you see..." Quigley laughed, "...is the Emerald

THE EMERALD HEAD CAPER

Head. You remember the electronic wizardry in the other room? Well, with it, I can appear in front of that head and speak to my workers. Their superstitions force them to believe my holographic image up there is their long lost God." He grinned widely as he glanced at the carving. "And it isn't stone, by the way," he added with a tone that smirked of condescension. "It's made of fiberglass, so I can make the green lights glow from inside it during my lordly appearances."

"But the maps..." Chuck began.

"The maps?" Quigley interrupted. "Don't tell me you came across those maps? Is that how you found this place?"

"Yeah," Marcie said, looking skeptically at him.

"Those maps aren't real," Quigley said, again amused. "I made them a few years ago. Oh, I used some old leather that was stashed here by the ancient indians when they created this once glorious temple that is now nothing but a ruin. I guess that made the maps seem authentic." He glanced about the ruins. "It is a very worthwhile ruin, though. It gives me the needed protection during my manufacturing."

"Manufacturing?" Marcie questioned. "What are you manufacturing?"

"A green rock we like to call an emerald," Quigley explained. "Sort of a rock, made of cocaine."

"Green rock?" Penn asked incredulously. "Rock cocaine! And you dye it green?"

"Isn't that a grand joke?" Quigley laughed again. "When the ancient Mayans thrived in this site it was famous for the way they cut and polished emeralds. That's why I decided to call it the Emerald Head. Now, of course, it's the head of our emerald rock cocaine manufacturing organization."

"But, why green?" Penn couldn't understand the rational in that.

"Simple. No one would look for cocaine when it is imported into the States with duty paid on it under the guise of uncut Emeralds. And that is so much cheaper then having to pay off the customs inspectors while trying to smuggle the stuff into the States."

"But," Marcie interjected, not believing everything she heard. "The old pirate? How did he get one of those maps, if you made them like you said?"

"The old pirate?" Quigley considered the question. "It sounds like you might be talking about my half brother, Alexis. He never did want to be part of this nice operation. He pilfered the map I made to record the location of this place. I made the map just in case I ever had to leave it in a hurry." He studied Marcie. "Is that where you got the map that led you here?"

"Half of the map," Marcie answered cautiously.

"Thorne Beusch had the other half," Penn offered. "He hired me to find the Emerald Head with his half of the map."

Quigley studied the group. "How interesting. You really weren't trying to find out what happened to his wife," he said at length. "So, what Thorne was trying to do, is interrupt this operation."

"How do you know Thorne Beusch, anyway?" Penn demanded.

"How?" He chuckled. "He's our step-brother. Alexis', and mine," Quigley responded.

"Beusch is your half brother?" Penn couldn't hide his surprise.

"You find that amusing, don't you," he smirked again. Then his expression turned sullen. "But I don't. I would guess he's trying to take over my part of this operation. It's a good thing I never told him where we operated." He frowned. "I will have to confront him about that when he returns."

"Returns? From where?"

"I think he's somewhere in Honduras, right about now. He's supposed to be making arrangements for another shipment to the states."

"You're a drug dealer?" Marc blurted out, as though suddenly aware of what was going on.

He peered at the trio. His tone changed suddenly. "That is true. But never mind. I already talked long enough. It's time I returned you to the chief of police in Belize City." He strode away, exiting the room through another door in the stone wall.

The guards ushered the group to follow him.

"Well," Penn asked no one in particular. "What do you suppose happens next in this little Emerald Head caper?"

"Your guess is as good as mine," Chuck responded, downcast.

"Shoot," Marc complained in disappointment. "That means there's no treasure, doesn't it?"

CHAPTER 20

The Guatemalan soldiers awakened in their campsite the next morning at about the time the sun penetrated the steaming jungle.

Guapito sat up, glanced at the sun, and jumped to his feet. "Everybody! Get to your feet," he shouted. "We must be on our way."

He grabbed his head. It throbbed with the sudden exertion. "Oh, mi cabeza. Such a headache." He spied his rum bottle on the ground beside his sleeping bag. "Oh, the hair of the dog. That is what I need." He quickly retrieved the bottle, feeling dizzy as he leaned over. He took a long swallow from it.

Satisfied, after letting the rum go to his head to relieve the hangover, he strolled to the Land Rover and climbed into the passenger seat. "Melones," he shouted, again sorry for his effort as soon as he shouted. "Get over here," he continued in a much softer voice in deference to the pain that shot through his head every time he spoke. "We must be going! Pronto!"

The others struggled to their feet. They stumbled around groggily, and filed into the Land Rover.

Melones, in the driver's seat, started the vehicle, put it in gear and lurched forward with a roar.

"Ay, caramba!" Guapito shouted. "Cuidado!" he said, softer, again, in deference to the pain. "Take it easy, Melones. My head, it hurts right now."

The vehicle moved ten yards forward in a roar, accelerating all the way, then suddenly lurched to a stop.

Harold R. Miller

Guapito hit his head on the dashboard.

The soldier in the rear again bounced off the machine. He landed on the ground, barely missing a muddy puddle remaining from the rain.

"Melones!" Guapito asked, straining to remain calm, holding his head to stop the pain caused by the sudden stop. "What are you doing? Why are you stopping?"

Melones shook his head. "I did nothing, mi sargente," he dutifully answered. "The Land rover, she stop alone." He stepped on the clutch pedal and then fumbled with the key switch to restart the vehicle. The motor turned over and over and over, without so much as a cough. In desperation, he got out and lifted the hood. He stuck his head into the engine compartment and fumbled around with some wires.

Guapito, impatient, anxious to get his invasion started, reached over to turn the ignition key and the starter once more.

The Land Rover, still in gear, without anyone pushing on the clutch pedal, leapt forward a foot or two under the power of the starter.

"Madre de dios!" Melones shouted as the vehicle knocked him to the ground and rolled on top of him. Fortunately, the vehicle had a high center, and he managed to crawl from under it after it stopped, none the much for wear, except for some mud. He was shaking, though, from the residual fear.

"Melones!" Guapito shouted. "Quit your fooling around. We must get on our way. What is the matter?"

Melones shook his head, slammed the hood shut, and climbed back into the driver's seat, and again fumbled with the starter. After several minutes of continued grinding of the starter motor, he glanced at the gas gauge. "Oh," he said with realization.

Guapito followed his glance.

The gauge showed empty.

"Idiota!" Gaupito yelled, impervious in his anger to the pain shooting through his temples. "It is out of petrol!" He removed his hat and slapped Melones across the head half a dozen times before the pain of the exertion forced him to stop.

"Out of petrol," Melones agreed sheepishly. "Si. I think it is out of petrol."

THE EMERALD HEAD CAPER

"Idota!" Guapito continued. "Now we must walk!" He climbed out of the vehicle, tossed his knapsack to Melones for carrying, and trekked off into the jungle out of view in front of the Land Rover. He was too upset to be patient and worry about his squad's welfare, or whether or not they followed.

But they followed. They had no other choice. They scurried to grab their gear, and disconsolately fell in behind their sergeant.

"I hope we do not meet any of the Belize army today with the head aching as mine is," Guapito could be heard saying from ahead, in the jungle. "I will feel sorry to have to shoot them. It will make my head hurt even more to hear the noise from the guns." He paused. "Melones!" he shouted.

"Si, mi sargente?" Melones returned the shout, on the run to catch up.

"Bring me my rum!" Guapito ordered.

* * * *

Quigley carryied a six cell flashlight loosely in his hand, although it wasn't turned on, as he led Penn and the trio of teenagers down another corridor inside the ruins.

The walls in the corridor were of plaster, and lights were spaced every twenty feet apart, providing dim lighting. The buzzing of hovercraft engines could be heard from somewhere down the corridor.

The group rounded a sharp corner, and entered the end of a ruined tunnel. The string of lights ended, and Quigley turned on his flashlight to show their way. The bouncing ray of light illuminated the tunnel as they rounded yet another corner.

At the corner, the plastered walls ended, replaced by the rough sides of tunnel made through the ruins. Jungle roots and growth penetrated the walls, and became thicker as the group progressed into the tunnel.

They rounded yet another corner, and daylight shone through the jungle overgrowth at the end of the tunnel less than twenty feet ahead of them.

Penn peered around at the tunnel. He looked ahead of the group, at the end of the tunnel with the light filtering in through the growth that overhung it. His eyes fell on movement in the tunnel side wall near the tunnel entrance. He stopped abruptly. "Hey!" he complained. "We can't go down this tunnel! A Fer De Lance hangs out near the end."

Quigley shined his flashlight on Penn's face. "How do you know that?" he asked, amused.

"I recognize this tunnel," Penn replied with anxiety. "I almost got bitten by that snake!"

Quigley laughed as he shined his flashlight on the snake.

The snaked hissed and lunged from the side of the tunnel at some imaginary prey in the tunnel entrance.

"You mean my little pet?" Quigley asked with a laugh. He shined the flashlight on the side of the tunnel, and opened a small panel to reveal a row of lighted switches. He flipped a switch, and the snake stopped in mid lunge.

Penn stared at the snake. "I'll be damned," he said. "It's a trick."

"A simple mechanical illusion," Quigley explained.

"I nearly got killed by a bunch of Lancandons on account of some trick snake?" Penn asked. He wasn't sure if he was angry or relieved by the explanation of the trick.

Quigley laughed as he moved forward, pushed aside the growth covering the tunnel entrance, and stepped into the daylight. "It serves to keep any curiosity seekers from discovering my operation by straying into this tunnel." He brushed away a spider that fell on his arm. "The bugs and spiders are real, though. They like the cool shade of the tunnel. Come. They won't hurt you."

The group emerged from the tunnel behind Quigley, assisted by the two guards with the Uzis.

Quigley approached the riverbank and stopped. He glanced at his wristwatch. "A group of bees should be here in about five minutes. I guess we might as well relax until then." He took out a cigarette and lit it, as several crocodiles scurried off the bank into the river.

* * * *

Guapito, followed by Melones and the three soldiers,

trudged along the jungle trail. He put away his rum bottle after yet another drink, and heard Quigley's complaint from somewhere along the trail ahead.

"The bees are late," he heard Quigley say. "I will have to do something about this."

"You meet them here and not inside the ruins?" Penn asked.

"It takes too much time to go all the way inside by the river. This is much faster," Quigley answered.

Guapito stopped and held his hand up in the air to signal for the others to stop. He put his finger across his lips for silence, and signaled for his men to quietly disperse along the trail. He furtively moved forward, as his soldiers hid among the brush. When he reached the end of the trail, he peered through the growth.

Quigley, Penn, the teenagers, and the two guards with the Uzis stood around the cleared area at the edge of the river.

Guapito quietly stepped back from the brush into better cover as he signaled for his soldiers to quietly move up beside him. They gathered in a circle around him.

"I think we have met with the enemy," Guapito whispered, glancing back through the brush in the direction of the group he surmised to be part of a contingent of the Belizean army. "They are many," he exaggerated. "But we are Guatemalan!"

His whisper grew loud, and firm. He had to make his men feel brave. After another glance through the brush, he took his rum bottle from his pants pocket, took a swig from it, and wiped his mouth with the back of his sleeve. "With luck," he added. "I think they will be unhappy to have met with us, no?"

The others grinned and nodded their affirmation.

"Oh, glorious day!" Melones said. In his enthusiasm he forgot to whisper.

Guapito removed his hat and swatted him over the head several times. "Silencio!" he barked in a loud whisper. He took his .45 pistol out of his leather holster and held it at the ready. He glanced at it to be sure it was ready to be used, and frowned. He quickly rubbed the top of it against his pants leg to get rid of the mud caked around the slide, then raised it again, worried his men might have seen his actions.

Harold R. Miller

While the group waited for Guapito to make a decision, the buzzing sound of the hovercraft bees developed. It came from a distance, but got louder as Guapito and his men exchanged glances of curiosity.

At the river's edge, Quigley, with his hostages and the guards, stood idly waiting, listening as the buzzing of the hovercraft grew louder. "They are finally coming," he said.

Guapito decided to do something, at last. He again crept forward to peer out of the bushes at the group of his enemies. He grinned with satisfaction, finding they were watching the river, paying no mind to him. He was sure he had the advantage of surprise for his attack.

Melones sneaked up beside him and joined the watching. "They don't see us, no?" he asked. He startled Guapito, who was focused on the group.

Guapito jumped. He took off his hat and swatted Melones several times across the head. Realizing the noises might have alerted his enemies, he peered through the bushes to see what the men in the other group were doing. Fortunately, the hovercraft were nearing the riverbank, and their sound made listening to anything else improbable.

Five hovercraft buzzed into view along the river. They moved onto the bank and settled on the ground. The drivers opened the tops and stepped out, leaving the engines idling.

Guapito stared at the mechanical bees in disbelief. He turned to Melones beside him. "What kind of trick is this?" he whispered. "The enemy has trained monster bees?" He peered at them again. "But they do not look like real bees," he concluded. "Are they?"

"I do not know, mi sargente," Melones said with a shrug.

Guapito slapped him again with his hat. "Silencio!" he ordered in a stern whisper.

Melones ducked back, and the other soldiers exchanged worried glances.

It was just at that most propitious moment, when Guapito swatted Melones again, that one of the guards turned to the jungle with curiosity. He thought he saw something moving along the trail. He took his Uzi off his shoulder and approached the brush where Guapito hidl.

THE EMERALD HEAD CAPER

At the same time, Quigley signaled for his captives to come forward to the hovercraft. "One of you in each machine," he directed. "Behind the driver. And don't try to escape. The guards will be right behind you in the other two machines."

Meanwhile, the guard poked the barrel of his Uzi into the brush, just to look around, and the muzzle came face to face with Guapito.

Guapito was no less surprised than the guard, but it took him less than a second to recover. He took advantage of the guard's surprise, and ordered his men to attack. "Arriba! Attack! Fuego! Fire!" he shouted.

The soldiers dropped to the ground and began firing. The leaves and branches shattered all around. The soldiers were not good shots, especially when they had to worry about their sergeant being directly in their line of fire.

The guard, surprised and frightened, fled inside the tunnel for safety.

The pilots of the hovercraft, also surprised, ran for cover, following the first guard into the tunnel.

The second guard took up a position behind a tree, and began returning fire, although he wasn't sure what was his target.

Quigley stared in disbelief at the trail where Guapito's men were firing. Bullets whizzed all around him.

Penn took advantage of Quigley's confusion, and shoved the man into the river, at the same time signaling for the teenagers to follow him. "Quick! Into the hovercraft!" he shouted.

The trio lost no time in following Penn's lead, and each climbed into a separate hovercraft.

"How do you run this thing?" Marcie shouted to Chuck, looking at the handlebar control system and the gauges on the dashboard in front.

"I don't know," Chuck shot back. "Turn the handle grips, anything. But just do it!"

"Oh, wow?" Marc shouted in dismay, watching his sister as she grabbed the handlebars and sharply twisted one of the handle bar grips.

Her machine roared and lifted off the ground, slowly turning in circles. As she learned how to move the controls, the machine headed down the riverbank and onto the water, following Penn in a somewhat oblique manner.

Chuck, in his hovercraft, did the same thing, but managed to steer his machine to the river's edge without trouble, and then onto the river to follow Marcie heading down river.

Meanwhile, Marc fumbled with the handlebars and the throttle of his hovercraft. The machine lurched forward, heading straight for the jungle.

He struggled, twisted the handlebars to the right as far as he could, then back to the left. The machine veered one way, then the other, in a mad zig-zagging path, continuing toward the jungle where the Guatemalan soldiers were carrying out their ill fated attack. In desperation, he shoved the handlebars all the way over to the side, and opened the throttle full.

The hovercraft spun in response, slid sideways, bounced off a tree, and headed down the bank onto the water. It floated above the surface momentarily, zig-zagged some more before racing down stream behind the others.

One of the pilots realized what happened with the other hovercraft, and decided to give chase. He ran for his machine, climbed in, and raced off downstream in pursuit.

Quigley scrambled out of the river with a crocodile snapping at his heels.

He raced into the jungle with stray bullets splattering the leaves all around him as the sporadic shoot-out between the Guatemalans and the guards continued, none of them quite sure what they were doing, or who they were shooting, what there targets were, or where.

CHAPTER 21

Penn raced his hovercraft down the river. He glanced back to make sure the trio were following, and nearly smashed into a group of rocks for his effort. But everyone was following, all quite well under control, except for Marc, whose machine was still zig-zagging, half spinning, and generally out of control.

There was another hovercraft following them. It was the one driven by the lone pilot, and it drew within twenty yards of Marc. The pilot raised his pistol over the cockpit. He fired into the air obove Marc's head.

Marc's hovercraft went into a dizzying spin. He fought frantically to control the monster machine.

"Stop!" The pilot shouted to Marc.

Marc's hovercraft neared the side of the river and hit a jungle branch. The branch folded back with his push. When his machine spun off, it whipped back.

The pilot steered his machine close to Marc's, and when he saw the branch, it was too late. The branch swung back and smashed him in the face. It knocked him out of the hovercraft into the water, and his machine, with no one at the controls, spun wildly down the river until it was caught by another low hanging tree branch.

Penn steered his machine to the riverbank, pulling to a stop just off the water's edge. He hopped out of the machine and motioned to the others, who already followed, not needing any directions.

All except Marc. He tried to steer his machine to the bank,

but couldn't get there until after he managed to snag himself on another tree branch, went into another dizzying spin, and came to the bank sideways, hitting an abrupt edge, which nearly knocked him out of the machine.

He spun, throttle wide open, and steered the machine onto the bank where he careened off another tree, smashed between two tree trunks, and stuck fast. He scrambled out of the machine a little dizzy, but he was none the worse for wear, once his feet were on solid ground.

Marcie was the first to note the roaring of the river after all the hovercrafts were shut off. "What's all that roaring?" she asked.

"That sounds like a waterfall," Chuck commented.

"It is a waterfall," Penn explained. "It's the Thousand Foot Falls, the other branch of the river. I knew it had to be around here somewhere. That's why I got off the river."

As they listened to the roar of the waterfall, the sound was slowly overcome by another roaring. It was the sound made by a multitude of hovercraft somewhere up the river from them.

"I think it's time we got the heck out of here," Penn said. "It sounds like they're coming to look for us." He hurried to the river and shoved the hovercraft into the water, letting them float downstream in the current. "Come on," he told the group as he shoved Marc's machine into the water, after some effort, "Let's get some cover."

After thrashing through the raw jungle for fifteen minutes, they broke out onto a trail. "Well, thank God," Marcie uttered. "I don't think I could have taken another ten minutes of that stuff." She brushed the broken leaves and greenery off her shirt, then ran her fingers through her hair to clean it. She sometimes wished she had short cropped hair like her brother and Chuck. Branches and twigs wouldn't get stuck in short cropped hair.

"Well," Penn said, as he spied a fallen log beside the trail and sat down. "Might as well take a breather. I guess We'll be safe here for a while."

Marcie had no patience for sitting. "Great!" she complained. "Then what do we do? We're not going to just sit around here in the jungle 'til they get tired of looking for us, are we?" She eyed Penn as she spoke.

"I hope not," Marc said. "I'm getting kind of hungry."

"You know?" Penn responded. "I've been thinking about that. We could do a lot of damage to that operation back there, if we had a mind to."

Marcie was still exasperated from the recent experience. "How?" she responded testily. "By throwing rocks at it?"

Penn grinned with confidence. "No. By throwing water," he said.

"Hunh?" Marc asked as the others stared, wondering whether or not Penn lost his senses.

"Remember that main cavern, where that joker had that phony green head statue set up?" Penn explained. "It's below the level of the river, and if we moved the river bank just enough..."

"With what?" Marcie interrupted. "With our hands" She was still impatient.

Penn was undeterred. "No," he answered. "I was thinking we'd use gas, the gasoline they use to run the hovercraft, and a match or two."

"Then can we find something to eat?" Marc asked.

Penn, ignoring the question, got to his feet and set off down the trail, back in the direction of the ruins. Marcie and Chuck exchanged glances, shrugged, and followed.

"I sure hope this leads to something to eat," Marc said, as he brought up the rear.

"C'mon, Marc," Marcie said with sarcasm. "You just ate something yesterday. What do you want, anyway?"

* * * *

Guapito realized the lone guard who returned his fire was not going to be any vanguard of any Belizean Defense Force, so he gave up the battle and moved his men back into the jungle along the trail. He was tired and disgusted. His hat was full of bullet holes, and his uniform was torn.

The others of his meager band all looked as though they went through a beating, and they were just as happy as Guapito to return to the sanctity of the jungle. As far as they were concerned, a little more rest and recuperation before they had to do battle with the Belizean Defense Forces would suit them nicely. Especially if the rest of that Defense Force would be shooting anything like the lone contingent they encountered.

After retreating - a tactical withdrawal, Guapito called it - the soldiers reached a wide spot in the trail.

"Alto," Guapito said wearily. "We will take some time for a rest here." He sat on the nearest fallen tree.

Melones sat beside Guapito and retrieved a bottle of Caribbean White Rum from the sergeant's badly tattered and shell torn knapsack. He opened it and took a long swallow.

Guapito eyed Melones. He removed his hat to swat the corporal over the head several times, grabbing the bottle at the same time. "Idiota!" he shouted. "How can you sit and drink at a time like this?" He eyed the bottle. "I am the leader. I need this more than you do." He tipped the bottle to his lips and took a long drink.

"Si, mi sargente," Melones said dejectedly. "I am sorry. I was not thinking."

It was after Guapito's third drink, which drained the bottle without any consideration for Melones' anguished thirst, that he heard brush being broken by someone walking along the trail.

He listened intently to be sure he wasn't mistaken.

Sure enough, he heard it again. He got to his feet and silently signaled his men to take cover in the brush while he hid behind a large jungle bush just back from the log where he rested. The bush gave just enough cover for him to watch the trail without being seen. He secretly hoped the sounds weren't made by a Belizean Jaguar, or worse, by some more of the Defense Forces.

His concerns were relieved when he spied Penn traipsing along the trail, followed by Marcie and Chuck, with Marc bringing up the rear.

They passed his position without seeing him. After they passed, he stepped out onto the trail and peered after them in a somewhat confused state of mind. "Gringos?" he asked himself, scratching his head under his shell holed hat. He shook his head, and peered with interest in the direction the group went. He got an idea. What would happen if he had some Americans to use as hostages if he had to confront the Belizean Defense Forces again? They would be useful, he decided.

Meanwhile, Melones moved up beside him. "Who are they, mi sargente?" Melones asked.

Guapito jumped in surprise at the sudden intrusion of Melones' voice. He grabbed his hat and again swatted the corporal across the head. "Idiota!" he whispered loudly. "Silencio! I am thinking!" Having made his decision, he signaled for his men to quietly follow him as he furtively set off to follow Penn and the teenagers. He would stay discretely behind them until he could develop a means of capturing them.

Barely an hour later Guapito signaled his men to halt. He caught a glimpse of his quarry standing in the middle of the trail, not more than fifty yards ahead along a straight stretch.

Penn and the teenagers were studying some Belizean ruins. They were the same ruins with the tunnel they first found, near the stele.

"This has to be the same tunnel," Penn said, as he moved aside the brush that covered the tunnel entrance, and peered into it with some trepidation. He didn't like the thought of going into a tunnel again, even though he knew they had to, in order to enact his plan. "That's the same stone stele," he added, as he pointed to the stele Marcie noted before. "Come on," he said, stepping into the dark hole.

Marcie, Chuck and Marc dutifully filed into the tunnel, and disappeared from Guapito's sight.

Guapito quietly moved forward to the tunnel entrance. With great caution, he moved the brush out of the way and took a peek inside.

Melones moved up and stuck his head into the tunnel. "What do we do now, mi sargente?" he asked.

Again, his voice was a surprise to Guapito, who jumped, letting the jungle growth swing closed, slapping the unsuspecting Melones across the side of the head.

"Aieeee!" Melones complained.

"Idiota!" Guapito chastised him, again. He would have swatted him with his hat, some more, except Melones' head was wrapped in branches and growth, out of reach.

* * * *

Inside the tunnel, Marcie stopped. "What was that?" she asked in a loud whisper, hearing Melones' complaint filter down the tunnel. By the time it reached her ears it was almost faded out.

"What's what?" Penn asked.

"I thought a heard a strange noise," she added, still whispering. "Like a shout, or something."

"Probably another one of Quigley's tricks," Penn responded, continuing his trek into the tunnel.

"I sure hope so," Marcie said.

"So do I," Chuck agreed.

"Oh, oh," Marc responded, worried, as he glanced behind and hurried to catch up.

* * * *

Guapito stepped back from the tunnel entrance and looked for a place to sit. Finding nothing suitable, he settled on the ground.

Melones gathered himself up, and joined him. "What now, mi sargente?" he asked.

"Now, Melones," Guapito said. "I think we think for a minute about all this." He paused. "Where is the rum? I need something to help me think of what we are thinking."

"I will get it, mi sargente," Melones dutifully responded. He twisted his knapsack off his back and began rummaging through it to retrieve the last of the bottles of rum he was assigned to carry.

* * * *

Inside the tunnel, Penn and the teenagers reached the first fork. Penn signaled for quiet when enough light filtered into the tunnel from the end of it to let him see. He heard a hovercraft engine from past the end of the tunnel. The machine was started, and revved up several times. The noise faded as the hovercraft drove away.

Quietly, continuing their furtive approach, they crept to the end of the tunnel, where they carefully peered over the rim.

THE EMERALD HEAD CAPER

Below them was the room with the river flowing through it where they first saw the hovercraft. There were two hovercraft parked on the river's edge.

Penn pointed to the hovercraft as he whispered. "See that area near those hovercraft, where the wall is blocked off? I think if we open that up, the river will flood the whole place."

"Good idea," Chuck agreed. "But how?"

"Easy," Penn responded with a grin. "We'll move those hovercraft over to the blocked up section, make make some fuses with some cloth, light them, and bango! The explosions rip out the wall, and you've got the biggest flood since Noah built his ark. It's lucky they left some extra gas cans around. They'll be a big help."

"Oh, just great." Marcie complained. "And blow us half way to heaven in the process."

"Why do you have to sound so much like my ex-wife?" Penn argued. "She never could see the genius in my plans, either."

"Maybe because she had to look after you and your half brained ideas all the time, too," Marcie retorted.

"I think I could use a drink," Penn responded with slight despair.

"You don't need a drink," Marcie shot back.

"See! Just like her," Penn complained.

"I just want to know how we're supposed to get out of here without being blown up if you set off that gasoline," Marcie responded. "There's no harm in wanting to know that, is there?"

"Why didn't you ask that in the first place?" Penn replied.

"How?" Marcie pushed her question.

Penn pointed to the river. "That river has to flow out of here back out into the jungle. Otherwise, those hovercraft couldn't be coming in and out of here. All we have to do is follow it." He looked farther out into the room. "Come on," he said, as he moved out of the tunnel into the stone steps that lead down into the room.

It was easier than Penn expected for them to reach the hovercraft. They floated them along the edge of the water to where they considered would be the weakest spot in the wall. He took off his shirt and tore it into strips to use as fuses, sticking one strip into the gas tank of each hovercraft.

"Okay. Into the water," Penn directed the teenagers after he inserted the last strip of his shirt into the last gas tank.

"What about the crocodiles?" Marc complained.

"There won't be any around here. Too many people," Penn explained, as he removed his lighter from his pocket and lit the first fuse. Three seconds later, he lit the second fuse and raced for the water.

The others watched, still nervous about crocodiles, but seeing the fuses lit, wasted no time in following Penn.

* * * *

Guapito, at the tunnel entrance, made his decision. He got to his feet. "Enough thinking," he told his men. "It is time we liberated these poor people." He headed for the tunnel. "Come. We will follow those gringos into the tunnel, wherever it leads." He pushed aside the brush and boldly stepped into the dark tunnel.

Melones followed, but the other soldiers were reluctant. They weren't sure they liked the possibility of being trapped in such close quarters.

It was at that instant when the fuses lit by Penn, reached the gas tanks of the hovercraft and exploded along with the gas cans.

The force of the explosion blasted outwards, finding the tunnel to be a release. It blasted rock, debris, roots and all manner of things out the end of it as though shot out of a cannon.

Melones, followed by Guapito, were blown off their feet with the force of the blast. They barely heard the explosion before they were picked up by the blast. They were shot out of the tunnel and at least fifty feet through the jungle.

The other Guatemalan soldiers stared, astonished, as Melones, then Guapito, landed amid thick jungle bushes, followed by an assortment of charred and burning debris.

They were still staring, stunned, when Guapito gathered his wits about him enough to stand up, though admittedly with something of a struggle. His uniform was shredded and smoldering. He was covered with debris.

Melones rolled off a bush and landed beside Guapito. He looked just as beaten. He peered at his sergeant with a bewildered look. "Maybe that was not such a good idea, mi sargente," he moaned.

Guapito grabbed what was left of his hat and tried to swat Melones over the head with it, but it fell apart in smoking shreds. He looked at it, and sadly shook his head as he dropped the pieces on the ground. "Melones," he said, disgusted. "Maybe you are right this once."

"I think, mi sargente," Melones continued. "Maybe these people of Belize don't deserve to be liberated just yet."

Guapito peered at him, pondering the thought. "I think," he said at length. "I think that maybe you are right, again."

"Besides," Melones said, emboldened by his sergeant's support. "We are out of rum. We should go back to get new supplies."

Guapito began a light smile. "I think maybe you are right, again, Corporal Melones. Maybe we should quit this campaign for now, but only to regroup. All great military expeditions have to regroup, at times." He paused to think. "Remember, it is only because we must get new supplies." He turned around and slowly, while slightly staggering, headed back down the jungle trail.

Melones signaled to the other still stunned soldiers to follow, which they gladly did.

* * * *

The tunnel entrance wasn't the only place the force of the blast was felt. Penn and the teenagers were rushed along the river in the huge wave that flooded out of the growth covered river entrance to the ruins.

They swam to the side of the river, and, helping each other, managed to struggle ashore where they sat long enough to recover their presence of mind.

"Wow! That really worked," Chuck said with enthusiasm.

Harold R. Miller

"Amazing what a little gas can do, hunh?" Penn grinned.

Marcie wasn't quite so enthusiastic with their plight. "Well, what now, genius?" she asked. "An explosion like that must have let everybody this side of Belize City know something is up. They're bound to come looking to see what it was all about."

Penn glared at her. "There you go again. What'd you say your mother's name was?"

Marcie was about to answer, but she was interrupted by the sound of a horde of people yelling in a panic behind them.

The Indian workers were fleeing the temple in a mad panic. Some were running out of the tunnel entrances, and some were swimming down the river out of the entrance to the ruins.

It was only seconds after the last Indian ran out of the ruins and raced off down the trail that the ruins were shaken by another blast, then by a third and even greater blast than the first two. Pieces of rock and rubble were thrown everywhere as the ruins exploded upward like a volcano.

Penn and the teenagers ran to cover as pieces of rock and stone landed around them.

The ruins crumbled. The stone walls collapsed into pile of rubble. A huge cloud of dust billowed skyward.

After the dust cleared, the group got to their feet and stepped out from their refuge behind a huge fallen log. They stared at what was left of the ruins.

"Good grief!" Marcie exclaimed.

"Wow!" Marc said.

"I never expected that much would happen," Chuck added.

"Neither did I," Penn admitted. "Our explosion must have touched off all the chemicals they used in their processing." He grinned as he surveyed the ruins. "Some fireworks, hunh?" he added.

After he realized the scope of the destruction, he saddened, and sat on the log. "Well. So much for the Emerald Head," he said. "At least Beusch's money was real." He thought some more. "I wonder if this isn't what he really wanted? Not to find any phony Emerald Head, nor to track down his ex-wife, as Squigley claimed, but to get revenge on his renegade half brother?"

CHAPTER 22

Two days later Chuck, Marcie and Marc were in the passenger waiting lounge of the Belize International Airport. They were among a throng of tourists waiting for their departure flights.

The day before was spent explaining to the minister of the interior of Belize, just what took place in the jungle.

The minister was satisfied with the explanations, and forgave them for escaping their jail, especially since his arch rival, the chief of police, was taken into custody for being associated with the cocaine manufacturing process. He let it slip during the interview, that he used David McGaughy and Richie to keep track of the chief's activities. Their information corroborated Penn's, a fact for which he was grateful.

Penn entered the departure flight waiting room carrying a freshly opened pint of Myers's Rum. He waived it around as he approached the teenagers. "Well," he said. "So here you are. All ready for your flight, are you?"

Marcie eyed the rum. She frowned. "I see you are," she said.

"There you go again," Penn responded before taking another drink. "What'd you say your name...?" He was interrupted by the rasping voice of the dispatcher coming over the loudspeaker, intoning instructions in a slight Creole accent. The voice also announced the immediate departure of the teenagers' flight. "Continental Airlines flight number 456 for Houston is now boarding at gate number one. All passengers should proceed to that gate immediately."

Penn smiled to the teenagers. "Well, that's your flight."

"Ours?" Marcie asked. "You're not on this flight?"

"Nah," he responded. "My flight's on Tan Sahsa Airlines. I'm going to Managua." He grinned wistfully. "There's some things down there I heard about. There's this guy who wants me to sort of, ah, go look for them, somewhere near Camaguey."

"Things?" Chuck said. "Antiquities?"

Penn shrugged his shoulders in affirmation, then as an after thought, retrieved his hand drawn copy of the map and handed it to Marcie. "Here. Take this. Maybe it's something to remember me by, okay?"

Marcie fought to hide the misting of her eyes as she took the map. "I don't think we could ever forget you," she said. "Map or no map." She quickly hugged him, then hurried for the boarding gate.

Chuck and Marc quickly shook hands with Penn, and hurried after Marcie, clamoring up the boarding ramp and into the air conditioned mechanical bird.

The plane began its taxi roll, and Marcie glanced out the window at the terminal. The map she got from Penn sat on her lap. "He really was a pretty nice guy, wasn't he? In spite of his drinking," she said.

"Yeah," Marc agreed, sitting beside her.

"Do you realize that after all we went through, we never even knew his full name," Marcie added.

Marc was surprised by the realization. "Wow, that's right, hunh?"

"You'd think," Chuck said, "that with all the excitement we had, he'd want to take a rest."

The airliner reached the end of the taxi strip, turned, and accelerated to take off speed.

The map slid on Marcie's lap. She grabbed it. She glanced at it, and sentimentally unfolded it. A note fell out of it. She picked up the note and glanced at it. She did a double take to read it more intently, staring at it in surprise. "Oh, my God!" she gasped. "We have to go back! We have to stop him!"

"What?" Marc asked.

"Why?" Chuck asked.

THE EMERALD HEAD CAPER

"Look!" Marcie explained as she held out the note. "He wrote us a note saying good bye!"

Marc took the note and peered at it. "Oh. Wow!" he said, after reading it.

"What?" Chuck asked.

"He signed the note," Marcie responded, trying hard to hide her excitement. "His last name is Gwinn!"

Chuck stared in disbelief. "That's your last name!"

The airliner lifted off the ground and banked to the left in the departure turn.

"Where's Camaguey?" Marcie asked, trying to look through the window at the quickly disappearing terminal, fighting the tears welling up in her eyes.

"In the jungles of Nicaragua," Chuck replied.

"Oh, oh," Marc added.

Enjoy an excerpt from another action packed
adventure featuring Penn Gwinn.

P.I. ADVENTURES
IN
BELIZE

This book varies in format from the usual Penn
Gwinn series, in that it consists of a set of short
stories based on Belizean experiences.

As in all of the Penn Gwinn books, each story has a
twist ending, and all are exciting adventures.

FILE SEVEN

DRUGS & FLAMBÉ

It didn't have promise of being much of a case, but in Belize, when you need to work as a P.I. you take anything that pays.

At least I thought it wasn't going to be much of a case. It supposed to be a typical domestic. A rich widow – yes, there are rich widows in Belize – wanted to know just what her latest paramour was doing when he wasn't with her.

According to my client, he was supposed to be having a business meeting at the Fort George Hotel in Belize City. I was told he would be easy to find with the description given by my client – 6 feet tall, Garifuna black male, bald, with a well trimmed beard and glasses. Even in the tourist season, there weren't too many people who fit that description in Belize City. Flambé was his name. George Flambé.

I, too, struggled to stifle a laugh when I heard the name. Fortunately, I had enough tact to not ask the obvious question as to whether he was a red hot lover. I don't think I would have gotten the retainer, if I had.

I caught the late afternoon Tropic Airlines plane out San Pedro for Belize Municipal Airport to begin my hunt for the client. His meeting was scheduled for that evening, so I didn't expect I would have to hunt too long to find him.

As I got off the plane and headed for the nearest taxi, a myriad of thoughts ran through my mind without any specific relationship. Fogging, it was called when I was in college. It was something a typical college student learns to do in any class with a boring instructor.

Anyway, it was late afternoon, and I was on my way to

the hotel. A 5:25 I entered the hotel, and at 5:30, I located the subject.

If he were in a business meeting, I decided I would enjoy being in his kind of business. He was sitting with two of the sexiest Belizean women I've seen in quite a while. Apparently, they weren't the sexiest he'd seen in quite a while, because he gave them nothing more than a friendly hug when they stood for his departure half an hour later.

I thought that odd. Maybe they were his sisters? Or, maybe there was something more to his meeting than my salacious mind first thought.

I was still wondering about their relationship when Flambé left the lounge. It took five seconds for me to get my mind off the women, and hastily get off the stool to follow him.

He was in a hurry. He cleared the hotel entrance, and grabbed a taxi by the time I cleared the front of the hotel.

By the time I found a taxi, Flambé's taxi was at least a block away. "Can you follow that taxi?" I asked the driver as I scrambled into the front passenger seat. What the hell, I thought. Maybe he knew the other cab driver. Cab drivers in Belize City are a tight knit group.

"Maybe," the driver said, hastily putting the car in gear and driving off.

Three blocks later, after half a dozen turns, a lot of conversation between the driver and I about the men with the machetes at the Bellevue a few weeks ago, and still no sign of the other taxi, the driver stopped.

"No luck, I guess, hunh?" I commented.

The driver shrugged. "You know dat man?" He asked.

"I know his name is Flambé," I answered. "Why?"

"Da two men wid da machete at the Bellevue. Dey work for him. You were dere?" he asked.

"Uh, yeah." I was even more guarded with this response. What gave him the idea I might have been there?

"Dey be two guys wid da machete try fa da rob da taxi. Dey may be da same dat work for Mr. Flambé. Dey try to cotch my taxi dat night."

"Your taxi? You?"

He nodded. "Dat night dey hold up da machete fa da

window, but I go hard, leave dem stand in da street, true."

"Where was this? Can you remember what they looked like? Did you tell the police?" I hoped it wasn't too many questions for one time. It wasn't.

"In town, mon. 'Bout maybe ten in da night. Dey raise dey arm fa me fa da stop, so I stop. But I have da care, chu know? Maybe dey not good fare, I t'ink. An' I be right! I get away, fast lak." He stopped to think. "One tall, one short. Da one tall, he have dreadlocks. Da odder? Short hair. Short, lak maybe in da army, da Belize Defense Force, chu know? No. I doan call da police. I no fa da police. Every time I fa da police, dey cause tr'uble."

I had to sympathize with him on that last point. The local police are about as deep into graft as the Mexican police are reputed to be.

Although I never had a problem in Mexico, I did have to pay a bribe once in Belize City when I jaywalked. The cop wanted ten dollars, American, to prevent hauling me off to the local police station with a threat of two days in jail before the court resumed to hear my case.

I paid the ten dollar bribe.

"Do you know where they're from?" I asked. The descriptions he gave matched the men Gerald and I saw in the hotel room.

He shrugged and nodded yes. "I t'ink dey come from Orange Town by da way dey spik. Maybe, from Orange town, dey stay in the triangle, I t'ink. Lot's a bad men's, dey from da Orange Town, dey stay in the Trangle."

"Trangle? Oh, you mean the Triangle. You seem to know something about Flambé. What do you know about him?"

"Flambé? George Flambe? Mon, he a big drug runner. He be so big, when he wan' to bring in da drug, he make da airport. Right dere in da middle of da bak land, he mak wid de airport. A big plane, DC T'ree, dey call it, come an land wid da drug. Den take off, da airport, it be plowed over wid da tractor, no trace, no ev'dence, day say. Dat Mr. George Flambé"

"Do you know where he hangs out? Where he can be found?" I was thinking I was going to earn my fee the easy way.

"Orange Walk, I hear. Or, maybe da Trangle."

"Okay, then you can take me there?" I said.

"Da trangle?"

"Yes."

The driver put the ancient Toyota in gear and chugged off down the street. Ten minutes later, he stopped in a section of town known as the Triangle. It was so called because three streets crossed each other at angles, about two blocks apart. It was not the safest place in the world for a white American to be, even in the middle of the day.

"Dat house, dere," the driver said, nodding at a run down house, a condition common among most of the houses in that part of town. It was a condition left from Hurricane Hattie, which ravaged the town with high water and 150 mph winds a few decades earlier. The houses left standing were never repaired. Most of them weren't even repainted. "Five dollars," the driver said.

"Wait for me, will you?" I directed the driver as I opened the door of the cab to get out.

The driver shook his head. "No, mon. I no wait fa dis place. Five dollars." He held out his hand.

When a cab driver refuses to wait in an area, it's a sure sign a white man doesn't belong there. "I take it you don't think I should get out here?"

"No, mon."

"Why?" I glanced around. I knew why, what he was thinking, but I wasn't going to let anyone intimidate me.

"Because," he responded, nodding in the direction of the house next door.

I followed his glance. It led to a house raised ten feet off the ground, as most of the houses in Belize were in order to provide clearance for the invading flood waters of hurricanes. Sitting in the shade under the house were six locals, and they were glaring at us, but none of them were the men from the Bellevue.

"You're trying to tell me I should be afraid of some guys taking shade under a house?"

"Ya, mon. May be fa da better chu come later."

"Later? When, later?"

"I t'ink, may be, chu first get some protection."

"Protection? Who?"

"Not da who, mon. Da what."

I studied him, questioning his meaning.

"Chu may be go fa da gun?"

I wasn't sure he was asking if I had a gun, or if I wanted to buy one. I did have a gun. I have one of the very few permits to carry a concealed weapon in the entire country of Belize. If I hadn't helped prevent the Prime Minister from being assassinated in Dangriga, I wouldn't have one, but I didn't tell the cab driver.

I shut the cab door, instead of getting out, and sat back. "Okay. I suppose you just happen to have a gun or two for sale?"

"No, mon. Not me," he said. "But, may be some mons in Orange Town, dey sell chu one."

"And, I suppose you just happen to know who that someone might be?"

It was an interesting turn of events. Although I didn't need a gun, knowing something about the illegal gun trade might be useful, sometime. And, since Orange Walk was where Flambé probably went, I decided to play along.

His response to my question was a non-committal shrugging of his shoulders.

"I tell you what. You ask those guys if another taxi came by here in the last ten minutes, and then we can go to Orange Town."

The driver grinned, and stuck his head out the window to shout at the men under the house. "Sweet mons," he shouted, "Chu see da cab da two mons, dey fa da come? Orange Town boys, dey?"

It took several minutes for me to remember the Belizean term 'Sweet Mons' was a friendly greeting, meaning the person you addressed was a guy the women always went for. It was a compliment. It wasn't at all what someone in the States would misunderstand it to be.

The men exchanged glances, and several of them shrugged.

"Dey be here now?" The driver persisted.

Several shook their heads, no.

"Hey, Willowby," one of the men shouted. "Why wid da question a da mons, mon?"

The driver perked up. "Hey! Dat chu, Chester? What fa da chu dis part a town, mon?"

"What fa da mons?" Chester repeated.

"I jes' be fa dem. True. Not'ing more. Chu know where dey be?"

"Chu no say I tol' chu."

"No, mon. No worry 'bout dat."

"Day be fa da Orange Town. Dey here, but dey say may be the mon be lookin' fa dem. Dey say dey got fa da go, mon."

"Orange Town? True?"

"True, mon. Five minutes 'go, mon."

"Yah, mon? I tank chu fa da words, mon."

"Chu mak me fa da beer, now, mon."

The driver laughed. "Fa true! Fa true! One Belikin. Tomorrow, may be."

"Belikin!" the man returned with a laugh. "Hey! I no wan da belly ache. I wan da Heineken!"

The others joined in the laughter.

"Tomorrow," the driver shouted, as he put the car in gear and stepped on the gas pedal. The car lurched forward with a 'clunk' from the transmission.

"You think he was telling the truth?" I asked, after we turned the first corner.

The driver shrugged. "I t'ink chu go fa da Orange Town," he said, picking up speed. "Da mon chu want? He be dere, I t'ink. My fran, he no lie da me."

"You're certainly anxious to get to Orange Town, aren't you?" I asked.

"Chu get wat chu want in Orange town," he replied, turning his head to grin at me. He almost hit a stray dog for his efforts. If a heavy gust of wind from the coming storm hadn't shaken the taxi at just that minute, I think he would have run over the poor animal.

"What else can I get in Orange Town?" I didn't expect an answer, but I gave it a shot, just out of curiosity.

"Mos' anyt'ing," he answered.

"So, how much is that going to cost?" It wasn't that I was going to go to Orange Town to buy a gun, but the prospect of running into my subject was more than interesting.

"Umm, maybe, fa da Orange Town? Hmmmm, sixty dollars." He said it in one complete, rapid expression. It seemed a rehearsed response.

"So, you're trying to tell me I can get a gun in Orange Town? Without a permit?"

My questioning made him more cautious. He returned another non-committal shrug.

"All right. Maybe you don't know that much, but suppose I do want to go to Orange Town for a gun, then what? How much do you think I would have to pay to get one? If you happened to stumble across someone who would have one for sale, that is, not that you do know, of course."

If anything, the driver had decided to be cagey. "I t'ink, may be, dere be a lot of t'ings for sale in Orange Town. May be we go dere, may be chu find somet'ings you want. May be. De mon you want. He be dere, true."

I studied his nonchalant expression. "What other things do they have for sale there?" It was a shot in the dark, but information is information, it's an asset in my kind of business.

Instead of answering, he cast a glance out the window at the sky. "Chu go fa da Orange Town, I t'ink may be chu go now. Before da storm."

It was my turn to shrug. Why not? I'm into the deception deep enough already, I might as well continue it. Besides, maybe I could get some information on the machete men, not to mention the man I was being paid to investigate. It was worth a shot, but I wasn't about to pay sixty dollars for it.

"Sixty dollars for the trip is too much," I said. "Drop me off at the Millie's Car rental. I have some other things to get, so I might as well drive myself."

"Fifty?"

"No. I still think I need a car of my own."

He shrugged "Forty five."

"Twenty five," I countered.

"Forty."

"Thirty."

"You hard, mon," the driver said, sadly. "You hard. I no can go da Orange Town fa da no money, mon."

"Thirty five. No more." I pulled out thirty five dollars in American cash, and handed it forward.

The driver glanced at the money, frowned, looked forward, as though the answer was written somewhere on the windshield of his taxi. Shook his head, studied the money, then said, "Thirty seven fifty?"

I handed over the money without saying anything.

The driver took the money. With another shaking of his head in despair, made a U-turn and headed out of town.

The drive to Orange Town from Belize City usually takes about an hour. There weren't too many cars on the road, mostly because of the storm developing, so our time was going to be a little less, if the storm didn't hit us before we got there.

We were still ten miles from the town when a DC-3 airplane roared low over head. It wobbled, fighting the wind gusts. The pilot had trouble keeping it steady in the gusts. He dipped one wing, and kicked the rudder in the opposite direction, which put the plane into a slide.

"Now, there's a guy in a bit of trouble," I commented, watching the plane.

The driver ducked his head to look up through the windshield at the plane. He laughed. "I t'ink may be dat George Flambe," he said, sitting back.

"George Flambe?"

"I t'ink may be he be makin' a deliv'ry," he said, focusing his attention on the road in response to the increased wind gusts.

I studied the driver. "Delivery?"

He shrugged.

"Drugs?"

He shrugged, again.

"There's no air strip in Orange Town," I said. I had been to Orange town, and I couldn't remember any air strips that could handle a DC-3, even though the old Gooney Birds were famous for their short field landings in bad weather.

"He may be mak da strip, again."

"He makes his own landing fields?"

"True, mon. I hear dey mak da field in one day, wid da bulldozer!"

"Where?" I was beginning to think I was getting too cryptic in my questioning.

The DC-3 was within a couple hundred feet of the tops of the pine trees that grew in the flat areas of Central Belize. The pilot was still fighting the weather, and still descending. The field had to be close by.

I wondered if the plane could make a safe landing, with the darkening sky of approaching sunset and the gathering storm. The sunsets quickly turn to night in the tropics, and there were only a few minutes of actual twilight left.

"Let's see if we can follow him," I suggested.

The driver glanced at me as though I were crazy. "Now, I be da gud driver, I know dat, but I doan' t'ink I can follow dat plane. Dis cab, it no fa da fly, mon."

I laughed. "No, of course not, but we can see where it's going to land, right? And there's no jungle in this part of the country, so you can drive through the woods."

If anything, this taxi driver was a quick thinker. "One hundred dollars," he said without hesitation.

"If we find it," I said.

"No problem, mon," He tromped down on the throttle, heading in the same direction as the plane. It looked as though the pilot was using the road as a landing guide. He would be easy to follow.

I didn't question the driver's sudden confidence, but I rolled down the side window to keep a better watch on the plane, just in case. It was a few hundred yards off to our side. It leveled off its descent, and banked into a sharp turn. "He's making a turn!" I shouted against the wind from the open window.

The driver made a sudden turn. We bounced off the highway and into the fields. There were a few trees in the area, but not enough to worry about.

The field was once a productive farmland for the Mennonites, a religious sect that sought refuge from the oppression of the Catholics in the U.S. They settled in Belize half a century earlier. The fields were abandoned, though., and were overgrown with weeds. Even so, they are flat enough to drive on. They were also flat enough to land a plane, especially if the weeds were cleared with a bulldozer.

I wondered how the taxi driver knew this is where the plane was going to land. It was a question I would ask later. At the moment, I needed to concentrate on the plane's final approach, trying to judge where it would touch down, and trying to keep the weeds from slapping my face with my head stuck out the window.

The late afternoon's sunlight dwindled with the approaching storm clouds, so the pilot turned on the plane's landing lights., and a row of lights flashed across the field ahead of us.

The driver slammed on his brakes, and slid to a stop. "I t'ink we go no more," he said, turning off the engine.

I agreed. We came within fifty yards of the end of the cleared area, with the plane heading right for us. If we went farther, there was a good chance the plane would run over us if it overshot the new strip.

A row of makeshift landing lights flashed on, lighting up the side of the home made airstrip. The lights also illuminated a row of cars at the opposite end of the makeshift strip. Some were recognizable by their shapes as being some very expensive vehicles.

Another reason for stopping was the outline of a Ford van parked halfway down the cleared area. There were three men standing beside the van, all watching the plane's approach. They carried Uzi sub-machine guns slung on their shoulders and held at the ready.

"Jesus!" I exclaimed against the wind. I tapped the driver on the shoulder and pointed at the van.

His eyes went wide when he saw it. "Dey da smugglers," he whispered, as though we were close enough to be heard over the storm.

"Come on," I said, as I opened the taxi door and stepped out.

"No, mon," the driver said with an anxious shaking of his head. "No, mon," he repeated. "Not wid dem mons. No. Dey shoot before da question, mon."

I hoped he was wrong, but I had to see what the hell was

going on. I had to get a closer look. I stepped out of the taxi. Apparently, leaving the taxi was a signal for the driver to leave, but I was too interested in what I saw to pay much attention to the fact I no longer had any means of transportation.

I watched the plan and the men at the van. Was someone actually smuggling drugs into Belize by DC-3, on home made airfields? That would account for the near mid-air collision with that DC-3 over Ambergris Caye a while before.

I felt the S.I.S. had to know about such an operation, so I crept forward, keeping my head low among the weeds, feeling grateful for the height of them in spite of the fact I was cursing a few minutes ago with my head out the taxi's window.

The DC-3's engines coughed and sputtered.

I stopped. The plane was visible in the glow of the landing lights, and I could see it was in trouble. One engine was blowing oil.

It was twenty yards from the cleared area on its final approach, barely clearing a group of small trees left over from an orchard the Mennonites planted years earlier.

The plane's wing dipped dangerously low. It lifted again, but too late. The landing strut caught on the top of one of the trees. The plane spun like a flattened top. The aft section of the fuselage broke off, and a dozen brown gunny sack sized bags flew from the broken fuselage. Some split open. White powder, reflecting the landing lights, spread across the field like flour from a ruptured bag.

The rest of the plane cart-wheeled. The nose smashed into the field. One wing tore off, and the other sliced through the air like the fin of an angered whale. The fuselage balanced on the nose and broken wing for half a minute, before another gust of wind rose, blowing it over to smash on its top.

The engine from the broken wing burst into flame. The white powder flashed in flame, like finely milled wheat in a grain silo. The fuel tanks exploded, and pieces of the airplane flew everywhere.

The pilot scrambled to the broken end of the fuselage, intent on escaping the flames, but he had no chance. He was lost. His clothes were on fire. He screamed. He jumped from the fuselage. By the time he hit the ground, he was too badly burned to scream. He was charred.

The van roared from the side of the field to the plane. The men with it ran to keep up. That's when I recognized one of them. He was the subject of my investigation. The client's boy friend, Flambé!

The van reached the plane, and the van driver ran to the burning body of the pilot. The other men ran to the side of the plane. They fought against the heat of the flames to see inside. One man tried to enter the plane, but his efforts were useless. He had no more of a chance than the pilot.

I watched in disbelief. I saw burning planes, before, I plane crashes and burning bodies when I was with the intelligence agency in the Orient, but it was the sudden and unexpected turn of events that made this scene so horrible.

I stood open mouthed, staring at the wreckage, not knowing whether I should go forward to help, or should use my common sense and stay where I was. After all, they were drug smugglers, and they were well armed.

I decided to stay where I was, and my choice proved the wisest of the options, for two military police cars from the Belize Defense Forces roared out of the tall weeds at the other end of the strip. They turned on their lights as they raced for the plane. They slid to a stop near the plane, and six M.P.'s jumped out with their weapons in firing position as they advanced towards the men at the plane.

The men at the plane fired at the soldiers, and that proved a foolish thing for them to do.

The van driver ran behind the plane. He grabbed one of the brown bags that didn't open in the crash, dropped to his hands and knees, and crawled into the bushes for cover, dragging the bag behind him..

The firefight lasted less than a minute, ending with the three men from the van mortally wounded.

The soldiers were approaching the airplane, when I heard a crashing movement in the high weeds less than a few yards to my side. I held my breath and ducked. Was it the wind, or was someone running through the brush?

Seconds later a man shoved his way through the weeds past me. It was the fourth man from the van.

There are times when you feel like being a hero, times when you don't necessarily feel like one but end up being one, and times when you damn well should have better sense.

At the moment I had better sense than to try anything stupid. I drew back into the weeds in hopes the man wouldn't see me.

Three minutes later the fire from the plane set the weeds aflame. It was time I got out of there. I listened intently for sounds of the fourth man, but there were none, so I cautiously crept back to the taxi, or where it was when I left it. It was nowhere to be found. The driver must have lost his nerve in all the excitement, and fled. Or worse, the fourth man came across him and forced a ride. I considered that possibility, and discarded it. The fourth man would not want anyone to know he had been anywhere near tonight's action.

I shudder, took a deep breath, and with the glow of the burning weeds reflecting off the low clouds, hurriedly followed the taxi's tracks back to the road, and hiked down the road as quickly as I could, heading for Orange Town.

The wind was developing, and behind me was the ever increasing glow of the weed fire. I wondered what happened to the fourth man, hoping he wasn't on the road, as well, and hoping even more that he didn't see me as I saw him. I wanted time to think of what I was going to do about that vision, who I was going to tell, and how. The how was the hard part. Who the hell would believe me without thinking I was involved? Yes, it was going to take some thought.

Another twenty minutes and two miles later, the rain came. Like any tropical storm, it was a heavy downpour. It was just what I needed, to be stranded on a back road in he middle of Belize, in the middle of an approaching hurricane, without shelter. It was useful, though, in dousing the airplane fire.

The best thing to do was find some sort of cover, but since there weren't any houses around, the best cover was a nearby palm tree. It was one with a great spread of fronds. If I sat on the downwind side of it, at least the rain wouldn't pelt me too hard. But, how long could I do that? How long was this storm going to last? Hell, it could last for as long as three days. I wasn't about to crouch behind a palm tree for three days!

I managed three hours. I would have stayed longer had not a car's headlights flared in the rain. It was within fifty feet of me by the time I got myself together, realized it was a car, and ran to the middle of the road.

I damn near settled all my problems with that less than brilliant move. I saw the car in the rain, because the headlights were bright, but the driver of the car didn't see me until the last minute. I jumped to the side of the road to avoid being run over, even though the car had all four wheels locked in braking, trying to avoid me. It slid halfway off the road before stopping. The driver was just opening the door when I ran up to it.

"What the hell are you doing?" The driver shouted at me. "I damn near hit you!?"

"Yeah. Sorry about that. Uh, I mean, yeah. I'm glad about that. Ah, that you didn't hit me, that is." I was caught off guard. I expected the driver to be a man, but it wasn't. "Sorry to have scared you, though," I continued my apology to her.

It took at least half a minute for her to figure out what I was trying to say. Maybe she was nervous, maybe she was having second thoughts about picking up a stranded waif in the middle of a storm.

I didn't wait for her questions. "My car ran off the road back there about a mile. I wonder if you could give me a ride?" I blurted.

She became even more hesitant. I couldn't blame her.

"Look," I said, reaching for my wallet, as though she would be able to see any form of identification I could present in a downpour. "I'm a P.I., my office is in San Pedro Town, and I was run off the road by someone I was trying to follow. It's lucky I managed to get back to the road on foot. I've been fighting this storm for over two hours, and I really would like a ride." I handed over my wallet instead of trying to pull something out of it. "Here. Take at look. All my I.D. is in there. It should prove my point."

She took my wallet, shut the car door, and turned on the dome light. She also locked the car door. After several minutes of rummaging through my wallet, she opened the side window, and told me to get in the other side. She unlocked the door, and I climbed in.

She paid no attention to the amount of water I dripped on the seat cushions and the floor as she returned my wallet, while keeping the dome light on.

That was the first time I got a clear look at her. She was a white woman, about forty, with short cropped hair, no makeup, wearing jeans and a tank top. Even during a storm, the weather in Belize is warm. I surveyed the car while she put it in gear. It was an Isuzu Trooper, an older model, probably a mid 90's, but one that was distinctive in shape, and it was packed with luggage in the rear. My conclusion was easily formed.

"You're a tourist?" I asked her to ease the tension.

"Somebody's got to be," she said.

After putting the car through all four forward gears. She was going at least fifty miles an hour, which was a lot faster than prudence dictated for such a road, especially in such weather.

I wasn't sure I understood her answer, and I sure as hell didn't understand her recklessness, but what the hell? I was out of the rain, and that's all that mattered.

"Kind of a bad welcome for a tourist," I said, keeping an eye on the road, just in case she missed something.

I hoped she knew the roads in Belize. They could dead-end at a cross street, without warning. If you weren't careful, you could end up in a ditch where you thought a road should be. Or worse, you could end up in a swamp, with water up to your headlights before you got a chance to get out of the vehicle.

She didn't respond to my comment, but continued driving faster than she should have in the weather.

"You seem to be in a hurry," I said, struggling to watch the road through the rain pounding on the windshield.

She didn't answer.

Ten minutes later, I tried again. "Where are you going in such a reckless, mad hurry? You're a tourist. You don't now the roads in this country. They can be troublesome, deceptive as hell. What's the big hurry?"

She glanced at me. I was relieved she was at least somewhat human, in that she was listening to me, or hearing me, but I wasn't so relieved as to appreciate her taking her eyes off the road. "I've driven the road between Orange Town and Belize City at least a dozen times," she said flatly.

"Why all the luggage?"

"Just because you're a P.I. you don't have the right to question everyone who comes along. Particularly when they're being a good Samaritan."

She had me there.

I was silent for several more minutes before thinking of a rejoinder. "Curiosity?" I proffered.

"Hah!" It was a friendly laugh.

"So?" I wasn't going to let up, not while I had her talking. If you could call it talking, anyway.

"What you really doing out there in the rain?"

The question surprised me. "Half drowning, if you want to know the truth."

"That's not what I meant."

I shrugged, and sighed. "No. I guess it isn't."

"I'll answer yours if you'll answer mine," she said with a relenting sigh.

"I, ah, was sort of following someone, using a taxi, and, well, things came to a rather ugly end, and I ended up walking."

"Did what you were doing have anything to do with that DC-3?"

"How do you know about that?"

"I'm a blonde, but I'm neither dumb nor blind. Did you have anything to do with that?"

She slowed down to take a rather dangerous curve. It was a relief to know she was paying some attention to her driving.

"In a way, yes. But not directly. I wasn't aware that was going to happen when I started out."

"How did you start out? What were you expecting?" She asked.

"Jeez. You sound like a cop."

She reached into her purse setting between the two bucket seats, and pulled a wallet. She flipped it open. Indeed, she was a cop. Miami P.D. And a Lieutenant, at that. Lieutenant Charmaine Hill. She returned the badge to her purse with one terse comment. "And don't call me Charming, nor Charmy. It's Charmaine"

I stifled my grin and was silent for the next fifteen miles, until the lights of Belize City glowed against the storm clouds. "You're working?" I asked, at length.

She glanced at me, then slowed for the last turn into town. The traffic was light, due to the storm, and she had no trouble making her way to the Fort George Hotel.

"You're obviously on an expense account," I quipped as the hotel came in to view.

She didn't appreciate my sarcastic humor, and passed the Fort George, rounded the corner, and entered the drive for the Chateau Caribbean, next door. If anything, the fact that she preferred this hotel proved she was a cop. It was the one hotel in the entire country where all the off duty police and police types stayed. It didn't have the glitz, the glory, the tourists, and the souvenir hawkers who plagued the other hotels.

"You can do what you want, but I'm staying here," she said as she turned off the engine.

"You're not worried about the rising water from the storm?" It was a poor comment, a poor excuse for haranguing her confidence, but I couldn't let it pass. After all, the City of Belize is barely more than two feet above the high tide mark. Any heavy storm surge could flood the city, including all the hotels near the water. Excepting, of course, the Chateu. Its builders knew that, and put it on stilts.

"The storm will pass more than a hundred miles to the south of us. Nicaragua will get it, not Belize." She glanced at the sky as she opened her door. "The worst is about over."

We got out of the car, and hurried for the hotel office. I had to concede she might be right. The rain did let up. It let up enough for me to see the no-vacancy sign in the lobby entrance. "You have a reservation here?" I asked.

She looked at me as though I were the dumbest man on earth. To tell the truth, at that minute, I felt like I just might be. Of course she had a reservation. She was too smart to travel without one. I followed her into the lobby like a lost sheep, a condition I did not like.

The motel clerk is named Meredith. I knew her, or should probably say had known her quite well. She greeted the cop with a warm smile, then turned a cold shoulder to me.

"You have no reservation, Mr. Gwinn," She said icily.

"And we are full." She glanced at the cop. "Unless," she added with a dour frown, addressing her. "You are expecting a room for two persons?"

I hated her for that comment.

The cop laughed. "Hey. I picked him up on the road. I'm not responsible for him." She grabbed the desk pen and began filling out the reservation form.

I shrugged, turned away, and looked out the door. I waited until she finished registering before setting out the bait. "There is a lot going on in this city that you're not aware of," I said.

She glanced at me. Taking the bait? I wondered. "And I have a pretty good idea there are some things you would like to know." I faced her and smiled politely.

She studied my expression. She was an experienced cop. I could feel her aura penetrating my mind, seeking my meaning. "Meaning?"

"Meaning, you didn't just happened to be casually passing that DC-3. Not in the middle of a storm."

She took the room key from Meredith, thought for a few seconds, then suggested we go into the lounge to have a drink.

I grinned inwardly. It wasn't that I wanted a room for the night. I could always hang out with any number of friends in the City, but she intrigued me.

Or more accurately, her association with the DC-3 intrigued me. Her association meant she knew something about the men with the machetes in the Bellevue, and she sure as hell must know something about the fourth man I saw running from the wreckage. That is what fascinated me, what tripped my insatiable curiosity, and those were the questions I was going to ask.

There are some hotels that make their lounges a focus point of activity, with hype, or blaring music, or worse, blaring TV, all designed to make the patron feel as though they're in some other part of the world, someplace where they can forget reality.

The Chateau Caribbean hotel lounge is none of those. It is comfortable. It's probably the most comfortable in all of Belize City. The chairs are soft, casual, and easy to get into and out of, yet offer a relaxing feel. Each chair is positioned near an overhead fan, so the sub-tropical heat of the country is allayed. There's no bar counter with the usual plethora of potions and poisons gaudily on display in front of a back-bar mirror. Instead, there's a simple counter with all the bottles set under it. The music is the pleasant cacophony of local birds in the trees outside the patio, even in the night, even in the rain of an approaching storm.

I spent many an evening in the Chateau. It's one of those well kept secrets the travel agents are always searching for. Fortunately, they didn't find it, yet.

A very sprightly waitress in her early twenties arrived as soon as my new found cop friend and I sat in the chairs, facing each other across the knee high cocktail table.

I ordered my usual Korbel Brandy over ice, and she ordered a Long Island Iced Tea. Holy cow! I said to myself. This is a woman who must know how to drink. Either that, or she is really trying to forget something. I preferred the former.

It took no time to get into which it was. She grinned in response to my surprise. "Hey. So, I like a good drink, now and then. There's no law that says cops can't drink, is there?"

I grinned in return, and thought of her statement. "Why cops, and not off-duty cops?"

She took a minute to understand my meaning. "You mean why didn't I say I'm off duty?"

I nodded.

The waitress returned with our drinks. I signed the tab. We took the complimentary first sip, nodded our approval, and leaned back for serious discussion.

"You're a P.I.?"

I nodded over another sip from my brandy. I savored the taste while she tried to think of another question. Or, maybe she considered the the relevance of my profession to hers, how we could be of mutual help.

"About that DC-3," I began.

"Who's it belong to?" If anything, she was direct.

What the hell, I mused. "George Flambé."

"How do you know that?"

"I get around."

"What was it carrying?"

"I'm supposed to know that?" I feigned. She wasn't going to trap me so simply.

"You said you get around. Apparently you don't get around Orange Town too much."

I shrugged.

She leaned forward. I hadn't noticed until then that her light tank top revealed cleavage ample enough to hold any man's attention. She put her elbows on her knee and peered directly at me. She glanced at her drink glass, swished the contents around several times, and returned her gaze on me. "I guess we have to be honest, here, don't we?"

"Is there any other way?"

She leaned back, swished her drink around some more. I guess it was her way of focusing her thoughts. Hell, after drinking more than one of those things, she was going to need something to focus her thoughts. I considered ordering her another one.

"You're Penn Gwinn." It wasn't a question.

I raised an eyebrow over another sip of my brandy. I was proud of myself. It took a lot of control to keep from gulping it down in one swallow. Of course, I knew how she knew my identity. After all, she plied through my wallet before she let me in the car, but the way she pronounced my name indicated recognition. That was the surprise.

"Don't be so shy. You're well known outside the country. At least in law enforcement, and some intelligence agencies. Anyway, I'm supposed to make contact with you, and try to get you to help me. I admit, I didn't think it was going to be this easy."

"Driving through a storm and picking up a stray hitchhikers is easy?"

It was her turn to shrug.

"Okay. So I'm easy." I said with a grin. "Another drink?" I suggested.

She chuckled. "You may be that easy, but I'm not. Maybe a bit later. First, let's get down to business."

"Your place or mine?"

I thought it humorous. She thought it a comment worthy of a nasty frown. Well, maybe later, I mused.

"I'm with Miami Vice, Dade County."

"Really? What happened to Don Johnson?"

It earned me another nasty frown. I apologized before she could think of some nasty, and quite warranted, remark.

"I was trying to follow two guys who attacked a D.E.A. agent in the Bellevue Hotel earlier this afternoon," I began my explanation. "On the way, I saw the DC-3 flying low, apparently making a landing approach. I had an idea it belonged to Flambe, so I told my cab driver to let me out. I tromped across the fields where it was making a landing. The weather was too rough for it, one of its engines was throwing oil. It crashed and burned. I was on the side of the makeshift field, taking it all in."

"What was it carrying? Did you see anything?"

"Coke, I'd guess. From the looks of the powder strewn around before the fire."

"How many bales of coke were in the plane?"

Her question was a warning bell. "You seem to know a lot about that plane in order to be asking me such questions. Isn't it time you told me few things?"

"We're working one of the major dealers in South Florida. We got a tip he was bringing stuff in through Belize. We covered all the ports, and the Guatemalan border, but couldn't find any smuggling routes. None that tied in with heavy cocaine smuggling, that is. They found a lot of pot coming in, but no cocaine. I heard about you and they way you work in this country, the ties you have, so I talked my boss into giving me a chance to fill in the gaps by getting you to work with me. Or rather, by me working with you."

"Don't you think you're taking a chance? You're not even sure I am who you think I am. I could have stolen the I.D. I could be the pilot from that DC-3, for example. Or even one of the guys who were waiting for it, who got away in the firefight with the BDF."

"Some one got away?"

I wished I hadn't given up that clue. "I'm somewhat sure," I said.

"Okay. Sine you don't look like a Belizean, or a Colombian, either. It's your bald haircut and demeanor, your mannerisms. Definitely not the criminal type, not to mention your reputation, of course. And anyway, you fit the given description." She finished off her drink, and held it up for the waitress, ordering another one. "Who was that fourth man?"

She certainly knows how to keep to the point, I mused. "A man. Any man. What makes you think I know who he is?"

"Like I said, I may be a blonde…"

"But you're not stupid. I know."

"So?"

I sighed. "Suppose I find it's too much of a risk to tell you who it is? Or even who I think it is?"

"Suppose I call the S.I.S. and get them in on this?" She challenged. "I'm sure they would have some questions you would have to answer about being there in the first place."

"That would be the biggest mistake of your life," I countered.

She studied me while the waitress brought her drink. Although I didn't order one, she had the forethought to bring me another, as well. Charmaine and I spent the next few minutes in thought.

"The guy's with the S.I.S.?" she asked, at length, over a sip of her drink.

"Is that your guess?"

She smiled softly.

"I'm not the kind of person who likes to disparage a young woman's ideals," I replied. "You don't believe cops are honest? Even the Sissy Boys, the Belizean S.I.S.? They're the elite, you know. They wouldn't be mixed up in anything too crooked." Was it too much of a pitch? Probably not. Or, if she saw it as one, she certainly knew how to sidestep it.

"Crap."

Okay, so she didn't exactly sidestep it. I sighed.

"Who?"

"Whom?"

"Like I said, crap. Who?" She persisted.

I hesitated.

"Should I make another lucky guess? Or do I even need to? It was Stevens, wasn't it?"

"Stevens?" I asked, feigning surprise. I sure as hell wasn't going to let her know I agreed with her. I have known Stevens for over five years. I've never gotten so much as a hint of wrong doing on his part, up until this night. "What makes you think it's him?" I parried the question.

"He's up to his ears in the Miami scene."

"Are we talking about the same Stevens?"

"Does that need an answer?"

I sighed again. I seemed to be doing a lot of sighing while talking to this woman. "Yes. It was Stevens."

"He got away. Did he get away with anything? I don't suppose he dropped anything in his hurry?"

"Dropped? Like what? You wanted him drop his wallet, maybe?""

"Things like do happen. Did he?"

"No. Just one bag. I would guess it to be a kilo of cocaine. He didn't drop it. He picked it up."

"How was it wrapped?"

"Hey! There was a storm coming on, it was night, there was a fire in the weeds, and I was more concerned with keeping under cover."

"How?"

"You're certainly persistent, aren't you?"

"It comes with the territory. It's my job. How?"

I took a breath. "In brown paper, with a red band."

"Imported directly from the Peten region in Guatemala. That's their sign, kind of a logo for their shipments. And that's why we could never track the plane. It can fly under the radar from Peten to Belize."

She took another sip of her powerful iced tea, pondering her next question.

I felt like I was being given the 3rd degree. I looked around for the hidden rubber hose and the bright lights, which I was sure were to be brought into the open any second.

"How often does George fly in?" She asked, at length. "When do you think he will, again?"

"I don't think he ever will again. He's dead."

What makes you think so?"

"I saw him jump out of the plane while on fire. He never had a chance."

"It probably wasn't George Flambé flying that plane.

That's not his modus operandi."

I had nothing to say. She was right, of course, but I wasn't going to admit it. What she said about his modus operandi is true. He moe than likely had someone else fly the plane while he stayed out of the way, out of trouble.

"Where do you suppose Stevens has gone? I didn't see him on the road," she said.

She had an interesting point. I added something more interesting to it. "You came down here for my help. Are you going to listen to my suggestion?"

"Of course." She actually smiled. Lightly of course, but it was a smile.

"Then why don't we find out just where he is?"

She eyed me curiously as I got up and went to the lobby. She decided to follow me as I finished dialing Stevens' cell phone number.

"If he's anywhere, he'll answer his cell." He did. "Stevens?" I said loudly into the phone. "Hey! Where are you? There's something important you should know about.... No. I can't tell you over the phone.... What's more important, a night with your woman, or catching some smugglers?....All right. Nine in the morning. I'll be there. I hope that's not too late."

I hung up the phone, waited a few minutes, and dialed another number. The call was answered after a few seconds.

"Penn Gwinn for Mannie Esqueville, please," I said. "Yes. I'll hold on...... Manny? Penn...I'm fine, yes. Listen, I think I got the answer you want. I'm more than surprised, and I know you will be, as well.....two hours?... Yes."

I hung up the phone, ignored Charmaine's unspoken question, finished my brandy, grabbed her by the elbow, and guided her out of the hotel. We got in her car. I drove without asking for her permission.

"Well," she said. "You certainly do know how to take charge, I admit. It's just as I was told, watch out for you. You're a take charge type person." She smiled.

That was confusing as hell. What she did she mean by that?

"Where are we going?"

"Manny Esqueville's house. In Belmopan."

"The Prime Minister's house?" She was awed by the prospect. "You can just pick up the phone and drop in on the Prime Minister?"

"I have privileges."

"Well, I guess you must have. I wouldn't be able to do that, and I come recommended."

I gave her a discerning glance, and grinned.

"Don't get smart, okay? I meant, I have high recommendations, letters of introduction."

I shrugged.

We were silent until we approached the long drive leading to the Prime Minister's residence, when Charmaine finally broke the silence. "You're going to report Stevens?" She asked.

"Do you have a better idea?"

"I thought he was a friend of yours?"

"That doesn't excuse drug dealing."

"Okay. Let's go back a bit. What makes you think it was Stevens you saw? Not only that, but if it were, why would he be answering his cell phone when you called?"

"In the first place," I continued, "I recognized his walk. He has a limp, remember?"

"Well, yeah," she said, but added, "If you say so, but anyone can fake a limp."

I considered her answer. How could she know Stevens has a limp? He's had it for less than a week, when he sprained his ankle in falling off his ATV while chasing Caymans in the middle of the caye. If she knew about his limp, then she must have seen him since then? And if she has, then why?

"How long have you been in Belize, anyway?" It was a simple question. I got a simple answer, a simple lie.

"I was just coming in when we met, remember?"

"Surely, this is not your first trip here."

"Well, no. The last time was six months ago. That's when I dug up some information on the Belize/Miami connection." She was silent for a few seconds. "Why is that important?"

Oh, oh, I mentally cautioned myself. Go slow. Was she recognizing my suspicions? If so, she was one hell of a lot quicker than I originally thought. "It's not important," I answered. "It was just a question, curiosity, something to pass the time."

She glanced at me as though to add something, and changed her mind. "You never told me what you're doing here, by the way," she said, instead.

What was she talking about? Didn't she give my I.D. the once over before she let me in the car?

"I have an office here. On the caye, that is," I answered cautiously.

"San Pedro Town?"

"Yeah."

"Maybe we should have another drink before we go rushing into the Prime Minister's house with this."

"Why? There's something you want to discuss?"

"Well, I'm just not sure we have all the answers."

"What if I do, though?"

"Do you? I can think of a few things you don't have answers to."

"Like what?" She looked nervous.

"Oh, come on. How did you know the plane was coming in? You never explained that."

"How did you?" she countered

"Let's quit playing games. Isn't it a little odd that you would be driving through that part of the country at that hour? After all, it isn't exactly the most direct route into Belize City, is it?"

"I could have been lost."

"Could have been? Or was?"

"Same thing."

"Now, you come on." I enjoyed throwing that comment back at her. "You said you made the drive before."

She sighed. "We can't go to the PM with this."

"And why not? After all, if the S.I.S. is mixed up in drug dealing, shouldn't he know about it?"

She took a deep breath. "Because he knows me," she said.

"Knows you? Explain that."

She slipped her hand to her knee, and pulled back her skirt. I wondered if she was going to make some seductive ploy to persuade me to change my mind.

I did change my mind, but unfortunately, it wasn't the result of any seductive ploy. It was more of a hard ploy, hard as in a snub nosed .38 Chief's Special. And the end of the bullets seen in the chamber when she pointed it at me had hollow points. It was not a friendly sight.

"As I said, we're not going to the PM's. Or anywhere else with this information, for that matter. Keep driving, and go where I tell you."

"My guess was right," I said. I hoped to find something that would through off her concentration, something would give ma an advantage.

"Your guess? What's guess?" She almost sneered with the question.

"Did you think I was so lacking in the qualities of observation that I didn't see the remnants of weeds caught under your car door? They couldn't have gotten there if you hadn't opened the door when your car was in high weeds. That fact, plus the overall shape of this car fits the one sitting in the middle of the other car and the van at the end of the landing area. It adds up to a nice conclusion."

"And the conclusion?" Another sneer.

I glanced at the side of the road. We were closing in on the side of a canyon. It wasn't much of a canyon, more of a back water slough, but it gave me a thought. Maybe it would be something I could use, if the situation got out of hand. Or, any more out of hand than it already was.

"The conclusion is pretty simple, actually," I said. "The man I saw was definitely Stevens, but you didn't guess that. You knew that. You knew he walked with a limp, and used that as an identity factor. The only problem is, he never walked with a limp before a week ago, that meant you had to have been face to face with him within a week, not six months ago. All of it together means you're working with him."

"I have to admit. You're every bit as astute as they said you are."

"You should have listened to them when they told you to watch out for me. Only, I don't believe the 'they' is the same 'they' as what I thought. Your 'they' was the rest of your smuggling ring, while I thought it was the Miami Dade narcotics office."

"Aren't you taking a few too many chances? You're going to make it necessary to get rid of you."

"I don't think so. If you did, it would only make your position worse."

"Adding another murder charge to the others won't make a difference, not now. I don't plan on being charged with any of them, nor with anything else, for that matter."

"Others? What others?" I dreaded the answer.

"A few narcs. But why do you care? You're going to be with them, soon enough." She peered up the road. "There," she said. "Where those trees are, past this slough. Pull in there."

I sighed. I seemed to be doing a lot of that lately. "Whatever," I said. "But I think you should take my advice," I added. "Anyway, what trees are you talking about?"

When she glanced to make sure she chose the right place, I turned the wheel hard to the right, opened the car door and jumped out.

I hit the asphalt on the roll, which was a good thing, because it slowed my forward motion enough to make the two shots she fired in my direction miss me.

The third shot never came anywhere near me. It went through the roof of the car as it sailed off the side of the road, down the bank and into the swampy slough.

I didn't expect the scream. If I had, I wouldn't have been surprised by the way it was suddenly cut off when I ran for the high grass for cover. I was certain she would chase me with much more effective aim when she got out of the swamp. Her gun was a Chief's Special .38 carries five rounds.

She had two left.

I didn't need to run for the weeds, though. She wasn't getting out of the car. She wasn't coming after me. With more than a little trepidation, I peeked over the top of the grass. The rear of the upended car was visible, but she wasn't.

I crept from the weeds to the road, keeping a wary eye for any movement in the dark, but she wasn't in view. When I reached the car, I saw why. She was right, she wasn't going to be charged with another murder. She wasn't going to be charged with anything, not ever. Her head hung over the steering wheel in an ugly position, at an ugly angle. No wonder her scream was cut short. Her chin was across her left shoulder, the result of a broken neck.

I called the PM, and after explaining the Stevens Flambe and S.I.S. connection, I flagged down a passing car and rode back to town. I took a cab to the Bellevue Hotel bar, and went to the bar. I needed a drink.

Three days later I got a thank-you call from Martino Bayer, the new Chief of the S.I.S.. He thanked me for my efforts, and expressed hope we could work together in the future.

Yeah, I thought. We probably could, but not until after I got over the loss of a friend.

California looked good to me, at the moment.

Harold R. Miller has been a private investigator for
over twenty five years. His case files are the basis of
his action adventure novels.

Novels by
Harold R. Miller

The Belize File
The Australian File
The Philippine File
Thai Moon Saloon
The Emerald Head Caper

Breinigsville, PA USA
14 February 2011
255447BV00001B/1/P